To: Barbara

I hope you enjoy my book.

Love,
Anita B.
Morris

Phil 4:13

RED HILL

RED HILL

ANITA MORRIS

Book design by Maureen Cutajar
www.gopublished.com

ISBN: 978-1512299946

For my father and mother,
Ray and Lois Bobo.

IT WAS DESIGNATED a boom town, similar to Huntsville in the 1950's, ready to explode with population and economical success. In the 1920's, Red Hill offered the following amenities: ample employment in an ever growing wood production market, a rambling boarding house, a quaint whitewashed school, a silent picture theater complete with a massive upright for the silent pictures, an established general practitioner, a practicing barrister who shared his office with the doctor, a company commissary which permitted credit to the employees, a handyman shack, a tidy post office, a lively dance hall, and an antebellum styled non-denominational church building. Company housing was available and continually increasing as the new residents moved in to Red Hill.

Americans, even in the rural South, were gaining confidence after The Great War, and many were making life changes to improve their economical conditions. Most potential Red Hill residents were happily oblivious of the remounting tension in Europe. Young families, hopeful, were willing to relocate to break away from generational poverty. Red Hill seemed a fitting place to start. Rental cost for company housing was one dollar per room. All housing had electricity, but most residents chose to heat with coal or wood, especially wood which was free and available for use from a cull butt pile near the looming red clay hill located northeast of the wood yard. Some houses had running water, but others did not. Indoor plumbing was available, but some less progressive families preferred a well and outdoor toilets. After all, the South, in many ways, was still stinging from the devastating effects of the Civil War around fifty years before Red Hill's heyday.

Sadly, segregation was still stubbornly and wrongly embraced by the whole nation, but more noticeably in the South. The town of Red Hill was strictly divided between the white section of houses and the quarters, as they were still called-a leftover term from slave times. Obviously, the distinction was more than just Jim Crow jargon; physically, the company houses in the quarters were of poorer quality with all the tiny shotgun houses without indoor plumbing. Located directly in the center of the quarters was a small, yet appealing little church where African Americans of all denominations could worship and could utilize as a community center for reunions, meeting, dinners, etc. The quarters were located near the wood yard office and adjacent to the railroad tracks where the old company steam engine chugged across at least twice a work day.

Surprisingly, Braun, the name of the company, did provide equal pay and health benefits for all employees, regardless of race. It also rewarded pay raises and promotions nondiscriminatory. For example, Lee Earl, a young male engineer, was given a salary and was responsible for several white workers who were under his authority. Some grumbling occurred on the yard, but Mr. Lang, the plant manager at the time, squelched the disgruntling with clear explanation: all men were equal—maybe not in the world itself-but in the eyes of the company in terms of advancement, respect, etc. The men accepted Lee Earl and other African American bosses because deep down they knew he and others like him had earned their spots; and, if any other worker wanted advancement, he would receive a fair shake, too. But the black population seldom ventured beyond their unmarked, but clearly established boundaries into white areas except to work, to shop the commissary, to visit the post office, to pick up supplies from the carpenter's hut, and to collect their paychecks at the main Braun office. Fraternizing between the two races was a rare sight.

The name "Red Hill", according to oral history, was adopted by the early settlers who were startled upon arrival to the hidden paradise which was surrounded by massive pine trees (not unusual) and substantial banks of clarion tinted clay streaked with an occasion white seam of fine, grainy clay. The formidable red clay was impervious to rub boards, to Twenty Mule Team Borax, to strong bleach, and sun-scorched clothes lines; you could lighten its stain, but only time and frequent wear could fade the stubborn hold it had on clothes. It wasn't uncommon to see the uncompromising red in Alabama hills, but many housewives who battled the brick red stain after setting up their washhouses in Red Hill, swore that the vermillion here was much more sophisticated in its persistence than clay located in other areas.

The pasty clay was valued by many women, especially pregnant ones in Red Hill. Shy, bulging bellied ladies trekked daily up the steep, yet worn, side of the black yard hill to scrap out the sour white clay which was actually craved by the birth ripe ladies; yet, the daily mining of it was usually ignored and gently tolerated by the community, the workers, and the Braun company itself. After all, geophagy has been practiced at some time in every culture because of tradition, intense hunger, or vitamin deficiency. When the weather was inclement, or the eater was unable to secure the white clay, she generally substituted corn starch or baking powder in its place. Nowadays, the clay eating practice has diminished either because of better diet or social embarrassment. But, in the 1920's, its popularity was at its peak and no one seemed to mind.

The incorporated town of Red Hill provided a perfectly secluded and convenient hideaway for escaped residents of the nearby city's mental facility and self-liberated criminals on the run, many of whom had once been members of the Red Hill community or who still had kinfolks living there. Since oftentimes there can be a close connection between a majority of lawbreakers and an overindulgence of alcohol, the local bootleggers or rum runners were more than willing to hide, to feed, and even to protect these criminals. They allowed them a few spirits and then called the police station to pick up the usually inebriated offender. For more dangerous criminals, the bootlegger called in favors to some of his body guards and had them literally carry the miscreant back to the steps of the jail. He was a businessman first, and he was not going to allow riff-raff to jeopardize his livelihood!

Most of the wandering mentally fragile were not considered dangerous, and Red Hill residents even recognized some of the fearful unfortunates. A simple phone call was made to the mental institution, and the frightened, confused escapee was soon returned to the safety of his/her comfortable home. On one occasion later in the 1960's, a childlike resident ran away and knocked on the door of the current plant manager's house. The composed and quick thinking lady of the house recognized gentle Donstil and invited him in for lemonade and cookies as she calmly dialed the familiar number of the mental hospital. He was loved and accepted in Red Hill, but his need of precise medication did not afford him the chance to stay in his already chaotic home. The whole experience was not a trauma for either the offender or the offended. Actually, there was no offended.

Unlike Huntsville, which truly emerged as a boomtown, growing and expanding, Red Hill did not fulfill those hopeful predictions of the economic prophets who felt that it would soar like the Rocket City. The town did enjoy moderate population growth and a steady job market for Braun wood yard production. However, a depression, a drought, and another war that followed the "war to end all wars" rattled its chances to burst into a metropolis. The plant continued to prosper and to employ around three hundred people. However, by the 1950's, the war was over, and Baby Boomers wanted to live in the suburbs, not in an isolated swamp area. GIs relocated near college towns to further their education on the bill that allowed for such. Red Hill lost its school, lawyer, doctor, antiquated and never updated movie theater, dance hall, and a sizeable chunk of its younger population. The tiny post office continued to serve its patrons. The commissary provided general store items—no frills and choices like the new supermarkets in town. The church was still shared by the

Baptist and the Methodist faithful. The handyman shack was occupied now by two rather than a crew-Mr. Lloyd ("Big Un") and his son ("Little Un"). Red Hill resembled a dozen or more towns in rural Alabama—barely surviving.

The Braun Company, owned by Mr. J. Braun of Kentucky, felt that 1953 was time for Mr. Lang, the general manager of the wood plant in Red Hill, to retire. He had served faithfully for almost forty years, but Braun, being a business visionary, could see that he needed new blood with new ideas to boost this wood business. He had been watching a young man Ray Beaux, who Braun had met; and Braun, thoroughly impressed, had hired him after Beaux returned from war. He was employed as a butcher in a commissary in Morris, but he had showed great initiative and business savvy, the characteristics of natural born leader. Perhaps, he could be quickly and successfully trained as Lang's successor.

Mr. Ray Beaux had grown up extremely poor as the middle child of sharecroppers around the Great Depression era. He'd even experienced the loss of his toddler brother, Newton, whose death was directly related to insufficient diet and lack of prompt medical care. Ray had continually been forced to drop out of school at cotton picking time to help his family survive. Yet, after losing time of classroom instruction, he would return for a brief stint before crop planting time, and his amazed teacher would find Ray caught up and actually far advanced of his classmates. He had straight, stark-black hair, which he had inherited from his mother who was half Cherokee, and piercing electric blue eyes from his French father that beaconed out from dark skin, also attributed to his Native American background. He was quick, respectful, and resourceful, attributes which endeared him to his teachers who saw him sporadically in the school year. Because of the memory of gnawing hunger and great poverty, he had an unquenchable thirst for a world that could offer him more than near starvation. More than ragged clothes and shoes with cardboard bottoms fashioned from old boxes found in community garbage can could provide. He had brilliance coupled with drive.

Beaux dropped out of school, eventually, and his father gave his position up on the WPA highway contract to allow his son to earn money for job training. After all, the elder W.L., or William Beaux, was himself a fair farmer; he knew Beaux was a bright star in his family of five other children and a thin, often dissatisfied wife. He had chosen Ray to accompany him to the bank many times when he had to borrow money because Ray's affinity and accuracy with numbers were uncanny, and the swarthy child could negotiate respectfully with adult bankers, even when Ray was still in elementary school. Ray's fondest memories with his dad on these trips included W.L. buying him a hot dog as a reward for all his mathematical efforts to help the family. He and father alone enjoyed this significant adventure. Beaux's photographic memory and accurate recollection of important names and personal data both came in handy when he and his cash strapped pop returned to town. Ray maturely addressed the loan officers, the tellers, and even the president of the local bank by their names; he was not hesitant to volunteer a strong handshake and courageous eye contact with his social class superiors even when he appeared before them in his faded overalls and bare feet.

Beaux, now with a little cash from his WPA job, was able to afford a bus ride to Bessemer Trade School to enroll in classes of business, typing, accounting, and even welding. He completed each class with honors, and eventually began to weld before the war. In 1939, he courted and married the love of his life, Eula, who graduated Valedictorian of her senior class. Beaux had borrowed a suit from an uncle and again, fashioned shoes lacking soles with discarded cardboard to spiff up for her graduation ceremony. Her educationally minded, strict father was not impressed with the shabby, exotic looking man with the white flashy smile, but Elder Turner could not dissuade his fair and brainy daughter from falling hopelessly in love with Beaux. She eloped with Ray on the very day she was to catch a bus to an Alabama Teacher College, where she had been awarded a full scholarship for the entire four years. She never regretted the decision, not even once in the sixty-three years they were together.

The love struck couple hastily moved in with the elder Beauxs and blended with the rowdy brothers and one sister in a two room house. Eula was popular and was loved by her new family; her father had not quite forgiven her yet for spurning an opportunity to better herself with a college education like her eldest sister. Soon, in about two years, a child Rabon was born in the back room of the little shack where chickens could be seen wandering around underneath the cracked floor, and with a brave decision to improve their way of life, the couple quickly moved to Mobile where Ray had been accepted as an underwater welder who repaired damaged ships during World War II. The couple lived on peanut butter crackers and anything their parents back home could afford to send them. On Sunday, December 7, 1941, the little family was sitting around the tiny table in their sparsely decorated apartment located above a small Italian store. When the radio sadly reported the bombing of Pearl Harbor, "a date that will live in infamy", Ray announced that he was signing up with the Navy. He kissed his beautiful wife and son goodbye and he hurriedly enlisted and eventually served four years as a gunner's mate. Of course, his welding skills were appreciated by the government as well, so he continued to practice that skill, too. Eula knew there was no negotiation on his decision, and she supported him strongly, even traveling with her young son, to any port in America where her beloved might be during the war. An ignorant, young bride who had never been outside her own county would now eagerly load buses for exotic places such as New York, New Orleans, San Diego, etc. just to spend a little time with her Ray. So, yes, Mr. J. Braun was right; Beaux WAS the man for the job at Red Hill. He was still hungry.

After the war, Ray settled his reunited family in Morris where he bought a modest house near the newly constructed highway, and there he began his second career as a butcher. Once again, he returned to school, learning meat processing and financial management at the Averson Drawn School in nearby Birmingham. Quickly, he and Eula were managing a successful commissary for the wood plant in Morris—a sister plant to the one at Red Hill. Their only child, Rabon, often accompanied them to work. The family lay down roots in the cozy town; they became active in the local church of Christ, in the school, and in the community. People admired Ray and Eula's work ethic and their integrity. They made friends easily. They were themselves quite social. Ray even moved his baby brother in with them so he could encourage Al to take his GED and then later take a job with Ray for the thriving Braun Conglomerate. Life was good, but his career drive was not appeased in Beaux. He always left his options open to advancement.

In 1953, Eula awakened with intense abdominal pain. Ray grabbed her up, deposited her in the new Pontiac, and dropped Rabon off at his brother's house. Emergency gall bladder surgery was prescribed, a surgery which at that time required a ghastly cut from side to side like a secondary smile plastered on the sufferer's abdomen. As Eula drifted into anesthesia grogginess, she remembered Dr. Yoko asking her, laughingly, "Now, Eula, you aren't pregnant, are you?"

To which she replied, slurring her words, "No, sir, I've never been able to have but one child, and I don't use birth control either." And with that, she fell into the deep abyss of drug induced sleep.

She remembered later, or thought she remembered the doctor saying, "Oh, God, Nurse, she IS pregnant; I see the sac!" Upon awakened later in the fall afternoon, she kept this memory secret, feeling it was probably just a dream conjured up as she floated into sleep before surgery. However, Dr. Cara, a prominent physician in the 1950's, appeared at her side as she awakened from her deep sleep and gained her consciousness. He told her that, yes, she was indeed pregnant, but because of the close proximity of the surgical procedure to the baby's watery crib, the baby would self-abort. He prescribed complete bed rest when the disappointed Eula returned home, instructing her to call his office when she experienced excess vaginal bleeding or pain. Eula, logically, knew what the respected physician said, but emotionally, she reveled in the fact that she was pregnant after twelve years of barrenness. Her fervent prayers began right then in her hospital room; Ray joined her in those prayers as did their concerned families and friends. Her healthy daughter Jansey was delivered by a proud and surprised Dr. Cara on September 16 of 1953. In March of the next year, now Dr. Braun came calling to the Morris commissary. By June of the next year when Rabon had finished the school year, the Brauns were traveling highway 31 toward Red Hill, Alabama. Beaux's drive was revived.

The Beauxs moved into the wood inspector's house while the manager's house was being repainted for the new boss. Beaux did not delay in assuming his new position as plant manager at Red Hill. He hurriedly scheduled a meet and greet with the entire yard crew the Monday he arrived, leaving Eula and her sister Mae (who had moved to Red Hill with her husband to run the Braun commissary) to set up the household temporarily. Beaux clicked across the railroad tracks and into the black yard, cutting across to the cylinders, around the cranes, and eventually halting near the old steam engine's crew. Ray was dressed in starched work khakis, shaking hands and introducing himself as his blue black hair gleamed in the glaring sun. He paused for introductions and even fielded questions. The working men just followed him as he went so that when he arrived at the railroad track hut, he had a sizeable crowd behind him. As they stood around, a pale yellow Pontiac wheeled in on what seemed like two tires, dust blowing here and there; it was Mrs. Beaux. The new mother opened the heavy door and wielded a hand crafted white oak picnic basket full of steaming, cathead biscuits stuffed with deer sausage and accompanied with homemade apple jelly. She spied two sawhorses and the men, amazed at her quickness, located a piece of plywood to serve as a table. She, grinning and talking, flapped a red checkered tablecloth over the top, set out some paper napkins, and dropped the loaded basket onto the table. She waved goodbye, gave Ray a peck on the cheek, and jumped back into the car with her two children seated inside. The first day stamped a positive impression on the men. Even Beaux was surprised at his wife's resourcefulness.

J. Braun was more than pleased with his selection. Orders were coming in daily, and Beaux was exploring the idea of shipping Braun's products overseas. The men were offered overtime hours on the weekend when production was so overwhelming. Triple time and a half overtime pay was unheard of in the mid 50's and early 60's. Beaux increased minimum pay at the Red Hill plant, with J. Braun's approval. The morale boosting move forced the other four plants to do the same once the word got out. Red Hill residents were more than satisfied with their new boss and his innovative ideas. Although he did not dwell on his difficult past, the men sensed that he had been where they had been and his memory was still painfully sharp. Little did they know how many times the slender Beaux had cried in his sleep because of his gnawing hunger.

Ray Beaux knew what it meant to live in insufficient housing. Once he moved into the manager's company house, he conducted an impromptu tour of all the company houses in Red Hill, ordering updates and repairs; the Lloyd boys took notes and knew they had job security as the handymen for the company. He and his son cleaned up around the quarters with pendulum-like sling blades visible above the tall grass and brush, and Beaux's old trusty Toro push mower, operated by Beaux alone, thinned out the undergrowth between the rickety houses. The "colored" church was freshly painted and beautiful handmade pews replaced the concrete blocks used by the congregation for seating. Beaux employed his now forgiving father-in-law to make each one. Weeds were sprayed with creosote and pentachlorophenol (both of which are now declared as harmful and illegal to use) to discourage their future growth and the growth of bugs and other pests. Red Hill had never looked better, nor had it ever had such community pride. Beaux even scheduled Red Hill reunions and political rallies in the nondenominational church, which had also been renovated and updated with a Kraco sound system.

Beaux had once dreamed of becoming a medical doctor, but his raging poverty had squelched that dream long ago. However, he did have an opportunity to do some "doctoring" on the workers and residents in Red Hill. Braun dutifully provided company and family insurance, workmen's compensation, and even a skilled company physician, Dr. Davies; however, minor injuries were oftentimes treated in the back of the Braun office, and by Ray Beaux. The twenty-five mile trip into town to secure medical help was not desired by many of the injured; they trusted Beaux to clean wounds, to irrigate irritated eyes and ears, to relieve pain, and even to temporarily set bones and suture gaping wounds. It seemed as though their confidence in his folk medicine skill bolstered his ability and his willingness to tackle minor mishaps. On occasions, he insisted that the patient see the company doctor even after he himself had repaired the injury quite effectively; he cared deeply for his workers and their families. He was also quite discrete if a quarreling couple's arguments turned to physical blows; he would stitch and clean gashes without asking any details. Obviously, the situations were not job related, but again, he was trusted by the Red Hill residents, and he would not jeopardize that earned trust.

Once, a Mr. Willingham was gashed by an errant peavy hook. By this time, Rabon was a licensed driver and was working for his father when the boy wasn't in school. The elder Beaux gently positioned the injured man into the 1957 silver Chevy, the company car, and told Rabon to rush him to Dr. Davies' office, which had previously been alerted of their imminent arrival. Rabon, a typical sixteen-year-old, was saturated with adolescent adrenalin, and flew from the parking lot, leaving the onlookers gasping for air from the overpowering clouds of dust. As the two men traveled the crooked road to town, Rabon sped unskillfully along at 100 mph; he conquered an abrupt hill, unaware of the magnitude of a sharp right curve with a deep ravine attached to its mushy shoulder. Inexperience overpowered good sense, and the frightened driver hit the brakes and the accelerator simultaneously. Rabon and Mr. Willingham, petrified with fear, became airborne, eventually landed against a grove of thick pine trees, which mercifully broke their fall from the bottom of the ravine. Once the lodged vehicle ceased its teetering, Rabon found his voice and spoke. "Mr. Willingham, are you okay?" asked the frightened teenager. "I just have a brush burn on my arm. I think I can climb out my window, and when I do, I'll open my door and get you out," the shaky speaking Rabon declared. He took charge even though he was unsure of his next move.

"Oh, son, if you'll pull my good arm with you, we'll go out—first you and then me—through the window. I'm skeered that if'n you open your door, the weight may shift and the trees may give way. We don't want that, do we?" the older man calmly offered. "Then, we'll walk across the street—can you do that, Rabon-and call Mr. Beaux to come and get us. I don't 'spect I've got any broken bones; I think I can climb out," he offered as encouragement. "The Wheats live across the street; they'll let us use the phone. They got a brother who works for Braun."

Rabon attempted to roll down the window, but the handle was smashed and was pushed into the steering wheel. Having watched too many karate movies, he kicked the window, and amazingly, the window popped out. He quickly climbed out and was then able to open the car door from the outside. He reached back in and gently pulled Mr. Willingham out, carefully avoiding the hastily gauzed right arm of the injured man. As the two victims cleared the wrecked car, the pines cracked and the company car tumbled to the bottom of the heavy underbrush which completely concealed the depth of the ravine. Both survivors, sweating like bullets, leaned over to see the once cherished Chevy morph into what looked like crumpled aluminum foil. Hesitating for a thankful moment, the two stalked toward the Wheat house across the road. Neither spoke until they reached the other side of the busy highway.

"Well, Mr. Rabon, son, you best call Mr. Beaux. Don't put it off no longer," Mr. Willingham offered as they ascended the dilapidated porch steps. Rabon rapped on the wooden door, and when Mrs. Wheat answered it, preferring to remain behind the rusty screen door, Rabon anxiously explained his predicament to the somewhat reticent lady, who eventually opened the squeaky screen door decorated with faded pink flamingos and reluctantly allowed him into the hall of the dogtrot home to use the phone. Mr. Willingham, still standing, waited on the porch until Mrs. Wheat motioned for him to take a seat on the fragile swing while she fetched him some cold water. She noticed the blood soaked gauze on his arm and pitied the black man. She assumed his injuries were incurred during the auto accident. This was not the first time someone had missed the sharp curve; fortunately the boy had not ended up in the bottom of the ravine like the last driver. Where did the boy get gauze, she wondered. Maybe an emergency kit in the car?

In about fifteen minutes, Mr. Beaux swooped in, driving the company truck. He walked across the steaming road and he, too, leaned over to see the "Silver Ghost", as he called it, resting in its personal burial ground. Then immediately, he jogged back to the porch to check on the passenger. He knew the driver was scared, but unharmed because he had just hung up the phone with him. He saw Rabon sitting in a ladder back chair in the hall of the house. He headed for Mr. Willingham who was beginning to recover now from the heat, the fright, and his weakness from the loss of blood. "Will, how are you? Did my boy scare you to death? I'll just take you and Rabon on to Dr. Davies. We'll worry about the car later. I'm awfully sorry about this, Will," Beaux shook his head. Now was not the time to dress down his son; now was the time to act. He reached over the chain of the wooden swing with his strong, tanned arm to pull Will to his feet, but instead, Mr. Willingham stood up on his own power, looking his boss straight in the eyes.

"Mr. Beaux, I've had enough fast drivin' for one day. I 'spect you can clean up this gash and sew it up like you did Hosea's lip when his girlfriend bit it last weekend. I ain't a gettin' in no car to go to town today. I want to go back to Red Hill. Please, Mr. Beaux. Your son's done 'bout dashed me into eternity today," the strong, pleading man trembled as he presented his case. Will knew that all work related injuries had to be treated by Dr. Davies, especially if he were to qualify for workman's compensation. Will pleaded," My arm don't hurt, and I ain't a-gonna lay up in the quarters and not work. You fix me up, and I swear I'll be back on my shift tomorrow. You can 'splain to Doc, can't you?" Beaux nodded, looked down at his feet, and grinned. He didn't utter a word, but Mr. Willingham knew that his boss would honor his wish. Mrs. Wheat and Rabon helped the weak but smiling victim to the passenger's side of the pickup. Rabon, well aware of his position in this threesome right now, leaped over the tailgate into the back of the truck like a large pet dog, leaning against the window and for once, keeping his mouth closed. The blue Ford headed north to Red Hill. Will showed up for work the next morning, his newly wrapped arm supported by a strong blue sling. Rabon was grounded for a few weeks and time rolled forward like the old steam engine, slow and sure. Unfortunately, Rabon continued to exceed the speed limit even where there was no emergency.

Red Hill residents worked hard and played hard—literally. Music was an integral part of the weekends. The Rash family, a large, extended group, "played music" Friday and Saturday night. That's what the residents and the musicians called their outside concerts on the weekend. Despite the fact that the community center/nondenominational church would have been available and more than adequate for the gathering, the Rashes preferred to stage the events at various musicians' houses, sometimes spilling the crowd and the band onto the broom swept yards in winter and summer alike. Those individuals who were not musically gifted were more than willing to prepare culinary delights for the lively audience and the performing band; Red Hill ladies used the event as a venue for trying the newest recipes for pimento cheese sandwiches, southern desserts, and creamy dips while adding chips, sweet tea, and the latest pickle rendering from the most recent Home Demonstration Club meeting.

The Rash family not only played instruments well and sang beautifully; many of the older members were luthiers. The fiddles, guitars, mandolins, and other stringed instruments and even simple woodwinds were fashioned from mahogany and ash wood which had been used, saved, and shared in the family. Highly sophisticated wood carvings of deer, sheep, fish, and various wildlife faces and bodies were formed on the extremities of the instruments. However, paramount to the construction was the absolutely accurate resonance and melodious sound produced by the hand crafted unique treasures. The Rashes would not consider compromising carved beauty for accurate musicality; they were artists in both the visual and auditory. Eager audiences arrived early with cane-bottom chairs and loaded picnic baskets in hand to get coveted sites. The concerts began around seven and had no finishing time. Listeners left when they needed to put children to bed or prepare for an overtime Saturday, but there always remained a faithful few to usher in Red Hill's breathtaking dawn as the musicians sang in the sunrise. Many Red Hill children were rocked to sleep with the grand music of the Rashes.

The Rashes were a tightly knit group and seldom allowed an interloping musician into their harmonious circle. However, the exception was Rabon Beaux, not because he was the boss's son; he had an excellent musical ear. He played guitar, ukulele, mandolin, fiddle, saxophone, piano, and even sang adequately. Rabon first approached the eldest Rash brother, Ed, when, while working in the black yard the first week his father was hired at Braun, he commented on a Gibson guitar in the passenger side of Ed's old truck. By listening to the sophisticated manner in which Rabon talked about the hallowed instrument and music in general, Ed knew the thirteen-year-old would be able to hold his own in the group. He invited Rabon to the regularly scheduled practice on Thursday evening at JT's house. He had heard the tales of the boy's love for fast cars and his impulsive nature, but he sensed in Rabon an abiding knowledge and love of music; he wanted to see what he was made of, as older people said when determining the depth of someone's commitment to a certain talent.

Rabon arrived early, bringing an assortment of instruments: his grandmother's Kay guitar, a handcrafted mandolin, an Arthur Godfrey ukulele, and a cheap Woolsworth harmonica. The Rashes gave each other knowing looks and announced the first song, "It Wasn't God Who Made Honky-Tonk Angels" by Kitty Wells. Only a few bars were played before the Rashes were completely at home with the young musician. He had snatched up his guitar, tuned it, and kept the pace from the first of the song. Before even realizing the time, the group had practiced way past Rabon's curfew, and like a slight, unobtrusive apparition, Mr. Beaux appeared in the back yard, walking down from the only white house in the settlement. "I'm sorry, dad. I just got into the music and these guys are so cool; I just forget the time. I'm putting up my guitar now," the red-faced boy explained. His dad, wordless, but not overly disturbed, got in the car with Rabon, and the two became shadows as they slowly backed out of JT's driveway. No one seemed angry; Beaux appreciated his son's musical talent which came from Eula and her family. Beaux could only sing four notes, and certainly couldn't play an instrument. He did admire and support those who did, so Rabon was not punished for slightly extending his curfew. However, he was strongly reminded to watch his time a little closer from now on.

Rabon also wanted to learn how to make stringed instruments, so Ed and Joe, the elder brothers, invited him to the handyman shop after the Lloyds had locked up for the day. The father/son team had given the Rash brothers a key and just reminded them to relock when they left later at night. Rabon latched on every word and on the slighest move the elder craftsmen modeled. He had his father's hunger, but not for business advancement. He wanted to know how instruments were built correctly and beautifully. He was in the right place at the right time with the right people to apprentice wood carving and luthiering skills. His mind was quick, and he listened and watched intently as the older gentlemen explained every detail. Rabon then began to design and to craft his own ideas. He was a gifted child especially in the field of art. The carving and constructing of musical instruments just added another dimension to his artistry. He continued the desire as he grew, eventually building twelve string Spanish guitars and decorative zithers, but that desire had been birthed and reared here at Red Hill in a scattered carpenter's shop with two unskilled Braun workers who altered his life and encouraged him in music and visual art-both of which remained dear to him throughout his life.

Red Hill was a low crime area as were most southern, rural locations during the '50s and '60s, but it also provided a haven for pranksters and small town crooks—mostly young, inexperienced drivers who had something to prove on the weekend. The Small brothers were such individuals who took great joy in flying through Red Hill streets, screeching tires as their old Buick barely rounded the hairpin curve by Uncle James's little company house, and finally, straightening up their latest hotrod for the stretch to the commissary. Upon reaching the wooden store, the devious fellows pulled the car around toward the left side of it and barreled headlong into the creosoted lumber walls. The continual and increasingly harder force scrambled, bent, and dropped the canned goods which had been neatly stocked on wooden shelves by Mae and her husband Chuck Bell, kinsfolk of the Beaux family.

After the Smalls tired of that activity, the driver, Oz Small would back up the souped up, old jalopy and purposely aim for the back of the commissary where the boxes and other garbage items were stored in a wire compost area. He rammed into this until most of the contents were scattered onto the neatly mowed and groomed back. The final piece of the weekend ritual was to cut doughnuts around the gas pumps; this time with Swig at the wheel. The Red Hill run became a common routine on Friday night. Each Saturday morning, reluctantly, the Bells would reorganize the chaotic cans, pick up the trash in the back, and begin their day. Obviously, the clean up was wearisome for the young store managers. No one was sure exactly how to amend the situation, but the situation actually corrected itself in a gruesome manner.

One cold, misty Friday night around midnight in March of 1959, Oz and Swig raced down the paved road from the two mile sign by the highway, and they barreled around the slight, subtle curve by the Simpsons' farmhouse as they had done numerous times in the past without incident. The old car swerved, and Oz, under the influence and with his reaction time out of sync, jerked the heavy steering wheel too far causing the metal monster to exit the road and ram into a Braun branded utility pole. When struck at such a speed and with such a force, the pole cracked and fell straight over the car's roof, penning the unsuspecting Oz and his passenger and brother Swig in the vehicle. Horrifying screams permeated the midnight air, and even though the accident was about a mile out of Red Hill, Ray Beaux, a light sleeper, awakened to a human's horrendous yelps of agony.

Beaux grabbed his pressed khakis laid out for the next day's work, slipped on his shoes, and literally ran down to the accident, not even bothering to crank his car. He ran as quickly as any track runner could. When he arrived, breathless and sweaty, on the grisly scene, other sleepy Red Hill residents had begun to arrive, wisely choosing their vehicles to get them from their cozy beds to the scene of the accident; some still dressed in jersey pajamas and terrycloth robes. All stood aghast as they stared at the gnarled mess in the grass clumped ditch. There were no ambulances or paramedics in rural Alabama at the time. The situation would have to be handled by these same people who stood in their night clothes. The shocked looks on the still sleepy faces of the bystanders were similar to those viewing a horror picture for the first time. Everyone stared at Beaux for a directive.

"Fix it, Mr. Beaux. You know what to do. They ain't got a chance without you a'goin' in and getting them out," Mr. Cross, a shy railroad worker who trusted his boss implicitly, hollered across the mumbling crowd. Beaux knew the victims' injuries were well beyond his self-taught medical skills and possibly beyond those much more educated in medicine than he. It appeared that Oz was driving and may have been killed on impact, but it was difficult to determine with mangled metal and mangled humans co-mingled.

Ray Beaux looked through his flashing blue eyes at the crowd, scanning for a solution. He recognized the majority of his railroad crew in the motionless group. "Come on, Railroad! Let's move the pole over and maybe we can see what we need to do," Red Hill's faux mayor declared. Mrs. George, an onlooker who was known for her organizational skills and her continual quest for cleanliness, volunteered to heat some water and borrow some towels from the Simpsons who were viewing the scene from their lean-to porch. She was willing to carry out the gory task of cleaning whatever wounds were visible once the men's bodies were liberated from the twisted car. She ran toward the farmhouse as Mrs. Simpson disappeared inside to gather towels and to heat water.

Mrs. George quickly returned to the accident scene, armed with her cleaning supplies provided by the Simpsons. About the same time as she returned, the railroad men, brawny and reliable, had just rolled over the broken pole into the clear side of the ditch. The six men next gingerly pulled the elder Small boy's limp and bloody frame from the grasp of the shattered windshield glass and steering wheel entrapment. Beaux checked the almost unrecognizable Oz's pulse and his caved in chest for any sign of breathing. Although Beaux silently acknowledged the glaring truth that no life remained within the young man, he gently moved him, with the help of some of the crew, to the dew laden grass near some early daffodils on the Simpsons' manicured lawn. Ruby George, anticipating the grisly outcome, had thoughtfully borrowed a clean white sheet from Betty Simpson's fresh laundry basket which she willingly relinquished as she, too, had predicted the worse. The sheet was lovingly placed over the very obviously deceased troublemaker. None of the weak quality of his character mattered now; he was Mrs. Small's beloved son, and her agony would be so great that to honor her, Ruby would shield the deceased adolescent from the cruel cold of the night.

After a moment of modest respect and mute sorrow, the chilly crowd now shifted its interest to Swig, hoping a glimmer of life would appear in him despite his visually obvious, massive injuries and his possible undetermined internal damage. Quickly, the overall morale of the townspeople boosted when Mr. Beaux breathlessly announced, "Swig's breathing and he's coming to!" Again, the valiant crew stepped forward ready to remove or to extract whatever trapped the passenger who had just awakened and had begun to scream soundlessly, thrashing his bloody head from side to side as if being physically slapped by an invisible and angry hand.

"Son, Son, it's Mr. Beaux. I'm here to get you out of here and to the hospital," Beaux spoke clearly as he patted the trembling hand of the battered boy who routinely rattled the commissary cans every weekend and was most likely headed that way with his now dead brother this fateful night. "Just lay back and Mrs. Ruby will clean you up a bit; you don't want to mess up Old Blue, do you?" Beaux chuckled to lighten the mood by mentioning the old company truck by its familiar nickname. Beaux remembered that he had arrived here by foot, so he'd have to send someone back to his house to retrieve the makeshift ambulance for Swig. The debris was removed, but Beaux's untrained medical sense still warned him and prevented him from moving a broken body. Ruby lightly patted the bloody places and then wrapped the young offender in a clean, but faded handmade quilt that she always kept in her car. She knew he could easily suffer from shock if he remained here cold and unattended. Before Ruby shut her car door back, Beaux asked Ruby's husband, Darrell, to bring the company truck (Old Blue) to the accident scene. He was to pick up Eula, too, who would drive the Georges' car, leaving Rabon to stay with Jansey. He knew his bride was awake as she always was when he slipped out of their four poster bed; they operated as one person.

Beaux continued to pat Swig's hand with his own small but powerful hands, an act which seemed to have a calming effect on the frightened boy. Swig ceased jerking his gashed and swollen head, instead choosing to slump his whole body over on Mrs. George's lap. She placed her hand knit sweater under his wobbly head to cushion it and to keep it from becoming damp from the night's dew. Beaux released Swig's hand and gently checked his body for broken bones, lacerations, and anything that might cause additional injury if his body were to be moved. As Ray moved closer in with his own white, ironed handkerchief to wipe the fountain of blood pouring from Swig's head, Beaux and Ruby noticed the handkerchief had all but disappeared into the crimson crater with a nauseating, sucking sound. The massive head injury was not a positive sign and both of them knew it all too well. He might survive, but what would be his quality of life with this damage to his brain?

After a silent prayer and against his better folk medicine judgment, Beaux with Mr. Cross, the railroad crew's strongest member, slid the boy's fading body into the car's back seat, now allowing Swig the opportunity to stretch out. Swig, remaining partially conscious, did not utter so much as a grunt or whine during the life threatening move; but in his gut, Beaux truly felt the move would provide the lone survivor a more comfortable place to lay while "Big Un" Lloyd drove down Sipsey Road to fetch Dr. Gwin, a community doctor of little note but whose proximity gave him an advantage over Dr. Davies. Lloyd and most of the bystanders sensed there was little chance of survival now after witnessing the distressing head wound scene. The little more than a child was in the balance between this world and the next; his brother had already narrowed his options.

Dr. Gwin drove his own red Ford Falcon, following Mr. Lloyd to the accident scene. He was quite familiar with the victim and his brother; for, he had sewn them both up numerous times after fist fights with their father or other rowdy relatives. He knew the boys had escalated their drinking since Oz had his driver's license, and he was also aware that the erratic brothers frequented the Mayfield's drinking parlor in the Moore's Mill community. Old Mr. Mayfield never passed up an opportunity to sell illegal whiskey, regardless of the partaker's age. If the fellow had the cash, he would provide the poison. Dr. Gwin had predicted that this dreadful day would come to his sunny little wife just this morning at the breakfast table as they discussed the empty bottles accumulating in the Smalls' cluttered yard which adjoined the Gwins' property. "Honey, I'm afraid that the next time you see them boys, it'll be them lyin' acorpse," she declared to her husband as he shook his head at such a waste of young lives.

When Dr. Gwin pushed himself from his compact car onto the Simpsons' property, he could tell from the Red Hill folks' stricken faces that the scene was as bad, or worse, than he and his missus had sadly predicted. One white lump lay on the dew laden grass while another was casually casketed in the back seat of the wrecked Buick; that one was also swaddled in cover-Mrs. George's tulip printed blanket. The corpulent doctor tottered over to the ditch, ignoring the first white lump and concentrating on the flowered one. "Son, can you hear me?" Gwin asked. He could see the mammoth head wound. He began to examine the crumpled body. There appeared to be a few broken ribs, some contusions, and some mild lacerations, but the doctor knew Swig's internal injuries were quite likely but undetectable here without x-rays. He repeated, "Son, Swig, can you hear me? You know me, Doc Gwin? I fixed you and your brother up just about a week ago. Now, we're fixin' to move you to the back of Mr. Beaux's truck. We're going to put a mattress back there and blankets to keep you warm. Mrs. Ruby?" She nodded. "Mrs. Ruby's goin' to ride with you and we'll get you fixed up at the hospital. I can't do no more without some tests, okay?" the country doctor asked the nonresponsive young man. "Mrs. Simpson", he beckoned the woman who now almost leaped from the porch steps to assist the doctor. He continued his orders. "Mrs. Simpson, you and your husband get your top mattress and put it on the trunk of the car. Gather some blankets and a pillow, too. Don't' worry about the mattress. It can be cleaned up and returned to you. I have no time to argue!" The farmer and his wife wordless obeyed and Ruby held up the blankets.

Mr. Beaux positioned the company truck side by side with the Smalls' Buick. The doctor's plan was to slip the mattress under the victim and then have the railroad crew gently place the mattress in the bed of the truck. That was the best he could to do to fashion a makeshift gurney. Then, he requested Mr. Beaux to drive while he accompanied him while Mrs. George rode in the back. It was a long shot, but it was the best idea among them. With the car and crew now in position, Mr. Beaux spoke, "I want you all to pray for this young man, regardless of what he's done. And pray that we can get him to the hospital in time." With that being said, the doctor spoke again, this time addressing the railroad crew.

"On count three, Beaux and Mr. Cross, you two lightly lift Swig. At the same time, James and Slim, you slide the mattress under him, and then all four of you position yourselves at the four corners and slowly place the mattress in the bed of the truck. Ready? One...Two...Three ". The procedure took less than a minute. Beaux and Dr. Gwin hopped in the cab, and Ruby climbed over the tailgate and sat next to the low moaning child. Now, to get to the hospital without incident, the doctor thought. He knew there wasn't a snow-ball's chance in Hell that Mrs. Small wouldn't be childless in a few hours. The blue truck sped away leaving the worried crowd to return home and wait. Beaux had already told Lee Earl to get the word around about no work this dreary morning. Now, the waiting began.

The crowd dispersed, walking as if in a trance. Eula stood near the cold body of Oz as Mr. Simpson called the funeral home. She was thinking. Who's going to tell Mrs. Small? It was a rhetorical question. She asked Mr. Cross, who was standing beside her, "Would you take me up to Mary Small's? She needs to hear the truth from me before some gossipy neighbor drops by. She deserves that much respect. Then, you and I will carry her to the hospital to see her re-maining child while, hopefully, he is still alive." The dreaded plan, although right, drained the morning's energy from Eula, but she revved herself up again to face Mrs. Small. Mr. Cross opened the door of his dusty green Impala and robotically, Eula got in. He walked around the front of the grill and seated himself. Off the unlikely pair headed to bear news which would render unfathomable emotional pain, but the two accepted their mission passively and without discussion. Red Hill strength was indomitable.

Swig lived! The homemade ambulance crew delivered him speedily and safely. Dr. Gwin was later publically recognized for saving Swig's life. He was not unscathed, of course. He had suffered two broken ribs, a punctured kidney, some bruises and scratches, and the head wound caused overwhelming memory loss and petit mal seizures partially controlled by phenobarbital. He was mentally unable to finish school, and he lived peacefully, sharing a home with his grateful and loving mother without carrying on any additional vandalism. His elder brother was buried at Bethany, and his mother consoled herself with the reality that at least one son survived. Swig and Oz's father loaded his twenty-two, tied a string to the trigger, and fired the weapon under his chin upon hearing the news about Oz-his favorite son of the two. He wasn't mourned; his passing simplified Mrs. Small's life. Rumor had it that Swig "found Jesus in the cornfield while pulling field corn and he got saved". No one actually verified the facts of his conversion. An old neighbor summed it up this way: "Well, it don't matter. He'll go in through the fool's hole anyhow because of his condition!" Red Hill residents paused and reflected on the wreck and its severe consequences as they polished off their lunches before the whistle blew, but then they decidedly moved on. After all, he wasn't really *from* Red Hill. If you lived past the two mile side toward the highway or further, you were not truly from Red Hill. You hadn't actually earned a place in permanent memory.

Wrecks, murders, rapes, robbery, incest and other dastardly behavior sometimes characterized life in Red Hill but no more common than in any other small town or large city. Interrupting everyday humdrumness, the hint of evil was easily spread and thoroughly discussed like the possibility of off-brand mayonnaise replacing the leading favorite—debated and generally rejected. Red Hill was not a place of violence; it was a place of simple living. Problems were just considered part of the world which had been introduced by distasteful choices in the Garden. Excesses of the basest nature of man caused unlawfulness. "Temperance in all things" directed one toward sound advice, regardless of religious fervor or the lack of it.

One of the strangest events involving both murder and secrecy actually occurred prior to Mr. Beaux's employment; yet, Red Hill residents continued to talk about it years after the fact. A lean, lanky man named Amos Beam moved to Red Hill after he had interviewed well and was hired by a then young Mr. Lang, Beaux's predecessor. He and his wife Laura, an extremely devout Pentecostal woman, moved into one of the best company houses on the front street.

Amos and Laura already had five children when they settled into House #14, complete with indoor plumbing and recent renovation. A short two years after establishing themselves as residents, two more Beam children were added. Laura's firm and quite vocal religious views were somewhat eschewed from that of the average charismatic believers in Red Hill or nearby Bethsaida. Her particular creed drifted away from the general Pentecostal beliefs and differed in the following issues: the refusal for medical treatment, the rejection of birth control methods, and the total, absolute sovereignty of the preacher. Finding the nondenominational church group inadequate, Laura had urgently and quickly proselyted around twenty or so residents, forming her own church, and she convinced one of the young, handsome male members that, through her holy vision, God had called him to preach the Word. Even though he was the "ordained by Laura" minister, it was obvious to the community and to the some of the members that Laura controlled the emotionally charged church and the young preacher like a twisted and perverted puppeteer. Oddly, though purposely in control, Laura willingly yielded without question to the preacher's final say in every situation-once she had convinced him of "his" stand on that particular issue. She was a woman of dual nature-divinely subversive and submissively controlling.

Because of Laura's blind loyalty to her personal Rasputin, who just happened to possess a matinee idol countenance, she acknowledged him as the absolute authority on any subject ranging from tips for planting corn, to the improvement of personal hygiene practices, and even in the realm of sexual experimentation outside the bonds of holy matrimony-especially Laura's. In her mind, she justified her extreme dedication to her lover by rationalizing:" I am presenting

myself a living sacrifice to a man of God. It cannot be a sin or a taboo." Guided, or misguided by her own delusional thinking, Laura
continued frequent clandestine meetings with the Reverend Pallister
and soon found herself pregnant. She knew it was the Reverend's
child because she had been over-nursing the last spawn of Amos as
an excuse to abstain from her husband's sexual advances. He had
kindly rolled over in the crumpled, feather bed and cared for his own
needs without disturbing his tired spouse. He recognized that she
was overworked, and yet, strangely, her energy level was amazing
high, especially in church activities. What drove her, he wondered.

Amos was not a Pentecostal church member or any other kind of
church member, but he was a spiritual man in his own way. He gladly
stayed at home during Laura's church meetings to care for any sick
child or newborn too young to be out, (Seven children made odds
high that each service someone would be sick or newborn). When
the church was first formed, Laura paraded all the children into
church, but after laboring through that unsuccessful task a few Sun-
days, she thankfully left some or all of the children with Amos, who
happily adjusted his chore schedule to meet the needs of his own little flock while his zealous wife walked down to the little Spirit-filled
church building fashioned from Braun scrap lumber and planted on a
weeded and vacant lot near the commissary. He noticed when Laura
returned home perspiring even in winter and animated in her speech,
the trait of exhilaration did not transcend into the bedroom; only her
extreme exhaustion was lasting.

As spring melted into summer, Laura's precarious condition was
becoming more obvious as the basketball bump straining her cotton
sack house dress distorted her extremely thin silhouette. No one suspected anything sinister; after all, the woman was obviously fertile.
Surprisingly, Laura seemed more content with her new life in Red Hill
than in the two years before. The innnocents of the community were
openly complimentary of Laura's calm demeanor as she worked in her
postage stamp sized garden behind the over packed little house. Amos
dismissed his inner doubts and continued to work faithfully every day
at Braun. He commented on Laura's renewed, pleasant nature to his

friendly co-workers. He proudly showed off his delicious lunches lovingly prepared by his affable wife. He talked more to the curious men on the yard; they got somewhat of an insight on the reserved man himself. He shared humorous stories about his many children and listened patiently to other men as they talked. But then, the majority of the Braun workers did not attend Reverend Pallister's church, so they were blind to the emotional frenzy of his preaching and the glazed eyes of his most devout sister.

But, as August came to Red Hill with an exhausting blast of dry, summer heat, Laura lost her sunshine smile and was miserable as her belly swelled to beach ball proportion. As residents passed the Beams' wide porch daily, they saw a different Laura, lethargic and enfeebled as she stretched her sweaty frame across the rickety swing while the seven little ones played in the dirt-packed and garbage strewn front yard. The once thriving garden she had so lovingly tended had shriveled up from intense heat and deliberate neglect. She had lost that attractive, yet illicit maternal glow, replacing it with a deep scowl. Her flaccid arms and legs were now stick-thin and her face was drawn and haggard. Her numerous children were carelessly left to their own devices, eating whatever was available and scuffling in the yard as Laura barked ineffective edicts. Amos, dutiful as ever, returned from work to face an ill tempered wife, brawling offspring, an insurmountable pile of soured laundry, a urine smelling house, and an absence of any food for the family's supper. He collectively hosed the children off and, with a dingy dishtowel, he hastily patted down the bigger children and ordered them to the commissary to get bologna and bread while he bathed the smaller ones in a #2 washtub, drying them all with the same stiff towel which smelled of mold and mildew. "This, too, will pass," he thought. Not soon enough for Laura.

On August 31st, a premature, but refreshing, fall breeze greeted the early risers at Red Hill. Many residents enjoyed their morning Chase & Sanborn on the screened in porch, but at the Beam house, Laura was ranting and shaking her sleepy husband by his wide shoulders. "Go get somebody-anybody. My water's done broke and I'm havin' this youngun!" Laura yelled, her ripe body convulsing in labor pains. The pains were rhythmic and fierce. Mrs. Barr, strolling on the main road for her morning walk, heard the woman's pleas and bravely stepped up on the porch. Laura's screaming subsided long enough to address the concerned neighbor. "Oh, Mrs. Barr, please help me. This one's harder than the other seven. Could you stay with the children, or could you just get them out of here?" Laura's voice morphed into a kind one as she begged her neighbor for help. The anguished woman arched her back and screamed again before speaking. Where'd Amos go to?" she roared as her voice changed back to a diabolical growl.

"Oh, Laura," the kind voice spoke. "Don't worry. I'll get my grown daughter who's visiting this week to help me. I'll take them back to my house, feed them, and you just worry 'bout birthing little Number Eight!" Mrs. Barr assured the frantic soul. She roused the older Beam children to help her carry the smaller ones back to her house in the old boarding house by the community church. She remembered Laura's question about Amos as she led the sleepy caravan of children out the door, "Your husband is next door at the Mills' using the telephone to call the midwife at Bethsaida. She brought in your last two, right? She delivered mine, too. She will be here soon. Breathe deep and pray, honey." Mrs.Barr grinned to herself. SHE, who had only delivered two babies to term, was rendering advice to someone delivering her eighth! She paused slightly, but remembered her overwhelming task at hand and like Moses, she delivered the children back to her Promised Land to feed them well, to bathe them, and to give them a little extra attention which they probably all desperately needed. Thank goodness her daughter Carol was still visiting! Seven mouths to feed, seven bodies to bathe, and fourteen legs to keep on her property and out of Red Hill's street!

The mid-wife soon arrived in a long, red late model Cadillac almost before Amos returned from the Mills' place. She was well known, respected, and compensated quite well for her excellent service. The infant was already crowning when Amos brought in the traditional, but unnecessary, towels, hastily boiled some water, and was immediately dismissed to the porch as was the custom at that time. Meanwhile, in the untidy bedroom, with one last push and a blood curdling scream, little Piety Ann Beam was ushered in as Red Hill's newest native resident. Amos breathed a sigh of relief. Each child's birth was faster than the child born before. The wise Indian woman hoped for Amos's sake that Laura would consider slowing down on her church's strict adherence to the Biblical command of being fruitful and multiplying!

The Cherokee mid-wife grunted as she placed the curly blonde headed, blue eyed child into the exhausted mother's arms. She recognized Laura and Amos as half-breed Choctaw themselves whose ancestors had settled around the Luxapalia River in nearby Frank County. Wisely, she kept her tongue, but she knew Piety Anne was going to cause a stir in this little community that joined her own property by the swamp. She held her dark, withered hand out to Amos and he flipped out $60. As most Native American people are able to do, she had sized up the financial situation when she had served the family twice before. She laid the cash on the cluttered kitchen counter and wordlessly, exited through the bashed kitchen door in the back of the unkempt house. No use squeezing blood from a turnip, she thought. This family, she thought, as she headed her luxury vehicle back to the murky swampland, would have enough conflict over the birth of a child, who was obviously not Amos's, without the additional burden of cash flow. The father's identity was of no concern to her. Still, even in her secluded lair, she had overheard Red Hill talk as the women, searching for healing herbs and edible plants, wandered near the border of her land. She could have prevented this unwanted birth if Laura had come to her early in her pregnancy, the old Indian thought. Church people!

Amos appeared thrilled with the little stranger's birth. He lovingly cradled her and displayed no shock, disappointment, or anger at her unusual coloring, choosing instead to rock Piety Ann for about an hour, before reluctantly surrendering the baby back to her recovering mother. He soundly planted a kiss on the sweaty forehead of his bride. She grinned weakly and both mother and child fell asleep. He sauntered toward the porch and seemed lost in his thoughts. Laura was left to begin the nursing process and to ponder her predicament. Surely, Laura thought, Amos knew, and right now, she didn't care. She had birthed a child of her beloved reverend—a holy child of a man of God. She actually thought herself as forgiven—no, not just forgiven-blessed and honored for Piety Ann's existence.

Laura, young and full of life even after eight births, easily recovered and her "lying in" was brief with so many other responsibilities to tackle at home. Life began to return to the familiar patterns prior to the pregnancy; Laura's cheery attitude returned and she diligently cleaned, cooked, cared for the children, and regularly attended her beloved church. She ceased worrying about what Amos thought; he seldom spoke but remained devoted to Piety as he was to the whole Beam gaggle. As Baby Piety Anne became old enough to venture out of the house, Laura insisted on taking only this infant to church, choosing to leave the other seven hanging onto the stair railing, crying after her as she left them in Amos's care. It seemed to neighbors that Piety was the pick of the litter –even over her own husband, Amos. And when the residents took one glance at the angelic baby, suspicions immediately loomed in their minds like dark storm clouds forming over the edible clay mountain in Red Hill. Who was this baby? The Pallister genes were quite recognizable in those individuals who had them. Many of the elderly residents remembered Old Mrs. Pallister, Billy Pallister's irascible mother, who, even in her advanced age, was still alarmingly beautiful with her long blond tresses and her piercing blue eyes. Yep, there was definitely a resemblance to Piety, they surmised.

Around the first of the New Year, scarlet fever ominously swirled into Red Hill, indiscriminately sweeping up children and adults alike; it left many sorrowing families with an empty chair at their dinner table. Some victims died almost overnight while more unfortunate others lingered as they contracting secondary illnesses such as pneumonia and dysentery in their weakened state. Gravediggers struggled to plunge the many shovels into the frozen Alabama dirt. The robust Braun foreman, Gregory, reported to work at 6 as usual, but by mid-morning, his congestion was unbearable, forcing him to take an early

lunch break at 10. By suppertime of the same day, Dr. Gwin had pronounced him dead. Panic and fear spread through Red Hill. Others
fell like tall, formidable oak trees which had been suddenly struck
with a strange and foreign blight, quickly deteriorating to skeletal
remains. Family members, shocked and broken, wandered around the
mud-frozen streets of Red Hill, mourning their losses together in
small groups around an outside fire on the community center/church
landscape.

The self confident reverend pounced onto the awaiting stage of
the already escalating health drama. He succumbed to his own car-
nivorous ego when an opportunity arose to incite controversy and to
share in the limelight surrounding it. He couldn't resist the opportunity to grandstand. Of course, Laura encouraged him. She fueled
his self serving power. "Come on, Brother Billy, you know you have
the answer; God talks to you every day! Tell them what they need to
do to save their families from the wicked curse of sickness," Laura
shouted, plenty loud enough for the gathering group to hear. She had
blatantly continued her tryst with Brother Billy, but now, in addition
to her usual look of unnatural lust, she also wore a defiant look that
unsuccessfully camouflaged that unbridled passion for the young
man of the cloth, a fact that was equally obvious and repugnant to
the conservative residents. Many Braun workers felt pity for Amos as
he continued to quietly work and care for his large family, but their
attitude toward Laura was quite the opposite. As a crowd, mostly of
his congregation, gathered, the red-faced handsome preacher began
to speak with confidence. "Tell it, O, Man of God," Laura commanded. That affirmation was the only encouragement he needed to
snatch the stage.

"If you have enough faith in the Lord Jesus to heal you, you'll not
need no doctor nor his fancy magical healing tools and vile medicine.
Medicine and science is of the devil—diviners!" Billy began. " Pray
and wait, I say!" the reverend continued indignantly, shaking his fist
and left leg in an Elvis fashion as he rattled the pine steps of the
nondenominational church, the center of Red Hill community life.
Laura, at first enjoyed the hype of the tragedy, but soon she felt her

neighbors' judging eyes burn through her thin, dark hide, so she guiltily returned home from the impromptu rally to pray for her own children waiting at home. She shared the preacher's dangerous advice with Amos who chose wisely to stay away from the mob. She reinforced Billy's admonition--the illness was the work of the devil; only prayer and the reverend's intervention could stop the death train. For the first time in their marriage, Amos turned his weathered face toward his wife's and yanked her ear to his straight, tight mouth. She knew he had never been a violent man, but she was unnerved by his glare. He narrowed his coal black eyes and began to speak in a low voice.

"You're crazy, woman. You don't think I know nothing, but still waters run deep, and I know what you're doing, you and your godly preacher," he whispered in her ear. He started to continue, but checked himself, let go of her reddened ear, and stalked away. Laura was left speechless, slipping into the children's adjoining bedrooms to check on them as they rested without incident.

Night fell hard on Red Hill that night and after the "revival" broke up, people scurried like startled mice into their tiny holes to take refuge from the January wind. Down the road, dim lights were visible in almost all the houses of the frightened residents. They had partially heeded the good reverend's advice; they were indeed praying, but rather than depending on their own levels of faithfulness for healing, concerned parents were welcoming the house calls of Dr. Gwin or Dr. Davies who equally provided encouragement and life giving medicine to the fever victims. Both worried physicians drove into Red Hill, dividing the cases between them to ensure that all the victims' conditions had been analyzed and treated with various medical options: prescription drugs, injections, hospital referrals and professional advice. Only at the houses of the faithful few of Brother Billy's church were the thick, wooden doors slammed in the shocked faces of these two medical heroes. "Our faith will save our loved ones!" they declared. Of course, Laura endorsed her lover's gospel, but her faith had not actually been tested yet; the Beam children had not shown any signs of scarlet fever. Her husband was not in agreement with Billy Pallister and expressed that concern to Laura, but he could not dissuade his wife from her religious conviction. Fortunately, at this point, it wasn't an issue.

Little Piety Anne awakened around two in the morning with a deep sounding cough accompanied by a phlegmatic rattle. Laura, startled, rushed over to the handmade wicker crib which was positioned at the footboard of the massive oak bed. The infant was twisting and turning; Laura touched her fevered forehead and confirmed her suspicions; the fever had hit the Beam household. Soon, the other seven Beam children one by one joined in the barking chorus first began by the youngest. All seven children slept in two four poster beds in the kids' room. The oldest three slept by the door; the youngest four slept near the fireplace. The putrid smell of sickness seeped through the walls, the floors, and even into the kitchen. Children moaned, cried, coughed, and vomited in shifts. Amos rocked some, switched to those who were worse, while Laura focused only on Piety.

"Oh! Amos! Laura anguished as if starring in a daytime soap. "We've got to pray for more faith. We will win this battle over Satan if we can get more faith!" Laura rationalized. Amos was never opposed to prayer, but he didn't feel that his precious babies' lives were totally contingent on his or Laura's measure of faith. He gently placed three of his stricken children onto the quilt covered couch and headed straight for the front door. He knew Dr. Davies was next door at the Mills'. He'd seen his headlights when the exhausted doctor pulled in about thirty minutes before. He was tired of medical care choices being dependent on the advice of a shyster preacher.

Laura, anticipating her husband's next move, protested loudly, "No, no, Amos! Calling the worldly doctor with his witch potions would just prove our lack of faith in God. It's the devil in them children; he's a'testin' us!" she declared, almost hysterically. "I'm calling Reverend Billy. He's a holy man. You heard him yesterday afternoon. Maybe he could call a few of my sisters in the Lord to come and pray with us—a prayer vigil. Yes, that's what we need. A prayer vigil right in this house! Amos, stoke up the fire," Laura prescribed with resolve. Before Amos could grab her hand, Laura raced out the door and into the biting cold to share her plan with Reverend Billy who was still at the church after the rally. Amos flopped lifeless onto the tattered rocker. Laura didn't even bother to use the phone next door to summon up her own church angels for fear the doctor there would attempt to block her mission. Soon the bald, winter yard filled up with Billy and his ardent parishioners. Amos was beyond irate, but again, remained silent in his rage. His rage, sensed by the congregation, garrisoned them away from the front door. The shouting and praying faithful, instead, safely chose to encircle the front yard as they rocked back and forth not unlike some mentally disturbed individuals who were experiencing sudden anxiety.

Loud moaning, wailing, and simultaneous prayers formed dissonant chords which echoed in the swampy bottoms of Red Hill. Neighbors felt a mixture of pity and disgust for the Beam family as the vigil languished on into the next day and the next. Amos continued to part through the religious wave like a man running the gauntlet as he left for work exactly like the other male members of the hard working community. The Red Hill women not involved in this twisted carnival-like scenario wisely kept their doors sealed and the faces inside their homes, rather than to watch the lunatic circus unfold in Laura's yard. Meanwhile, Billy and the raw-boned pale pianist, Lucy, led the devout prayer warriors who afforded Billy his easy life by sacrificing even to the point of half-starvation, and he continued to fuel the mostly women crowd into emotional bedlam. The unnerved community just wanted the depraved band to dissipate. It weighed on them all like an improperly fitting winter coat, heavy and uncomfortable. At wit's end, Mrs. Gray and Mr. Wheat, two well respected, logical residents and loyal Braun employees, earnestly petitioned Lang to declare this unnatural display of a perverted religious caucus a public nuisance, calling on the introverted Mr. Lang to insist that Mrs. Beam allow one of the doctors in to treat her stricken children.

As much as Mr. Lang agreed with the caring and concerned neighbors, he was also aware of the delicate balance between disturbing the peace and disturbing the Pentecostals-especially this group. Unfortunately, he was not afforded the opportunity to finalize his decision to Gray and Wheat. As early dawn approached on that frigid January

Saturday, almost a week into the faith farce, each Beam child, including Little Piety defied the corporate and individual prayer requests and returned untreated to their Maker. Suffering the inability to breathe, struggling to live without medical aid or even professional medical advice, seven little dark headed angels and one little blond cherub breathed their last—their breathing becoming so shallow that it was virtually undetectable. In a burst of passion or anguish or both, Laura tore out of the fever infested house screaming, "It was Amos. It was Amos. He had no faith. He killed my babies!" As she rushed out into the freezing arms of her church sisters, who were not so consoling, they, too, realized that Laura was hysterical and was using religion as a powerful whip to beat down her already shattered husband. During the hooplah, Dr. Gwin slipped in the back through the Beams' kitchen to verify the actual condition of the fallen babies. They had unnecessarily perished from this earth.

Even Laura's church members were appalled by her declaration of Amos's responsibility for the Beam children's deaths. They gently pulled away from her emaciated body, and mumbling under their breath, tucked their tails and headed home like beaten dogs. Laura now stood alone in her empty yard. "Brother Billy, Brother Billy, come tell them the truth. It was Amos. It was Amos and his unbelief that took my babies from me. You know if he'd been a church going man, we'd still have our angels. Tell him what God told you; tell him!" she shouted and her lone voice echoed throughout the settlement. But, for once, the usually boisterous Billy Pallister shunned the limelight, choosing rather to hide in his church office like a cornered, rabid animal. There was dead silence for what seemed like forever, but which was probably only a minute or two. Cutting the cold silence, Mr. Lang now stepped up to the raving mother. Billy peered out his office curtains, craning his neck to hear without being seen. What would Lang say?

"Now, wait," Lang, physically repulsed by the devastating scene, began. "They just didn't get the help they needed, Mrs. Beam. Don't blame your husband who's hurting as bad as you are. Perhaps they were beyond the doctor's help from the beginning; we don't know. We do know that they are not suffering as they sleep on the Savior's breast." Mumbles of agreement could be heard from the Grays and the Paters who were still standing across the road near the swamp bank. "Let's just all go back home and get some sleep. This is awful, but it is over. We'll make our plans in the morning. Doc, can you help us with the precious ones?"Lang asked Dr. Gwin, who was now joined by Dr. Davies, both large men weeping like children the age of those who lay lifeless in the Beams' unnaturally quiet house. Almost on cue, Dr. Gwin then loaded his camera and quickly snapped a final picture of each of the little ones, as was the custom in some rural areas. Next, with the help of Mr. Pater and Mr. Gray, two lingering neighbors, the silent group organized themselves to commence stacking the little, limp bodies up on the porch for transporting them to the nearest funeral home; for the poor often chose to bury their dead without embalming them to save heavy funeral costs. Grizzly duties for these men, for sure, but necessary. Mr. Gray and Mr. Pater stepped forward and lovingly lifted the tiny, still warm bodies of the eight little ones. Laura collapsed on the swing and Amos pulled her upright and joined his wife, his posture wooden and cold. Amos noticed a shadow coming stealthily down the commissary road. It was Billy Pallister. Amos, almost leaping up, fled the porch, slamming the door behind him. His demented looking wife remained motionless on the icy swing. Amos was ready to slam the bastard off the porch if it became necessary. Even in his intense sorrow, rage also had a place in his broken heart.

With the group dispersed and the children stacked in the naked bed of the company truck like concentration camp victims headed for their undignified burials, the Beam property became even deeper in silence and pain which encircled the house like a diabolical aura. The noisy truck pulled out, headed for the funeral parlor, and the smell and sound of pervading evil and quiet became even more profound. Pallister was headed for the Beam house. Amos suddenly lost his will to attack the preacher. Pallister, sensing the initial anger dissipating in Amos, mounted the steps and chose a stance directly in front of his lover. "Laura, don't blame Amos," he began in a ragged voice. The man ain't no Pentecostal, but he is a good man and the father of your

fallen little ones. Respect him and go inside. Dr. Gwin done struck
their likeness for you so's you'll have a picture of them afore they're
buried." Billy's unnaturally soothing tone similar to that of an undertaker's finally had its desired effect. It calmed Laura and reminded
her that she had an immediate purpose. She would have guests soon
and her house was a mess. Her lover had spoken and she was to obey.
He continued, "I'll call some of the women of the church to help you
pick out burial clothes for your younguns and for you and your husband. They can help you mend or iron what you need. They'll be
bringing in food, too. You must get your house in order like the
woman in Proverbs 31," he concluded. Laura nodded her greasy head
and even smiled gradually. Billy patted her arm and walked to the
Mills' house to use their phone. He avoided all eye contact with
Amos out of fear or out of guilt.

By lunchtime, not just Laura's church members, but several of the
Red Hill ladies appeared with steaming dishes of food, clean linens
and towels, and even used clothing to help cover the bodies of the
dead. Laura, in a fog of sorrow, led them through the hastily tidied
up house, and suggested chores for each lady to tackle. She was ab-
normally calm. Most of the women wept as they worked, but it was
mostly sorrowful relief that their own children were safe in cozy beds
and this ragtag carnival was lowering its perverted tent and was permanently silencing the crazed crowd. Overall, Laura disgusted the
true Believers, but they, nevertheless, wanted to serve even if it was
out of respect for Amos and the departed Beam clan.

Lang, generally traveling afoot somewhere between and walk and
a run, quickly reached Amos, who had escaped the house and had
walked down to the artisan well by the commissary. When Lang
spotted the humped over Amos, he was methodically washing his
tear-stained face with the pure waters of this natural well-a pristine
liquid which bravely rushed out of creosoted saturated surrounding
swamp sludge. Lang cleared his throat; Amos looked up unapologeti-
cally. "Amos, it's not your fault. Dr. Gwin should have been called in
to see your kids immediately. They are where they are because your
wife foolishly allowed a corrupt man, pretending to be a man of God,

to guide her. She and that snake oil salesman Pallister are up to no good, Amos. You know I didn't have to let him into Red Hill; he doesn't work for Braun, but you're a loyal employee and I did it to help keep you here. That and the other kicked-up-a-notch Pentecostals. I try to keep the employees' wives satisfied because I know that makes my employees happy. As a whole, I have no beef with the whole congregation; they are clean-living and honest. Several of the members your wife recruited asked me if they could build a church on that empty lot, and I agreed. Why, you know, I even gave them the scrap lumber to build it with." Amos nodded and looked away at some unknown site. "I can revoke his Braun privileges just as quick as I granted them because I'm bending the rules letting him stay on Braun property without rent cost." Lang finished, pausing hopefully for a word from the silent giant. Uncomfortable time lapsed, but finally, Amos parted his dry lips to speak. He slowly lifted his hulk of a body until he was upright and eye-to-eye with his boss.

"Now, Mr. Beaux. I don't' want to take away nobody's church even though I'm not a church going man. I 'spect it'd be best for me and Laura just to git a little place outside of Red Hill and I would look fer another job. She's a getting' a little too old to birth me any more children—too old to have had that last one, for that matter," he added. He didn't call Piety by name, Lang noticed, but he chose not to make a comment. He chose merely to listen to a man who was seldom acknowledged at all and whose pain was immeasurable deep.

"Amos, don't go making decisions you'll regret later. Times are hard. It's not easy to find another job when you don't have an education. Don't get me wrong. I know you are smart, and you've got a good work record, but, I recollect you told me that you dropped out of school after your third grade year right before the cotton came in. Am I right?" Lang pressed on. Amos nodded, wiped his face again, and started toward the road. "Just wait, son. Wait until after the funerals, at least. You'll make a better decision then," Lang encouraged.

Amos wanted the funerals scheduled as soon as possible. Embalming was not necessary in the state of Alabama at this time if the family buried the body within twenty-four hours of the death. That step saved tremendous burial costs for rural families, so that was a common practice. Besides, because the children had died of scarlet fever, the local city undertaker was unwilling to even dress the children, so Laura and the ladies of her church met the funeral director at the church just prior to the funeral to dress them for their final departure. The women believed the children could no longer infect others and their own children were on the mend now. The epidemic had ebbed in Red Hill. But the drama had reached a horrifying crescendo.

The questions now that lurked in everyone's minds were: Where would the funeral be and who would conduct it? Laura's church was too small to accommodate the potentially large crowd, so Billy suggested that he himself conduct the funeral in the nondenominational church at Red Hill. Mr. Lang had encouraged the couple to select Mr. Gaddy, the Methodist circuit riding preacher, to conduct the funerals, but Laura, even in her apathetic mood, insisted on Billy Pallister. There would be no coffins because there was no money; the Beam children would just be placed on quilts which would then be wrapped around them before they were placed in their individual graves. Although the odd practice was slightly unorthodox, the coroner and other county officials waived their concerns because of the extreme circumstances surrounding these babies' deaths. After all, Red Hill was not a priority on the minds of county officials or politicians.

Laura now returned home to dress for the funeral. She had lost her accusatory furor and her passion, choosing rather to stumble through the sparkling house, locating her one Sunday dress and her broken heeled shoes. Amos had lost or hidden his inward rage, and he nervously reached for Laura's hand as they started for the church building together. Suddenly, Lee Earl, the cylinder opener at the plant,—a gentle, shy, coal black man with a kind heart and a mild drinking problem—tapped on the ravaged screen door. (His drinking was overlooked because it never interfered with his work.) "Mr. Beam, Suh, I's come to pay my respect and tell you that I made your chillins' coffins so's yore babies could have a decent burial. I's been making coffins all my life and selling them, but these is a gift to you. You've always been good to me and treated me like I's white. I ain't forgettin' that. I'm sorry you been cheated out of seeing your babies grow up," the baritone voice continued. "Now, they's not fancy, but I carved them out of pretty yellow pine and Ella, she padded each one with white cotton balls and sewed a top for them. Mrs. Lang gave her the material. I don't want them babies to be in the ground with no protection 'cept a quilt. Would this hope you out on your finances, Sir?" The mountain of a man finished his monologue and breathed deeply, starting again. "I'm agonna stay on the pole yard while the rest of my crew attends the funeral. That's sumthin' I can do." Lee Earl concluded and backed his way off the porch, avoiding direct eye contact with Laura, as did most Red Hill residents. Amos just tipped his hat and mouthed a thank-you to his generous friend.

Suddenly, Amos stood up as if realizing something for the first time. "Lee Earl, I can't let you tie up your inventory like that. Me and the misses is goin' be moving soon and we can pay you once we get ourselves settled," he trailed off.

"Naw, sir, Mr. Beam. Yous ain't gotta worry 'bout that. I don't 'spect I'll have this big a order for a while. And I carved me up several when I was off with the flu, so I'm ready for business," he reassured his friend. Amos grabbed Lee Earl by his strong shoulder, drawing him near to his own bony frame. "The railroad crew is gonna take them caskets to the cemetery unless you have somebody else in mind. It ain't but about a mile from the church to the cemetery," he finished. Amos then did the unthinkable: he grabbed Lee Earl, hugged him, and cried into the stronger man's chest. Unable to speak, Lee Earl patted Amos and smiled as Laura looked aghast at her husband. Shocked over male tears, the hugs, and the unselfish black man, she quickly dropped her eyes to the ground to stop her own tears. "Mr. Beam, you have them church women bring them babies down her to the carpenter's shack so's we can fill up them coffins," Lee instructed as he started out.

"The only way I'm goin' to accept your unselfish gift, Lee, is if you'll carry my baby, Piety Ann, to the church and to the gravesite. I don't care what people think; I want MY friend holding the child from my old age," Amos declared. "Someone else can take over for you while you come to the funeral," he suggested as he stepped backward. Lee Earl smiled and nodded. He would do that for the only white man who had treated him as an equal.

Lee Earl again finished backing out the squeaky porch door and finally headed toward the road. Before he cleared the yard, he slowly turned back around to face Amos who was standing on the top front step. "Mr. Amos, I done this for YOU, nobody but you and them babies," he emphasized the words so that Laura could not misunderstand his meaning. Emphasis was duly noted by Amos and by a few nosey neighbors who had witnessed the touching scene. Laura clasped her husband's husk dry hand and together they sat back down on the swing together.

By one that day, the seven railroad crew members, dressed in white shirts and starched overalls had made their way to the commissary to meet and walk together for the funeral scheduled at three p.m. The eight little coffins filled with the fallen Beam doves were lined up on the Lloyd's carpenter shed porch. Who was going to carry the eighth coffin? Shortly after Kendrick, the assistant engineer, took a head count, he saw Lee Earl running toward the store. He, too, was dressed in a white shirt and starched and ironed overalls. "Wait, y'all. Mr. Beam say he want me to carry little Piety's coffin. I made it 'specially pretty to match her blond curls. Mr. Lang say he gonna use Lucien to cover the cylinders." There was no hint of prejudice in the pallbearers' eyes; this was what Amos wanted and this was what he got. They received the massive African American co-worker with handshakes all around. Each man lifted a coffin and began their sorrowful walk toward the church.

Red Hill residents had filled the nondenominational church, and the Gothic styled sanctuary had been lovingly decorated with what little greenery the elderly Mrs. Barr had growing in her homemade greenhouse. She had nursed two poinsettias left over from Christmas and now they were displayed on two stands near the preacher's podium. The railroad crew had deposited their assigned coffins in order of the children's ages and now the somber men were seated on the front two pews. Laura and Amos took their places behind them. The

Rash brothers played two familiar hymns first; then the mighty Brother Billy Pallister stepped up onto the pulpit area. Even this the day of the funeral, several neighbors and well meaning relatives had once again gently suggested that the Methodist circuit preacher would better suit the melancholy occasion as he had the gifts of flowery speech and memorized scripture. Laura would have no ear to any suggestion contrary to her own choice. Amos's emotions were too anesthetized to protest. So the charismatic and controversial gospel guru slithered up the squeaky pulpit steps to deliver his message of comfort. The two nearest Pentecostal churches completely shunned Billy's sect and refused to attend the funeral, choosing rather to support Amos at the gravesite.

"Now, faith is the substance of things hoped for, the evidence of things not seen," he began. "This, my people, today, stands as evident of those of you who are lacking in faith. Oh, ye of little faith..." Pallister railed on mercilessly about the community's overall weak faith without actually calling Amos out, but the message was quite clear and its insinuation angered the audience. Everyone knew why he was hammering away about faith, and the crowd grew hostile trying to maintain the dignity of the situation, but ending up deadened and just staring mindlessly out the big eyelid shaped windows. Even Laura's church sisters and brothers were appalled at their own minister's attack on the emotionally shattered husband of his lover. Nothing was mentioned about the children who were permanently housed in their pine and cotton counterpanes. Billy's message had a not-so-hidden agenda. Pallister was refueled for his captive audience. Any earlier grace he'd extended to Amos had been lost in the hype.

The religious ranting continued for about forty minutes; then it abruptly ceased when the quitting whistle blew, interrupting the preacher's thoughts. Lee Earl perked up at the familiar sound because he had purposely shut off the timer to avoid this very thing. Its interrupting noise awakened the daydreamers, confused the speaker, and eventually led to an unexpected closing prayer by R.D. Rash, a lay preacher who also sang with his brothers in the bluegrass quartet. The damning text had ceased, and the railroad crew unanimously stood up and walked to the front, each one heaving a crudely constructed

yellow pine box which housed a Beam child. Lee Earl followed behind and gently lifted the tiniest, smoothest casket which held the
remains of Little Piety Ann Beam. In single file the sober looking
men marched the bodies out the front door, down the stairs, and into
the nearby church cemetery. The family followed; the friends fell in
behind them. Eight neatly dug graves were lined up near the small
creosoted bridge that lay between the church and the old school. The
sobbing crowd stood still as Reverend Pallister walked to the center
of the group. The audience anticipated further condemnation for
their lack of faith, but, thankfully, they were spared from such.

"Ashes to ashes, dust to dust. So a life is like a vapor," he declared.
That was it! Pallister stood, arms folded and nodded to the railroad
crew. Each man singlehandedly put his assigned coffin into the proper
hole, with Lee Earl's as the last one lay in the icy ground. Another
quick prayer was offered by Mr. Lang, and the large troupe dispersed
like oil in a sea of degreaser. The graves would be covered up later by
the same railroad crew members after the family and friends had left
the makeshift cemetery. Amos and Laura led the path back to their
home which would soon be filled with sympathizing people and delicious food—the traditional southern way of mourning.

Pallister headed toward the Beam house, but Lang, gritting his teeth,
snatched the preacher's arm. "Don't go where you're not wanted. Haven't
you caused enough pain? If I were you, I'd be looking for another church
to pastor far away from Red Hill. This godly, little community don't like
you, and you've helped to break a strong and good employee of Braun. I
believe you've outstayed your welcome. I'm not running you off, but you
should see the handwriting on the wall, Billy," Mr. Lang dropped his
grasp and stepped away from the shocked preacher. Lang headed to the
Beams' place where he would meet his wife who was already serving up
steaming plates of southern cuisine. Billy stood alone in the abandoned
street as he pondered his next move. Perhaps, Lang was right. There
would be another lonely parishioner in another fleabag town, he
thought, haughtily. His god would provide. (And who was his god?)

Life slowly commenced again in Red Hill. Initially, the tragedy
was hashed and rehashed on the commissary porch; but, as most

tragedies do, the horror lessens in time, and other local gossip heartlessly replaces even the most horrific of events. Wisely, Reverend Pallister and his piano player married, jilting Laura Beam completely. Then, he got called into a new ministry on Murrow Road where the congregation provided a nice brick parsonage, a hefty salary boost, and no questions asked about his seedy past. The standard of living for this sanctimonious asp improved greatly. His continued crusade of FAITH HEALS ALL was embraced and exalted in his new progressive church. The new Mrs. Pallister soon birthed twins-two identical boys, and the family was complete. Billy's future looked bright; he had already made friends with the young, single church secretary who was still stinging after a recent jilt at the altar. The Red Hill house of Pallister was quickly enveloped in the ever present curtain of kudzu. Billy had dragged his twisted ministry up the food chain of churches. All the past had been forgotten, forgiven, or ignored by his new parrish.

Amos continued to work for Braun, choosing to peel poles in the back of the black yard, a mindless and monotonous job. He seldom spoke, but wasn't rude or unfriendly; for he had always been reserved in his public comments. He abandoned his early dream of leaving Red Hill and its heartbreaking memories behind. He renovated the house, removing the hurtful traces of trinkets, toys, etc. that would remind him of his lost children. He painted and repaired the porch for Laura who spent most of her time there, hand sewing or just staring into nothingness. Always slender, now her body was gaunt. Amos took over the cooking duties as well as other household chores now left undone. She never mentioned Pallister again, nor was she tempted to visit his new church. The little church in Red Hill was abandoned and years later cleaned up and used as a polling place. Laura backslid from any church attendance and discontinued even reading her tattered Bible or offering up a prayer anymore. She lived a mummy-like existence shrouded in apathetic disconnection. She had no friends; she had been convicted, condemned, and was sentenced to living-dead. Home Demonstration Clubs continued to meet each month, but Laura was not on the invitation list and was not missed—the ultimate Red Hill rejection. Her once unbridled passion for Billy Pallister deteriorated to apathetic catatonia.

About six years after the children's deaths, on a bright autumn September Saturday, Amos excused himself from the breakfast table. Without actively acknowledging him, Laura waved her husband away with a limp, stick thin arm. He further announced that he was going to take a little drive in his new Ford after work. He did not offer Laura the opportunity to agree or disagree to accompany him. She had, on occasions, ridden with him, but again, she consistently dissolved into the interior of the vehicle, unable or unwilling to respond to his small talk. She has borne her self-inflicted punishment in silence. Amos continued to treat his wife kindly but distantly like one would treat a demented cousin at a family reunion.

Amos had secretly been pursuing the same route via rub board dirt surface several times a week without anyone's suspicions; after the tragedies of his children's deaths; in totally ignorance of his plans, the men on the yard had given Amos a wide berth. Only Lee Earl, his best friend since the funeral, had been in on part of the secret. Amos had been consistently stalking the everyday activities of the Reverend Pallister for a while. Before he left in the couple's only vehicle that morning, he re-explained his travel plans to a disinterested Laura; he needed to leave straight from the wood yard to see a man about sharpening and repairing company saws, knives, and other cutting tools before he closed the shop. In actuality, he had quickly swapped his work cap for a worn straw hat, draping it purposely over his left eye and speedily exiting at the quitting whistle. He was heading the long finned car in the direction of Bethsaida, not the most common or the easiest route to leave Red Hill's unpredictable swampland. He had concealed the nature of his mysterious exit by parking his car front first near the base of the eating clay mount. Then, he headed out by way of the black yard and around the old school until he ended up on nearby Murrow Road by way of Bethsaida.

After reaching his destination, he slowly pulled up and parked under the grove of pine trees slightly south from the Pallister's new home place. Amos had daily noted the time when the little Pallister boys returned home from school on bus #48 which also continued on to Red Hill with the other riders. That was generally around 4:20 pm. Usually the noisy little fellows joined their mother who was already pruning and picking vegetables in the quite expertly tended garden near the parsonage. The Reverend Mr. Pallister seldom showed up until later, Amos noted. Often, Billy was parked by a late model, sporty green Pontiac in the parking lot of Shell's Grove church where he was employed. His new young church secretary coincidentally owned a late model, sporty green Pontiac. Perhaps he was helping her build her faith now.

The Pallister boys, Amos had noticed, generally worked the more sparse rows in the garden farthest from the highway. Their smiling mother would greet them with loving arms, and would point to separate water jugs which lay at the beginning of their designated rows. She then extended her hand and shared some fresh muscadines which she had squirreled away in her bulging apron pockets. She had always been working in the three middle rows each time Amos watched her. If the Reverend was home rather than out saving lost souls, which Amos noticed was not very often, the holy man would tackle the two, longest, and grassiest pea rows nearest to the road. Amos observed and made note of this pattern which seemed to be kept almost to precision, so his confidence was bolstered with each additional trip. Never a man to move or to act impulsively, he had mentally justified his final act of bloody revenge during the long, loveless nights while he lay fully awake beside a skeletal corpse. He was ready; he had earned his right for payback. He had no children to stroll beside him in the garden.

Today, this day, his misguided strategy was ready for execution. He was jovial, self-assured, and the tormented Amos was even whistling a favorite old spiritual, "We are Climbing Jacob's Ladder". As he turned the Ford onto Murrow Road this particular fall day, the driven man panicked, silently acknowledging the extreme risk of his actions. His breathing grew shallow and frequent. Yet, in his tortured mind, he was justified and even sanctified in the knowledge that right was going to prevail because of his imminent choice. He relaxed and continued his path, crawling out from his shadowed hiding place.

He readjusted his straw hat brim over his left eye to avoid any obstruction to his vision yet kept it down just enough to blur his identity. His crank style car window was already rolled down flush with the driver's side door, allowing the slight breeze to cool the black interior of his vehicle. His left hand was not positioned on the steering wheel, but instead it was poised to his side, armed with an A-5 sawed off Browning shotgun which was highly effective in its shorter range, lower muzzle velocity, and wider spread of shot. He had personally forged and cut its steel barrel, specifically tailoring it with a handmade spreader choke. He kept the vehicle at a crawling 10 mph-not completely stopped but more like a rolling stop to get off just one clean shot at Pallister, to gun the high powered engine, and to escape down Murrow Road until he could figure out his next step. He had tried to talk himself through a thoughtful plan beyond his initial, violent action, but his confused mind had stalled out; it had taken all his lagging energy to get this far. No, he would just deal with the here and now. He could think and strategize later. What did it really matter after his action anyway?

As usual, Mr. Palliser was at the left corner of the pea patch nearest the road—an ideal position for Amos to get off an accurate shot. He quickly raised his lean left arm and aimed the short barreled gun out the open window. While he mumbled some phrase to himself, he aimed, fired, and hit the unsuspecting holy man—his mouth wide open— square in the chest, splattering the hoe handle with the massive blast of blood. He fell forward on the hoe, the blade slapping at his sunburned forehead as Amos revved the escape car and raced away from the grisly scene. Amos glanced back only once, like Lot's wife, to see the screaming children bouncing up like Mexican jumping beans around their mother who soon fell over her obviously dead husband. Amos jerked his head partially around for one more look but stopped himself short of a total turn. Did I hit her, too, he wondered? He questioned himself although he knew she was not near her husband when the shot went off. Then, as if to reassure the reluctant killer, she wriggled to the ground beside Billy now and her hysterical children formed a human tent over her body. Amos hammered down on the accelerator. He could not shut out the screams from the mother and children and from his own children's screams in his disturbed head which was tormented by the mental picture of his babies hopelessly scratching at the ceiling of their coffins.

Amos sped up to over 80 mph and had free reign of the newly scraped road. He was clammy with nervous sweat, but he felt confident and exonerated at the demise of the dishonorable clergyman who captured the attentions of his wife and eventually murdered his seven children and Billy's own daughter, Piety Ann. He could acknowledge her illegitimate heritage now. However, he didn't blame her for her parentage. She was just an innocent baby born to evil adulterers.

When Amos failed to show up at work the following day, Mr. Lang called the local sheriff, who was a personal friend of his. The sheriff sauntered across the pole yard toward the cylinders. Lee Earl was working inside in the dangerously high temperatures, so the lawman waited, leaning against the shed near the cylinder doors. Lee Earl was casually questioned by the county sheriff, but the authorities showed little interest in capturing a possible perpetrator. Lee Earl could only verify that Amos left work at 4, and he didn't show up the next day for work, nothing more. Laura couldn't even recall the reason her husband had said he would be late from work; she provided no useable information when she was questioned. Even Mrs. Pallister, who later in the year moved to Berley and remarried, was unfortunately stricken with the inability to positively identify the shooter. Police officials conducted a half-hearted search for the black Ford and eventually abandoned the investigation, but most residents and police officers agreed that Amos was most likely the assassin; yet, they collectively determined that the broken man had suffered enough without a physical prison to bind him. Amos was never seen or heard tell of again, as Southerners say.

As for Laura, she moved back to her parents' old place near the Byler turnoff, but in just over a month, her rail-thin body was found swinging over a caned bottomed straight chair with a cheerfully printed flour sack wrapped over an exposed pine beam and fastened tightly around her bony neck. She was buried alongside her eight children; Lee Earl did NOT carve her casket. She had no funeral service. The county pauper's fund covered the cost of the pine coffin and a tiny headstone. An inexpensive carnation spray attached to a handmade plaque which read: "Faith is the Victory" had appeared on the fresh grave shortly after the diggers covered up the wicked cavity in the blood red soil. Red Hill moved on as quickly as Amos disappeared down Murrow Road.

As in most southern communities, there were stories as humorous as Amos's was sad in Red Hill. The incorporated town had a handyman shop referred to by residents as the carpenter's shop; it survived until the year 2000. It was a crudely fashioned, creosote shack with an unsteady porch, a front room, and a long side room on its right. The little cabin was filled with a variety of hardware, electrical, plumbing, and building tools and supplies. The Braun carpenters, a father and son team, the Lloyds, were responsible for all the maintenance of every company and resident building. They were gifted men who repaired, rebuilt, and constructed for the company. The father, who was Lilliputian in statue, was nicknamed "Big Un" due to his age, and the rotund son was called "Little Un" for the same reason. The two worked uncomplainingly and effectively, making house calls at all hours and in all weather. Yet, the work load never decreased. There was always a leaky roof, a rotted porch, an electrical short, or a frozen water pipe. In addition, there were heavy items in need of relocation, which required strong arms and reliable vehicles; the Lloyds had both. They worked hard; they drank even harder, a nip or two during the day and a pint or two through the weekend. Again, the imbibing was overlooked because their love of firewater never interfered with their good, honest labor and their impeccable work ethic.

The Lloyds were not alone in their thirst for homebrew, and no one cooked up white lightning up like S.V. Perry. Silvanus, who worked on the yard crew, chose to live outside Red Hill and pay for his own home, perhaps to avoid open exposure of his side job to the Braun executives. Red Hill residents and those beyond the Two Mile Sign alike knew S.V. produced the cleanest whiskey around. He himself was impeccable groomed even for a grimy job on the wood yard.

His work clothes were starched and pressed; his car was as clean as one that would drive the grand marshal in the Northway Christmas parade. Still neat at the end of the workday at whistle time, S. V. stopped at the commissary almost on a daily basis to purchase the following items in the following order: malt, yeast, and sugar. He'd place the items on the worn counter, smile his million dollar smile at Mr. Bell, and say "Mr. Chuck, charge it to me, please Sir. I've got some cooking to do." No questions were asked; he paid his bill on time. Partakers of his concoction did not experience the gastric problems that many homebrew drinkers suffered when they bought from the Mayfields up the highway. The Mayfields were incidental in personal hygiene and production cleanliness. It was rumored that old Mr. Mayfield kept the whiskey uncovered which made it vulnerable to stumbling varmints, a mistaken outdoor toilet seeker, or to an old tractor battery or two. His special recipe was said to have been responsible for numerous Monday sick days at Braun. The mysterious ingredients did not deter his loyal customers, however.

The elder Lloyd was happily married, but his son was in his late 30's and still a bachelor, living at home with his aging parents. It wasn't that he was opposed to marriage; he just had not met the right one, as he would say. One April at the spring meeting, Little 'Un spied a female visitor briskly fanning with a funeral fan and unpleasantly warbling the revival hymns across the squeaky wooden pews. She possessed about the same amount of unattractiveness as Little Un. He suddenly got religion and began faithfully attending the Methodist services throughout the entire week which led up to the nondenominational Easter Service on the following Sunday, (although he was actually Primitive Baptist in his faith). He was distracted from the foreign doctrine and flowery text of the Methodist circuit preacher; his concentration was on Freida, as he had discovered was her musical sounding name. Junior Lloyd was unlearned in the polished matters of courting and also sadly cursed with a marked speech impediment; strangely, he waited until Easter Sunday when almost the entire population of Red Hill was in attendance at the sunrise service on the groups of the church to introduce himself and to move into defending his intentions if she were to indicate any interest.

"My, my, my name is Junior Lloyd, but most people caw me Little 'Un," he stammered as he lightly tapped Freida on the shoulder, startling the stringy blonde creature into turning around to face her nervous and inept pursuer. He drew in a labored breath and painfully continued, "And your name, I heered, is Miss Fwreida. Mrs. Barr told me you play the piano and sang jest as purdy as you look. So, Miss Piano Player, can I stand by you during the service and maybe sit by you at the sunwise breakfast? My momma made baloney biscuits," he trailed off, realizing he was talking too fast and too much, but at least, he had controlled his crooked speech for most of his monologue.

Freida was not familiar with anyone's romantic inclinations toward her ever, for she had never even received so much as a noncommittal nod from a male other than her father. She was, as the Bible put it, "tender-eyed". Her crowning glory was her ability to adequately play the piano unless she attempted to improvise chords which signaled a musical train wreck when she misplaced her fingers from the "home keys". Her singing voice was similar to that of a dying calf in a hailstorm. But Freida was quite flattered by this man's attention—any man's attention, and she answered him softly and accompanied her answer with a kind smile. "Why, Mr. Lloyd, I'm glad to meet you. Thank you for your complimentary words. My whole name is Freida Gaddy from Burl, just right down past Bethsaida. My daddy is the preacher this week. And, yes, you can stand by me," she finished as she lowered her voice when her eloquent father began speaking. But then she continued in a whisper, "I don't have to perform today; the Adams Quartet is the entertainment. I hear they're very good. I'm free, so I can join you for the breakfast. I myself made a blueberry coffeecake. I hope you'll like it." This time she hushed completely as the Resurrection prayer was given by Mr. George. Little 'Un lit up like a marquis as he boldly grabbed her gloved hand. She assured him with unspoken permission through a gentle squeeze to his rough, pudgy hand. It was love in bloom even though it wasn't the prettiest bloom.

As her rhetoric loving father droned on, Freida's mind wandered back to last Sunday's services when she had overheard one of the church ladies refer to her as "the preacher's spinster daughter". She had lately realized that her matrimonial chances were diminishing with each unwanted pound and each new wrinkle. Mr. Lloyd's obvious interest in her had restored her hope in seeing the puffy third finger of her left hand encircled with a gold band. After all, she wasn't perfect, either, and he seemed very kind. She also acknowledged her weariness of the circuit riding her father so enjoyed.

Little 'Un joined Freida that Easter Sunday and every Easter Sunrise Sunday until his death many years after that first clumsy introduction. They had married a year after their first meeting; her father had performed the simple but touching ceremony in the quaintly decorated house of Little 'Un's parents. A succulent feast was provided at the reception; both of them loved good food, and Mrs. Lloyd, Sr. was more than happy to prepare enough items for all Red Hill residents and Reverend Gaddy's small church family. It was a casual but joyous celebration. Red Hill residents were pleased with the union of the hard-working carpenter and the church pianist.

The Lloyd Jr. couple moved into one of the best of Braun's company houses, located about a half a mile from Little 'Un's parents. Life was simple and content for the newlyweds. Little 'Un slowed down his drinking and cut back on his workaholic schedule. Freida only played the piano (thankfully) for public Red Hill events such as revivals, funerals, weddings, political rallies, company picnics, and at Christmas; she gladly retired from the circuit ride while her father, a widower, reduced his circuit schedule and remarried a younger woman who swiftly bore him three strapping sons to keep him busy. The remainder of her time was identical to other Red Hill homemakers who completed daily chores, involved themselves in church, civic and school activities, and updated the local gossip at Home Demonstration Club meetings. Life was good for the Lloyds. Or, so it seemed.

In the South, when the temperatures drop in winter, the desire to even stir from cozy wood heated homes requires great effort. Southern people are not equipped for snow travel or for cold weather clothing. Because of that fact and his expanding girth due to Freida's culinary genius with even simple foods, Little 'Un returned home hungry, tired, sore, and cold from daily exploration under a house or even underground for a frozen pipe. He had little to say and wanted to do even less. Freida understood and sympathized with her easy-going husband's weariness but she was begin to tire also, not of the frigid weather outside, but of the stillness of her home and the frigid-ity of her bed. She lost her once ravenous appetite and became withdrawn into herself. Her understanding of her husband's fatigue did not reduce her daily boredom.

In the past, after her mother's death, she had served as her socially mobile father's hostess and accompanist. Father and daughter had traveled in an old Ford to quite a few towns and communities, spreading the Word and sharing a song or two. The traveling had afforded Freida the opportunity to meet people, to dress fashionably despite her awkward size, and to be exposed to different life styles. Now, she felt trapped in a well decorated house that she kept surgi-cally clean, a closet of clothes impeccably laundered, and a table full of meals that steamed sumptuously every day.

Halloween of 1964 was unseasonable cold. Freida pulled the Priscilla curtains closer around the window frames to block out the howling north wind. As her dull, but loving husband slept, she decid-ed that she must liberate herself from the house, regardless of the plummeting temperatures outside. She molted her lacy pink house-coat, grabbed some wool pants which were baggy now after her tremendous weight loss, and added her husband's faded but warm flannel shirt to her rag tag outfit as she dashed toward the front door which was covered in heavy plastic. As she quietly pulled on the sparkling crystal doorknob, the door squeaked slightly and she called back to her slumbering husband, "Honey, honey, I've just got to get some fresh air. The heat is just stifling in here. It's only around seven. I'll be right back in a jiffy." She guiltily caught herself speaking more softly than usual to avoid awakening him at the potential cost of him finding her gone and causing him worry. Relieved and exhilarated by the lack of his response and the blast of cold air as she continued opening the door, Freida picked up her speed and literally ran down the steps to icy freedom. The last step was wider than the other three and had become slick as the rain had solidified, turning it into a mini skating rink. Freida's heel slipped forward, forcing her to grab the railing to avoid a fall. "I must be more careful," she reminded herself. As she steadied herself upright, she glanced down at her feet and realized she still had on her pink fuzzy house shoes. "I'll be fine," she assured herself to no one in particular. "I have on socks!" Freida rationalized. She continued her conversation with an invisible entity. "After all, I'll be home shortly. I won't get cold." She was correct in part of her prediction.

No one was outside in Red Hill on a night as cold as this one. Most all of the workers had endured freezing weather all day and had basically followed Freida's husband's schedule after work: bathe, eat, warm up, watch tv, and commence snoring in front of the Ashley wood heater provided in each company home. Not tonight, she thought. Freida squinted a little and spied a faint light near Uncle James's storage shed. She quickened her step, abandoning her own advice about safety. She drew closer and decided to call out, "Is anybody there? Can you hear me?" She knew Uncle James was at work, for he was one of the few Braun employees that chose to work the night shift, serving as a watchman for the preserving cylinders. "Why would someone with a cheap flashlight be wandering around an old widower's property on a brisk winter night?" she questioned aloud.

The stiff grass crunched beneath her chilly feet; nevertheless, she moved on, intoxicated with the possibility of something out of the ordinary shaking up her ordinary life. As she neared the back of Uncle James's dark and neglected house in front of the shed, Freida discovered the source of the weak light. As she had initially suspected, it was extending from a small, cheap, dim flashlight, and it was held by a shadowy figure that recognized her when it later addressed her by name. Surprisingly, she was totally unafraid.

"Freida, is that you? What are you doing out here? You'll catch the death of cold. Can you see me?" the Yankee accented voice without a form kept speaking. She heard rattling noises as if this form was gaining proximity on her; her heart began to race. Then, the lightning bug beam of the fading flashlight dimly illuminated the stranger's face. "It's Virgil, Virgil Jones!" he declared as if that name spoken in a hint of a Yankee accent would spark her complete acceptance and recognition. It accomplished neither. Awkward silence permeated the night air. The many stars shone like beveled glass in the completely clear Alabama sky. The dim flashlight was almost an insult to the nature light from above, but even the sky's light did not aid in Freida's recognition of the figure.

Freida drew in a quick breath after a while and her brassy voice broke the silence, shattering the barrier between the two. Her desire for adventure overrode any fear she might have of this man. "I'm sorry, but I can't recall your voice or your face, what little I can see of it. Perhaps if we stepped into the little shed, we could be a little warmer and I could think a little clearer. I've met so many people on the Methodist circuit with my dad", she attempted to explain and then suddenly regretted her words. "You idiot", she mumbled to herself, he could be a rapist or a murderer!" Her vivid imagination had been fueled by the daytime dramas she allowed herself to view once her daily household chores were completed. She assured herself that since the friendly specter had known her face and her name she was probably safe. Regardless, the man pushed open the dilapidated door of the rotten shed and pulled on a light cord. The naked bulb forced additional light into the small building and centered it on the stranger. "Oh, you do look familiar," she acknowledged. Still, she was unsure of the man's identity. Then, it came to her in a flash! Virgil Jones, the salesman, who lived with them one summer-the summer she lost her precious mom.

"Freida, I was a Bible salesman in seminary when your pappy, the Reverend, took me in and let me live with y'all the summer that your blessed mother passed away. You was just a little squirt then, weren't you?" he continued, motivated by the streak of recognition in Freida's eyes. "You're a grown woman now with a fine, full face." He spoke" full" as if it were a compliment, but Freida's mouth turned down slightly as she thought of her present weight which was still hefty, even after her recent weight loss. "How's your pappy? Is he still preaching? Now, that man could testify how the cow ate the cabbage, couldn't he? I bet he still can." Virgil Jones finally finished his first round of conversation as fast and as consistent as a Tommy gun. His salesmanship ability must have been enhanced by this gift of gab, or perhaps, his unfortunate clients may have just purchased his products to rid themselves of the Chinese noise torture he provided in his sales pitch.

Freida did vaguely remember her father frequently housing various summer Bible salesmen to help them financially and spiritually. The summer of her mother's death was still a blur of carnations, macaroni salad, and mobs of well meaning neighbors who followed the Southern tradition of sending flowers, visiting the home of the bereaved, and delivering the very best food available from their well stocked kitchens. She was often covered in sloppy kisses, was served a plate of steaming food, and gently nudged to the front porch steps while the grownups visited, mourned, and received encouragement from each other in this hallowed death tradition which was especially practiced through church people—and most especially in honor of a preacher's sorrow. That funeral ritual certainly contributed to making her the fat adult she was today.

The typical goal of a summer Bible salesman was to sell enough religious texts to cover the cost of seminary enrollment and to alleviate the cost of living expenses for the coming fall. Word was passed casually throughout America that the Bible belt was more sympathetic to those called into the ministry; so during the scalding, scorching summer, it was not unusual to see young men in outdated dark dress suits drumming throughout Red Hill and other conservative communities like it. Sometimes, a well meaning theology student from north of the Mason-Dixon line would find himself at a southerner's table eating squirrel, Bird's Eye, or even pickled okra for the first time. Afraid of rejection and the potential loss of a sale, he accepted whatever he was served.

Freida's eyes lit up and she smiled at Mr. Jones for the first time during this unusual pairing. "Were you the one daddy fed a peanut

butter, mayonnaise, and banana sandwich? That fellow was introduced to country lunch cuisine with a bang!" Virgil looked up and
nodded, poising as if to speak, but Freida began to snort and to
laugh—not necessarily an attractive combo to see or to hear. She
sucked in a heavy breath, gained some composure, and continued, as
snippits of her childhood that melancholic summer traveled from her
brain to her tongue. "Dad didn't have any food prepared and all the
food that had been brought in had been eaten or thrown out. Mother
had only been dead about two weeks, I believe. That was the first
time I had laughed since she was buried. Was that really YOU? Oh,
and to answer your earlier question, Dad is still alive. He's remarried,
and I have little brothers!" she laughed easily again with this stranger
for no apparent reason. She was starved for adult conversation; you
can't communicate with a husband if he's comatose, Freida thought
bitterly.

"Why, yes, that was me! I didn't think I could get that disgusting
sandwich down, but I was afraid that if I didn't, I might lose my
chance of renting that little garage apartment from your daddy that
summer," Virgil chuckled. "You know, Freida, your sainted daddy
wouldn't take a dime of rent money or for food costs that summer.
He said he was "entertaining angels unaware". Isn't that something? I
know his heart was aching from your mother's death and from worrying about your care," Virgil reflected on the character of the godly
man who gave him a chance. Virgil returned to the present, "What
ARE you doing out on this brisk night, girl? How will the shed own-
er take to us being on his property?" Virgil Jones asked the two
questions rapid-fire without even taking a slight breath. Freida
thought that he could wear out a person quickly, but then connected
that character trait to other aggressive salesmen she had met in various churches throughout the region.

"Mr. Jones, time has a way of moving on with or without you.
Who would have thought my aged father would have three small
boys under five?" Freida was only recently comfortable talking about
her father's new family. She resumed her newsy monologue. "You
know, I have changed, too, since that summer you were in our lives. I

graduated high school and went to college a while at Judson. All the while and after college, too, I continued to travel with dad, and as you may remember, I played and still play the piano. I had begun performing, I think, even before you came to the parsonage." She paused wistfully, and resumed her place in her oral autobiography. "I just got married about three years ago," Freida declared as her voice dropped in pitch and her wrinkled bow mouth drew up even tighter. "And as to the reason I was outside ......sometimes when I feel like I'm choking, I have to step outside just to breathe." She paused and stopped to recall the other questions Virgil had posed. "And to answer the other questions you asked? Uncle James lives here, but Braun owns all the houses in Red Hill. And anyway, he won't care; I do some light cooking, some laundry, and house cleaning for him on occasions because he's a widower. He wouldn't mind me being here. Besides, he's a night watchman. He won't be home until the whistle blows in the morning." She paused and boldly suggested. "Did you know there's a beautiful artesian well down at the commissary... if you want to walk a spell? And while we're walking, perhaps, you could tell me what YOU are doing in Red Hill anyway and why at this time of the night?" Freida chatted away, feeling liberated with each new sentence she added after she had hurtled over her marital status confession. Why was she so hesitant to reveal her marital status and why was she unwilling to elaborate on any of the details surrounding the courtship, wedding, and everyday life with her husband? It troubled her, but not to the point of providing more about this part of her life.

The two left the chilly shed, Freida reaching up to turn off the light while Virgil waited until she exited to pull the door shut. Virgil crossed the half-frozen ditch first and stretched his long arm back over to give Freida a helping hand on her jump. Then the unlikely duo walked in the middle of the vacant asphalt road toward the commissary. Freida spoke first, "Are you still selling Bibles?" she asked. He shook his head wordlessly. "I know Daddy would love to see you again." Then she plunged headlong into a treatise of her father's many virtues and their many religious travels on the circuit. At that moment, Freida actually considered telling Virgil more about her husband, but she stopped herself again without really knowing why she did. No, deep down she KNEW the reason; this human blast from the past had flattered her and had sparked a little excitement, maybe even a dab of passion, in her mundane Red Hill life. Instead of sharing her marital bless or lack of it, she chose, instead, to boldly grab Virgil's obviously willing hand before he could even answer her question about his employment. He conceded his command of the conversion, so she rattled on like an ADD sufferer who had inadvertently forgotten her medicine, totally uncharacteristic of the normally sedate Freida. It was as if she were breathing a new, experimental mixture of air which contained more oxygen than she was accustomed to; she felt recharged and mentally alert.

Freida logically credited her sudden mental, physical, and emotional clarity to the extreme cold and clear weather; she hadn't felt this alive or open in years. Had she really felt that stifled, or was it just the stark contrast of the night air with the suffocating atmosphere of her little world she had left behind earlier in the evening? She was mentally uncomfortable giving herself permission to answer that question honestly. But Freida wasn't so distracted or guilt-ridden that she delayed redirecting her mind to the present to revel in the moment for what it was, or for what she *thought* that it was—a temporary escape from the uneasiness and dissatisfaction in her melancholy heart.

Walking silently until arriving at the well, Virgil's mellow baritone voice split the serenity of the Siberian air, "You know, Freida, I never knew you'd grow up to be such a sensual creature. I knew you were innocently alluring back when you flittered around the dusty yard beneath my apartment stairs. It wasn't a sexual thought for me, then; it was more about knowing that I was in the presence of a luscious peach blossom which would eventually mature into a juicy peach." Freida blushed as the simple salesman waxed poetic. "I knew you needed a mother, but your father was doing the best that he could, and what he was doing to help you meet your potential appeared to be working. I have dreamed of you many times when I was on the road trying to make my sales quota," Virgil confessed as he held her hand even tighter as if it were a life line for him-a drowning soul. He was a master charmer; that was certain.

"And to answer YOUR question more fully", as he spread his tattered coat down on the frosted grass near the old well and then motioned with his free hand for Freida to join him on the thin fabric seat. He continued, "After leaving the Red Hill area, I immediately withdrew from the seminary and ceased selling religious literature and bibles. I don't think I'm cut out to be a pastor, Freida. "I am no longer a salesman at all for Marirose Publisher's, but I'm still in sales, trying to peddle vacuum cleaners for a sister company based out of Pasadena, Texas. And to tell you the truth," he added, avoiding eye contact with Freida's big interested eyes, "I'm not doing that well, and I actually came back to find your daddy. He's the only one who treated me like a son, and I was so hopin' to be able to count on him again to help me find some real work. I'm not cut out for sales either. I barely made it when I sold Bibles." His voice registered discouragement as it dipped to almost inaudible when he reached the conclusion of his autobiography. He purposely focused his eyes on his own smooth hands which were now both clasping Freida's musical hands in a most desperate grip. His seductive voice was far from the urgent one he had adopted earlier in the night. He appeared to have more to share but had suddenly just lost energy like an AA battery in a well loved mechanical toy. He scooted his hips closer to hers as they both sat on the dripping wet coat. Again, silence. Virgil, from his vast experience, knew well-timed silence had an almost magical effect on desperate women, and he strongly sensed Freida's despair and her motherly instinct to sympathize with his feelings of failure.

Freida was somewhat surprised but not really repulsed by Virgil's mini-life story. With despondency and boredom validating her delusion, she saw Virgil as a world weary, handsome man who paid her some attention and who recognized that she was, indeed, a treasure. He didn't seem to her as a weakling but just a man in need of a strong, loving female like her to guide him back toward financial success. Freida swallowed the thick lump which filled all the space in her dry throat, causing her voice when it commenced, to sound as raspy as a lifelong Marlboro smoker. "Why, Virgil, I'm sure daddy could help you. He has his own church to pastor and he still does the circuit, just closer to home now; since I've married, he is missing an instrumentalist. Do I recall that you used to strum the strings sometimes? Or was it the drums you played? It's a little foggy to me; it's been so long ago. I know a fresh, new musical addition would help out. You know, the right music can stir people even when a sermon fails. Don't get me wrong; Dad's a fine speaker and an adequate singer, but he can't play a tune on any instrument. Many of the little congregations he serves lack musical talent, too, but most of them would be willing to pay for some good music on that Sunday when you performed. A musician's salary wouldn't pay much, but it could be a start for you." Her mind was racing with job options. In a reversal of roles, she wanted to be the knight in shining armor. Freida branched out in offering her many job ideas and suggestions. "Why, Dad could surely use some extra help there at the house, too, when he runs an occasional revival or workshop. You know, there's plenty to do with his growing brood and his young, hassled little wife," she explained. Her eyes lit up as she spoke, "You know what you should do? You should come by the house tomorrow! Dad eats lunch with us at 11 on Tuesdays. That way, you could meet Little 'Un-I mean my husband, Junior Lloyd, too." Her voice had gathered strength and volume as she provided solutions without first consulting her father or her husband. Virgil just starred at her; he hadn't expected her to be so resourceful or so pushy, and he wasn't exactly sure how to respond. Before he did decide, she pushed forward, almost pleading, "Don't say no; oh, don't say no." She recognized her own urgency as stemming from something—a desire for anything—new in her dull life. Before tonight, she had disciplined her mind to disregard what was missing in her life; but now that she had a taste of excitement, through seeing and talking to Virgil again after all these years, and through tasting the alluring flavor as a grown woman and not a motherless child, a small glimmer of growing hope for positive change and real grownup passion sparked inside Freida; she refused to let that hope die even though that hope was foreign and perhaps even wicked.

Virgil cleared his now raspy throat, smiled slyly, and answered, "Well, Frieda, I guess I could do that. I don't reckon I've burned any bridges with the Reverend. We parted on good terms, I recollect. And, besides, I'd like to spend a little more with you and catch up on Red Hill news." He clasped even stronger on Freida's chunky hands; she didn't resist that firm hold, either. "I do still strum a pretty mean guitar, if I do say so myself. And if'n it was to help your daddy, I'd be glad to practice up and provide him with some music. And to get to meet the lucky man who calls you his wife? That would be an extra bonus! It's a date!" Afraid of being perceived as a little too forward and anxious, he reworded, "I mean that it's a *lunch* date." Virgil smiled, and, with freshly fed confidence, raised his head until it was even with Freida's. Without checking himself this time, he declared, "You know, Freida, little peach, I've never thought there was anything wrong with a man having a woman for a good friend, don't you agree?" He hoped for her affirmation, and she timidly nodded but avoided direct eye contact and began wriggling her hands away from his, but her body heat radiated in the cold air. In reality, both night travelers were lonely and desperate to fill deep gaps in their lives—his for money and hers for passion. She was much more afraid of her own reactions than she was of Virgil's actions. He, conversely, feared he had created a monster with an insatiable appetite, a most intense appetite unrelated to southern cuisine. But, he was a man and that passion was just an added perk along the way on his quest for financial gain.

Freida, looking at the sky, spoke again. "Oh, I better get back. Junior will be ready for bed, or he may have already moved his personal saw from the living room to the bedroom! He can ring the rafters with that snore." Virgil's laughter in response was a little too loud and he echoed in the cold, night air. Freida blushed so profusely that he could see the color in her rosy cheeks deepen under the dim street light near Junior's shed.

"Would you finish walking with me back to my house?" she asked as the two glanced back at Uncle James's house and shed. "That way, you'll know how to get there tomorrow for lunch." He didn't actually answer, but he arose from their coat seat, pulled Freida up by one

hand, and draped the wet jacket over his arm. He continued to hold
her hand, erotically rubbing his fingers in her palm, unashamed and
greedily, as if he expected her to vanish like a genie. She just as fiercely held his hand in a bulldog grip, and they walked toward the corner
of the main road where Freida lived, Freida guiding Virgil back to
her frosty, glistening yard. No one spoke, but as sages profess: "Silence speaks volumes." And if that is true, this protracted silence
could have replenished the County Book Mobile.

As the couple-and they were a couple-reluctantly approached the
creosote steps that led to the tiny screened in porch by the kitchen,
Freida again interrupted their silent reverie. "Well, I guess I'll see you
tomorrow around 11, right? I hope you like field peas, cornbread, and
meatloaf," she added hastily and hopefully. She knew only a thin wall
separated them from her sleeping spouse, and this fact made her a
little nervous. Virgil, as if miraculously stricken deaf and mute,
dropped his sweaty hand from hers and slid both freed hands down
to Freida's comparatively slim waist. Her amble hips accentuated the
smallness of her waist. (Unkind church ladies referred to her peculi-
arly shaped hips as those similar to "two pigs fighting".) Virgil boldly
pressed the unsuspecting but not protesting woman into his own
form, planting a wet, passionate kiss on her delighted and secretly
expectant lips. He took his time pulling his full lips away dramatical-
ly and slowly with his long, pink tongue still exposed after the lips
had separated. He felt Freida's furiously pounding heart next to his
chilled chest. This carpenter's wife was more than willing to play
with fire, and Virgil would easily be able to fan the flame to get what
he wanted. After all, nobody lost in this sweet deal, he thought with a
smirk on his icy face.

Their lips, dried and chilled by the weather, stuck in place just for
a delayed second; then Virgil turned on his heel almost clicking them
together like Dorothy in Oz or a German Brown Shirt hoping to
impress the Fuhrer. He walked across the crunchy yard and into the
distance; he was barely visible even in the brightness of the witnesses
of the glowing moon and stars. "Where will you stay tonight, Virgil?"
she half-whispered into the darkness of the corner. Virgil shone his

weak flashlight toward her wanton face; he could easily see the siz-zling desire in her eyes. 'I don't want you to get cold and lonely," she added, with a sultry tone, unnaturally low and slow.

"I'll sleep in your uncle James's shed tonight. It'll be dawn soon, and I'll clean up at the artisan well in the morning before the com-missary opens," Virgil called back in a quiet, but seductive tone. He anticipated her concern and fear for his safety and comfort and as-sured the genuinely worried woman. "Now, Freida, I've slept in much colder places than the shed since I've been down on my luck. Besides, seeing you again and knowing you're willing to help me gives me warmth enough for the night," his voice began to change in pitch as he turned away from her and headed toward his bed for the night. Freida's round, porcelain face sported fresh, hot tears.

Freida's practical side wanted to run inside and fetch him her own pillow and wedding ring patterned quilt; her passionate side wanted to run outside and down the road to share the shed space with Virgil. Neither side won; common sense served to remind her that any unusu-al noise or motion could alarm Junior. But her reasonable embrace of reality did nothing to diminish her intense desire to be with him. How silly, she though! I'm a logical, Christian woman with a faithful hus-band. But as the majority of the society knows, logic and reason vanish when love or even lust is involved. Southern mother wit declared that when two people were in love or in lust, the couple abandoned the seat of intellectual strength—the brain—to make wise choices. Or as some plain spoken Red Hill grandmothers contested:"It's a case of the tail ruling the head!" Blunt, perhaps, but painfully accurate in Freida's case.

As Virgil wandered back to Uncle James's shed, Freida shuffled back into the toasty warm house which now seemed emotionally and even physically cold and lifeless even though the buck stove radiated, displaying a deep red as the embers burned down during the pred-awn hours. She had been much warmer sitting on the cold, damp pea coat with Mr. Virgil Jones. She mindlessly stoked up the fire, adding a small, pine cut-off as a back stick.

She lightly closed the door and bolted it with the handmade latch her husband had fashioned. As she blundered through her tidy matchbox sized kitchen, she mentally chastised herself for making the situation even more tenacious by extending the lunch invitation to Virgil when Junior and her father would both be in attendance to witness the electricity between her and Mr. Jones. Why was she thinking of him as "Mr. Jones" now when she had met him, encouraged him, held his hand, kissed him, and yes, desired him? Perhaps, she thought, by choosing the formal name, she could will herself more formal and less passionate. Her moist eyes turned to size up Junior's status.

Junior had not so much as moved the daily newspaper off his lap. His snoring was steady and rhythmic like his life. He was reliable and predictable. But at the same time, Freida was not in the market for either of these qualities after tasting something erratic and erotic. She turned off the living room lamp, climbed into her side of the fluffy bed, and fell into a deep sleep without taking the time to remove her robe or house shoes. Soon, the bright morning sun cut like a sharp blade through Freida's flour sack curtains. Amazed to find herself in the same sleeping position as she had last night, she awakened with a start, fearing that she had overslept and ignored the alarm clock. Her fears were valid; Junior had already left for work. She hadn't even heard him take a shower or fix his own breakfast. She remembered that he had no need for a lunchbox because he would come home for lunch as was the routine today. Upon recollecting that fact, she bounced out of the heavy covers, slapped her flat feet against the pleasantly warm floor and raced to the kitchen to begin her lunch preparation. On the mustard yellow plastic tablecloth was a small handwritten note written on a discarded Sears catalog application. It read:" My Sweet Freida. You must have really been tuckered out. I didn't want to wake you, but Mrs. Barr's pipes done busted, so I reckon I won't get through with her problems in time to eat lunch. I cooked me a egg and some sausage for breakfast. I'm sorry I didn't wash up the dishes. Me and Daddy's gonna be tied up over there working during our regular lunchtime. Don't worry about bringing me lunch. I'll get a plug of bologna and a nickle's worth of cheese to tide me over. See you later this evening around 5. Maybe if it's not too cold, we could build a little campfire outside and roast some winnys for supper. Love, Junior"

Guilt flooded Freida after she put the sweet, chicken-scratched note down. He really was a good man, and he really did love her. He couldn't help it if his reliability was the source of her irritability. What would she do? Freida had no way to contact Virgil and cancel the lunch, but perhaps, it was better-safer this way. Her daddy would be here; that's who Virgil really needed to see. That is what she tried to convince herself of as she caught her wild, disheveled reflection in the chrome on the stove. In a quick decision, she decided to concentrate on improving her looks before she prepared the meal. She could whip up the simple meal in no time, and she wouldn't have to hurry to get lunch over in time for Junior to return to work when the whistle blew.

She flapped her bare feet once again across the kitchen and living room as she headed for her bathroom to "put on her face". She heard the screen door screech, and she stopped in her tracks. Surely, it wasn't her husband! "Freida, you here? Can I come in? I know I'm early, but I just wanted to explain myself to you before the Reverend and Mr. Lloyd arrived. As I lay in that cramped little shed for the remainder of the night, I realized that I overstepped my bounds." Virgil's familiar and now formal voice echoed as he advanced into the kitchen. Frieda couldn't decide if she was relieved or afraid that the early visitor was actually Virgil instead of Junior.

"I'm getting dressed, and it's already 9:00, Virgil. If you've got something to say, you'll need to talk to me in front of my bathroom door. Freida had never had another man in her bedroom except for her husband or her father, who, when she was a child, listened to her recite her prayers before pecking her rosy check with his weather cracked lips. Both men's images flashed before her mind's eye as she hastily slapped her makeup onto the sleep creased face that stared back at her in the medicine cabinet mirror. She couldn't let Virgil see her in the daylight like this. She attempted, feudally, to present herself as angry at Virgil catching her unprepared, but her heart raced as she picked up the faint scent of his body. "I've got lunch to get on the table. Daddy'll be here shortly. Junior won't be here; he's got to work during his lunchtime. Just come on out with what you're trying to say." Frieda feared the worst; her self confidence began to plummet and she sensed a break up even though there was no relationship yet. She had never been the recipient of male attention. "Let's get it over with. You regret the walk? You regret the hand-holding? You regret the kiss?" Her heart was pounding as she perspired off as much makeup as she applied in her efforts to "doll up" for his early visit.

"No, dear lady, it's none of that. I just want to say that I'm sorry. I mean, I'm not REALLY sorry, but I wouldn't want to injure you in any way," the pseudo-repentant, failed salesman explained. "It was the cold air, you being grown up and all, and I ain't been cared a whit for in a long time. I pushed you too far-you bein' a married Christian lady. Does your man know what he's got? I hope so,'cuz I sure do 'ppreciate a fine specimen like you, Frieda. Let's just enjoy the time we have together as old friends and I'll try to keep my mind off your-uh--body. If it's alright, I'd still like to stay and eat lunch and see the Reverend. I'm right hungry, and I'm broke, but I wanted to get this settled before we all sit down to say grace," Virgil wound down like an old grandfather's clock. He did, truly, feel slightly guilty, but as Red Hill residents like to say, "The truth's the truth when the world's on fire". And the truth was that Virgil couldn't remember his last meal or his last tumble with a woman, so if humble pie was on the menu, then he'd take a generous slice to get his way with the lonely housewife. He needed money and she needed him. Availability evened the odds.

Freida's heart melted, and her desire to decorate herself suddenly embarrassed and hindered her. She jerked off her crumbled robe, and grabbed the glass doorknob. She pushed open the bathroom door, bumping Virgil's forehead. She was half-way through the makeup process, but she had not changed her clothes from last night. She felt her cheeks burn with shame. She immediately acknowledged her lack of innocence in last night's activities. "It was my fault, too, sir. Don't take all the blame on yourself, Mr. Jones, I mean Virgil," she responded. Frieda had restored his formal title in hopes of re-establishing formal boundaries and distances between them even though she wanted

them completely abandoned. As she rattled on, Virgil found himself
more interested in her form than in her information. Freida's obviously pear shaped body under the thin gown stuck to her full figure
deliciously, he thought. He liked ample curves, and thank goodness
for static cling, which made them more visible.

Suddenly passion seized them both. Virgil did not find her
stringy hair, her one gold tooth or her corpulent shape in any way
repulsive; rather, he was drawn in by her rawness. To him, she was
beauty, passion, kindness, talent, and most especially, a wild ride away
from filthy lucre. His present allusions were thinly supported by lust
and unbridled want. Freida felt his hot glare burn through her skin
like a new candle through a bride's veil. He pulled her trembling,
willing body tightly toward him like the string on a Duncan yo-yo,
and she, without any hesitation, cooperated fully. Briefly, Freida
glanced out the tiny bedroom window that faced the main road,
jerked the curtain shut; and then, trance-like and still magnetically
stuck together, the steamy couple fell into the messy bedcovers.

There was barely enough time for Freida to compose herself, and
there would never be enough time for her to erase the slow smile that
gave away her awakened sense of satisfaction now as she magically
transformed herself from illicit lover to down home chef. She allowed
Virgil to dress her quickly, and he even attempted to help in the kitch-
en until he realized he was more of a liability than an asset. The heat
between them was much higher than the preheated oven readying itself for the cornbread. The unique gleam in her ocean blue eyes-bluer
than ever before—a sharpened color which satisfied women wear—
complemented her emerging beauty, and Virgil counted that change as
coup. He defended his actions to himself, swearing that the encounter
with Freida was his premier and his grand finale, all in one. He
couldn't allow himself to get involved with a married woman and especially with THIS married woman. He needed financial help more than
he needed additional trouble. He admitted to himself that Freida was
needier for sexual satisfaction than he was for financial relief.

Freida hand formed meatloaf, boiled zipper peas, and stirred up
dog bread (cornbread without eggs) while Mr. Jones prudently sat

and shivered on the rickety swing on the front porch as he anxiously awaited the spiritual advisor and mentor of his youth. Soon the rattletrap car pulled up near the ditch, and the beloved Reverend rolled out of the driver's seat. Virgil leaped off the porch to meet him. The two hugged and walked back to the swing to relive better times. Reverend Gaddy, being ignorant of the morning's activities, conducted small talk with Virgil before going into the kitchen to greet his beloved daughter. "Why, baby girl, you're looking unusually happy this morning. You've fell away more since last week. Don't lose too much, or Junior won't be able to find you!" her father laughed as he kissed his only daughter's cheek.

LUNCH WAS CARRIED out uneventfully. Old times were discussed and history was conveniently revised. Laughter rang freely in the Lloyd's house. The Reverend Gaddy listened to Virgil's tale of woe and willingly hired him as guitarist; of course, his own young, exhausted infant bride was daily consumed by the Gaddy boys' constant needs, so he assured Virgil there was lots of work to be done around the Gaddy place for additional income. The Reverend also promised to help Jones get a better job either on the Braun black yard or on the peeling yard near the base of Red Hill where the prepaid stock was stored—a weeding out place for new employees, but far superior to vacuum cleaner sales. This holy man, the Reverend Gaddy, unlike Billy Pallister, was respected and welcomed in Red Hill by his parishioners, the residents, and by Braun's boss, Beaux. Chances were fairly good that Mr. Jones's financial future was on the upswing. However, Virgil was even more convinced that the new development between the beloved preacher's daughter and the disinterested salesman had to be extinquished.......or, at least secretly managed. Reverend Gaddy would not cotton to his only daughter's indiscretions, and Virgil needed the Reverend's endorsement more than he needed Freida's involvement.

Freida started to relax as the meal wound down. The conversation had been light and pleasant, but as Freida daydreamed between dull accounts of the past, she knew that if she were to continue the dangerous relationship with Virgil, it would have to be airtight; for, she knew the Red Hill mindset would sympathize with her loyal husband as it would crucify her, forever damaging her father's influence on the people's faith in preachers and perhaps even in God. Loyalty to the trusting residents of this incorporated town meant more than just receiving a gold watch after years of faithful service. Loyalty was respected and valued. A nauseating knot built in her stomach as she knew tough decisions awaited her. But the lingering feeling she retained from this morning reinforced her determination to experience what she thought was true love despite the tremendous risks it entailed. And Jones would be back in her father's old apartment, too.......

"Mr. Jones, are you about ready?" the Reverend began as he patted his extended belly and stretched against the dining room chair. "My pretty daughter has filled our stomach, and we've filled the air with old times. It's time for us go on home so you can get all the leavening out of that dusty apartment," he chuckled at his own religious joke. Gaddy referred to the ancient Hebrew game of removing yeast from a Jewish home in an symbolic effort to eliminate sin and purify the area. The meaning was lost on the other two. He reached over and kissed his loving daughter on the cheek and continued, "Thank you, honey. I'm sorry Junior couldn't join us today." The reverend scratched his head and picked up his cap. He continued, a little shyly, "You know you and Little 'Un need to get busy making me and Luella some grandbabies. Now, I'm not picky. Boys or girls will be just fine. They'll have built in playmates with our rounders," he chuckled, slapping Jones on the back, and hugging his completely embarrassed daughter all in what seemed like one wide swoop while guiding the equally jovial Jones to the front yard. The men left a trail of dust as they sped off toward the Gaddy compound. Freida felt abandoned and discontented.

After her father's auto was no longer in sight, Freida's embarrassment quickly eroded to panic. She knew very well what could happen, or even what might have already happened. Again, she reasoned with herself by rationalizing as many other women have done.

It *couldn't* happen after just one time. Lloyd and I, she remembered, haven't had any success conceiving, so I might be incapable of having a child. She busied herself with a specific household chore that sparked no intellectual activity-washing the lunch dishes. With each plate she scrubbed, her unsettled mind would wander back to the morning exhilaration she had felt in her own bed. She attempted to block or even to discard the possible consequences which persistently intruded on her erotic thoughts. Logic, now, had been abandoned. When had she felt more alive? Now, she knew why battles were fought and kingdoms were captured in search of the feeling she now had about Virgil.

Her kitchen musings were abruptly halted with the grinding sounds of Junior's brakes as he stopped the engine of his rattle trap truck. She reluctantly greeted him with an air kiss as she stepped on-to the porch. He looked exhausted and frozen, but he wore a weary smile. She noticed a small package in his back overall's pocket, but she did not inquire of its contents. Junior cleared his throat, "Um, hey, baby cakes, are you rested? Man, Mrs. Barr's pipes were a booger to get to, but me and daddy finally got 'em working now. We poured hot water through them copper pipes until the ice melted. You know, it's a warmin' up now to what it was earlier, "he puffed rapidly and asked, "You know what I got in my back pocket?" He seemed more enthusiastic in his tone than in his usual after work mumble. She glanced at the Felix clock whose tail served as a pendulum; it was around three in the afternoon. He was early. Mr. Beaux probably gave him some comp time for working during his lunch, she presumed. What would she do until he characteristically fell asleep in his chair?

As before, she conceded in her mind that, yes, he was a good man. But after last night and this morning, she was no longer in the mar-ket for goodness. She didn't love him and hadn't loved him; he had rescued her from becoming a spinster and elevated her marital status from that of an old maid. He had been a bachelor with little hope of marrying until she gave him some attention at church. She had had no suitors. Her father was busy with his new life. Marriage suited everyone-everyone except Freida. She now recognized his steadiness and stability as dreary traits, and her life with him was just as barren and dull. She swallowed hard and spoke. "You know, dear, we had leftovers from lunch, and I'm still exhausted from doing all the chores today. Let's not have a campfire tonight. I know you are ready to be out of the elements," Freida spoke kindly with a veneer of empathy. She saw the wrinkled corners of Junior's mouth draw down in disappointment. "I just don't want you to take a cold," she assured him. "We can enjoy that on a warmer day, honey," she added with false kindness.

"Well, if that's the way you feel. I can just eat the leftovers early and maybe have some pie later," he suggested. "But you haven't guessed what's in my pocket, or are you too tired for that, too?" He sounded defeated, but continued, "Oh, it don't matter now 'cause it's just coconut bonbons-your favorites. We'll just wait until you're rested. They'll keep a while," Junior added thoughtfully. The loving husband peeled off his iced covered boots, damp woolen socks, and padded into the little den where he melted into his favorite chair, repeating his daily ritual earlier than usual. His fat, swollen body seemed to deflate as he sank into the candle wicking cushions in the overstuffed chair. He was, as southerners say,"Give out". Methodically, Freida served his early dinner still warm from the oven where she placed it after lunch. She positioned the tv tray directly in front of her husband's belly and centered the Blue Willow plate for his convenience. Junior inhaled his meal, wiped his face with his folded handkerchief, and starred at his wife, pondering her unusual fatigue. He thought she looked a little confused, yet her eyes were as bright blue as he'd ever seen them. Was there a glow on her plain face?

Suddenly, the exhausted and lethargic Little 'Un jumped from the chair as if he had sat upon Freida's stray pin cushion and shouted gleefully, "I know what's ailing my woman! You're in the family way! Ye-haw! That's it, ain't it? Why didn't I think of that already? Here, set down and let me git you a piller fer your feet!" Ignoring his own soreness from the day's labors, the renewed "father-to-be" (in his mind) raced to the couple's bed to fetch a fluffy pillow before Freida could deny or confirm his assumptions. He surged with newfound energy as he left the living room. "You are a'glowin, ain't ye?" Junior shouted, shaking the small framed house as he stomped toward their bedroom.

As the ecstatic husband stretched his pudgy arm across to his side of the bed, an unknown object fell and clanged onto the shiny, polished floor. It rolled under the bed and stopped its motions when it reached the base of the bedpost on his wife's side. Junior walked around, bent his heavy frame over, and picked up a small, cheap flashlight still emitting a fragile stream of light. "Where'd this come from, honey? I ain't never seen this, and I shore as heck wouldn't buy a piece of junk like this," the confused man commented. He looked foolish holding a fluffy pillow and a tiny, dim flashlight as he wandered back to the couch.

Simultaneously, Freida moved with nervous adrenalin to met Junior as he headed toward her. "What are you talking about, Junior? Isn't it yours? Daddy was over here today, but I didn't notice it in his pocket," Freida answered, pretending to be as confused as Junior over the flashlight. She conveniently omitted the mention of a third luncheon guest, which to her was the most important one and the one she needed to protect. "Maybe it was Mr. Beaux's flashlight. You know he came around earlier to collect the rent. It may have fallen from his pocket; you know how fast he moves," Freida, conjured, providing weak excuses which were blatant lies. She had thought them up quickly, but she was not confident of their strength and rightly so.

"Mm….," Junior muttered, confused. "Why would Mr. Beaux come to collect it? I pay the rent each month when I'm in the pay line on Fridays. (Employees were paid in cash, so they usually paid any company debts immediately upon receiving their pay.) "It wasn't overdue, and it ain't gone up," Junior offered, even more concerned. "And Mr. Beaux, he would never carry a lightning bug for a light!" he surmised, his seriousness lifting slightly as he remembered the reason for his trip to the bedroom. He refused to do or say anything that might upset the little mother. "I guess anyone can make a mistake. Maybe Mrs. Beaux was out when I paid it, or Mr. Whig didn't write it down. I'll get it to him," he concluded. "Don' worry about it, sugar. Even the remote possibility of becoming a father and the excitement of that reality took precedence over rental confusion or flashlight misplacement, and Junior gently pushed Freida back onto the couch. "You set back and let me put your feet on this here piller," he finished. Freida was stiff and uncoordinated as he lowered her to the seat and lifted her feet to the coffee table.

"You jest rest, and I'll git myself some of that chess pie I saw in the Frigidare. You ought to eat again," the excited man encouraged, but Freida shook her head. Junior smiled as he remembered. "Aw, that's right. Women are a might puny at first, ain't they? They lose their appetite. I know. I've heard the men of the yard talk about their wives when they wuz expectin'," he spoke knowingly. Having Freida's comfort secured, Junior explored the refrigerator for his wife's famous chess pie.

At first, Freida panicked and felt a need to fabricate some story that could explain her fatigue, but as Junior dug in the refrigerator for his pie, she realized that at least she had a built in excuse for resting and for avoiding his advances, giving her more time to recap the day's events in peace and form a strategy. She remembered the added mystery of Virgil's flashlight. She would have to find a way to dispose of it before Junior dutifully returned it to Mr. Beaux. She couldn't give it back to Virgil now because the possibility of Junior recognizing it again was higher since her father had rented the apartment to Virgil. The Lloyds visited the Reverend's place too often to return the flashlight before their next visit to her father's. Too risky. What would she do?

Heeding Scarlett O'Hare's advice, she postponed solving the problem until tomorrow. Freida opened the pages of the local newspaper and stared at the thin pages but she did not actually read it. Hours passed slower than it passed at a Red Hill political rally. Soon, Junior entered the next phase of his daily routine-slumber and snore. By dark, his layered eyelids were closed for the night, and his rhythmic snoring rivaled the sounds of the plant's old steam engine. Freida's body again began to yearn for what it hadn't had in her marriage. Grabbing the slender flashlight, boldly, the determined woman slipped off the cozy couch, dashed out the back door, and pushed Junior's truck into neutral, cranking it further down the road to avoid its rattling, tearing noise. "What am I doing?" Freida asked aloud as if someone would provide an answer. And even if someone had suggested a logical choice, she would have rejected it; logic still was not a welcomed guest tonight. Her raw emotion reigned queen for the day.

A short while afterwards, Freida pulled up behind the garage apartment of her new lover. She killed the motor before it could produce the tubercular sputter on its own. Her father's house was completely dark. The only light on the isolated property came from above the garage. Virgil may still be straightening up his new place, she thought to herself. The muted sound of Junior's truck dying caught Virgil's attention away from his chores. He pulled the burlap curtains apart to see Freida flashing the weak beam of his own flashlight up toward the window. Motioning her to come up the back stairs, he let the dingy curtains fall back into place as he marched over the clutter toward the door at the top of the steep stairs. Her heart was forcing its beat through her heaving chest as she ascended the unsteady steps two at a time. Virgil looked out over the Reverend's property for any sign of light, and then he quickly opened the paint-stained door just as she arrived in the doorway, a move which caused Freida to stumble into the messy apartment. She literally fell into his arms and clung to him until he peeled her off like a stuck wrapper on a favorite candy bar—overly sweet and greatly desired. He starred at her somewhat disapprovingly. But, he was, after all, a man, just as human as he was broke.

"What ARE you doing here?" Virgil asked with a stern tone. Even Virgil was taken aback by her forwardness so early in the new relationship. He regretted allowing his physical needs to supersede his initial plan for financial help. However, he did not regret creating this sizzling desire in Freida for him. He had not found anyone so desperate for love on any of his travels, and he prided himself in her immediate dependency for what he could provide. He glared at this hungry being as she spoke. Yeah, the old salesman still had it, he thought, arrogantly.

"I have recognized that my loneliness is unbearable. You helped me identify what was missing in my silly little life," she explained in a Judson girl manner. Virgil glanced down at the cursed flashlight in her swollen hand. Seductively, she slithered the plastic light across her leg and near her upper thigh imitating the slow slid of an exotic serpent. "Oh, that. It's your flashlight. Junior found it under the bed, and I told him that Mr. Beaux had dropped it when he came by to collect the rent," Freida spilled. But as she truly listened to her own flimsy story, she knew just how shallow and unbelievable it sounded. It was too late now. She was here, and she wasn't leaving-at least for a few precious moments. "He'll forget, Virgil. I'll think of something. Just hold me, please," she unashamedly begged her lover. When he reached for her, she, as the aggressor, strongly pushed him into a single wrought iron bed which had been hurriedly assembled in the middle of the scattered room. As his tousled hair fanned out over the moldy old pillowcase, she slipped her hand under it and tucked the flashlight in the pillowcase.

Reverend Gaddy's rooster crowed three times, causing Freida to sit up in the cramped but cozy old bed. She unbraided her thick legs from Virgil and snatched up Junior's car keys. "I've got to go. Junior will be up soon. I haven't fixed his lunch, and I'll have to feed him breakfast, too," she declared as she walked closer to a faded, advertising calendar that Virgil had not taken down yet. Freida, walking toward the garage apartment door, struggled to gather her hopelessly twisted clothes, which she had wildly pitched over the headboard last night. She hadn't wanted to bathe for fear she would diminish the musky odor that clung to her body. Freida stood at attention and remembered something, speaking as steadied herself in her stanch position. "Oh, today is the day Junior takes his mother to see her sister at the home. He sleeps a little later since he's going to be off work," she relaxed as she snatched one last kiss, and fled down the rickety staircase. Funny, she hadn't even noticed the wobbly steps last night. She laughed and raised her head to see Virgil wave and weakly smile from the other side of the dingy glass. Almost immediately, Freida was humming down the crooked road toward Red Hill and

Junior. Her lingering and unwashed sensual scent filled the rusty truck. She would finally take a bath when she returned home, she admitted, smiling provocatively at no one. She already regretted losing the intoxicating scent that drove her like the unbridled passion of lioness that paced her cage in hopes of the return of her king of the jungle; the unfamiliar emotion morphed Freida from a mild housewife to a wild beast. Virgil fell back, exhausted, on his earthy smelling covers, and dropped immediately off to sleep.

As she maneuvered the old truck, Frieda calmed down a bit to savor the clear, sunny morning. The cold winter temperatures were improving; spring would not be too far away. There had been no traffic thus far, but again she glanced back in her rear view mirror and noticed a vehicle gaining ground speedily behind her—soon tailgating Junior's old truck. She took a second look into her rearview mirror identifying the vehicle as a work truck similar to her father-in-law's which had lumber stacked on two piles in the bed just like this one! As it moved in even closer, she recognized the familiar orange Igloo cooler affixed on the back near the tailgate. It could only be the Lloyds' work truck. Freida's nerves tightened as she wondered why Mr. Lloyd alone would be headed back into Red Hill so early. No to be too obvious, she slowed down to 35 mph to allow the dangerously close truck to pass her. When she braked, Mr. Lloyd gunned the old truck, pushed in on his brakes, and pulled up even with Freida's passenger side. As old Mr. Lloyd moved in dangerously close to the side mirror, Freida saw a partial shadow on the other side, but the driver leaned forward and blocked her view; she had her suspicions as to the identity of the passenger, but the delusional woman persistently held on to the possibility that she was incorrect.

As the elder Lloyd pulled up, he jerkily motioned for Freida to roll down the window. She leaned over to reach the passenger window while continuing to steer with her left hand. "Pull over!" he ordered. Big 'Un was not one to order anyone around, but his stern look was convincing as the guilty woman stretched across the seat and then returned to steering, guiding the wheels toward the soft shoulder. When the two vehicles stopped and Mr. Lloyd shut off his engine, she exhaled in shame; Junior *was* with his father and was already advancing to her window while his father wisely remained in the driver's seat. Junior insisted on direct eye contact with his wife; his chocolate drop eyes registered hurt and defeat, which cut through Freida's own feelings and forced her to focus on the man standing before her that she had vowed to love until death—a promise that seemed to have been taken a lifetime ago. Virgil's sexy body and how he had skillfully shared it last night quickly faded into the background-at least for now.

In a split second, Freida was plagued with decisions: Do I face this right now; or, do I just push the pedal through this rusty floorboard and leave Red Hill forever? Maybe I should aim this piece of crap into the woods and end it all. Instantly, she fantasized warm thoughts of Virgil and the possibility of a future with him. Was *she* just a fling to the unstable salesman? Was she his heart's treasure, or was she just a tantalizing appetizer that temporarily satisfied his hunger until the main course came? Too many questions loomed with too few answers.

She was not given an opportunity to mentally play out her dreams. Her father-in-law joined his son in the window confrontation and spoke first with intense anger in his shaky little voice, "Freida, what do you think you are doing? Me and Junior was a goin' fishing early this morning before the Missus' appointment to see her sister, and what do you think we saw?" he asked but did not expect an answer or even an acknowledgment of guilt. "We drove down by the Reverend's house to see if he wanted to join us, but it was so dark and he has so many younguns that we decided to let him sleep. But as we turned around in your daddy's yard, we seen Junior's old truck pulled right up flush with those old steps to his old garage apartment where your daddy used to rent to people,'" the old man caught his breath to continue, but Junior clapped his big hands over his father's flapping mouth. Yet, the older Lloyd jerked his son's strong hands away and finished his tirade. "And..and..we heard noises!" He spit the words out like an unwanted bite of inedible dessert. "I've been around a farm, young lady!" Mr. Lloyd declared. "I know what them sounds was!" he spit out indignantly.

"Stop, daddy! I told you this was between me and my wife. I told you when you forced me into the company truck with the pwetense of going fishing that you was meddlin'. You had some wild idea about things that are none of yore bidness," Junior exhaled and turned his father around toward the pickup. "Now, you jest git back in that twuck and go fishing in the nasty little stream by the bridge, or wherever the Hell you want to 'catch fish' and leave me to wwide home with Fweida. I ain't a goin' fishing today!" Big 'Un stomped back to the truck, jerked it into gear, and squaled his tires getting back into the foggy road. Surprisingly, Junior's frustrating stutter was partially controlled as he spoke, but he was far too upset to control his speech impediment while he gnawed at his father.

Freida could see that all of Junior's energy and control had been depleted by that difficult monologue, but even in her disturbed state of mind, she admired her husband for standing up to his irate father. Glancing back at Junior, she regretfully conceded that his bovine brown eyes were deep pools of pain, drained of masculine pride, and replaced with indignation. With his almost toothless mouth wide open like an ancient swamp alligator poised to snap, Junior sucked in the brisk air as if to renew the physical strength necessary for opening the door on the passenger's side and perching on the splitting truck seat . Confused that he expected her to drive, Freida, after some difficulty, cranked the truck but caught the tire in some loose gravel which caused the truck to hesitate before bumping back onto the road again. She glanced over at her husband who was starring out the side window and breathing rapidly.

Freida cleared her throat and mentally prepared her defense of half-truth, but then thought better of it, and just shut her mouth. Starring down at her wet, grass stained house shoes, she prayed to her father's God for strength and guidance. She felt unworthy to call him her God as she drove her husband back to Red Hill. Unexpectedly, Junior broke the silence and ordered, "Pull over. I'll dwive." With no resonance in his voice, he sounded like one of the visiting preachers who persistently droned on and on until someone walked the aisle for repentance in the nondenominational church on a fifth

Sunday—*drop shots*, as Mr. Beaux labeled them. Freida obediently pulled over at the next convenient spot as Junior exited the passenger side. She then slid over to his warm seat, wondering what would happen next. Junior gently closed his door and returned to the completely empty road. As he steadied the truck, his dry lips parted as if he were about to speak, but this time his voice failed him, lacking the stamina that he had possessed earlier when he confronted his father. He paused to gain composure, but sadly, his second attempt was not much better. His voice was barely audible, but it *was* audible; even in a dead silent cab with only two passengers, a broken radio and no traffic to camouflage the awkwardness, it was faint.

"I want to speak first, Fweida," Junior claimed as if he had to vie for the spot. "I've got a few things I want to say. I ain't much for flowery words, and I know I ain't worth killin' when I git in of a evenin' adder all them calls about busted pipes and 'lectricty shortin' out, and I ain't been acting lack a husband should and thankin' you fer havin' food on the stove when I git home and clean, ironed clothes to wear, and a neat house with a fire going…" Junior trailed off as if to gain more steam to finish. He struggled to control his speech impediment. "I.. 'ppreciate you not wunning up the ticket at the commissary. I know you give up a lot of culture and sech when you give up the pianer and stop travelin' with ye daddy," he breathed easier and gained vocal strength. "Well, what I'm a buildin' up to is, I reckon," he searched for the exact words, but strong emotion and generational ignorance dammed his thoughts. "Let me put it this way, honey," he boomed with confidence now as he reached the home stretch of his twisted soliloquy. "I don't mind if'n a man picks some fwuit from my twee," he paused, laboring to finish, "but I do want my twee back!" Even though the air itself was cold, Junior was drenched in sweat, and his usually tanned face had yellowed in the heat of his intense stress. He was through talking. After all, even in his broken speech and with incomplete education, he had created the perfect metaphor; and, if the circumstances had not been so melancholic, it would have been hilarious. And believe it or not in later years after his heart was thoroughly healed, Junior told it on himself and eventually joined in the yard crew in a hearty chuckle. But at this moment, there was no humor in the pitiful figurative statement.

Freida understood the simple statement from her simple husband: he loved her, he wanted her back, and most of all, her Junior had forgiven her indiscretions and even understood her unhappiness as she had recently developed a wandering eye. The couple returned home. The tsunami was over, and they had both survived. Junior dutifully drove his mother to the nursing home in town while Freida familiarized herself again with her own surroundings. She knew she and Virgil were through; he was just a tasty tidbit in the romantic past. She had quenched her sexual thirst, and she would no more imbibe from that fountain. She was crestfallen, but resolute.

Mr. Virgil Jones never accompanied the Reverend on the circuit; he applied for the sawyer job at Bert's sawmill about thirty miles from Red Hill. He was ready to leave the area when he realized all opportunities for fleecing the reverend had disappeared. He'd miss that steaming woman, but it was time for him to move on. A cousin of Virgil contacted Mr. Gaddy by phone in an attempt to locate him; he knew Virgil was an expert with saws, so he wanted to see if he would be interested in a job at the newly formed sawmill. Mr. Gaddy, who had allowed Virgil to remain in the apartment until he found employment, suspected nothing and kindly informed his daughter's ex-lover of the Bert's job. Reverend Gaddy even drove Virgil to the worksite after the former Bible salesman packed up his meager belongings and took his damnable flashlight with him. He took the sawyer job, but within the month, he had left Bert's and moved in with his cousin in Gargan, Alabama. Gargan had desperate, lonely, wealthy women, too. The Reverend regretted losing his guitarist, but sensed that the timing was right for Virgil to move on. No one talked about Freida and Virgil, perhaps, because it was so brief, so secretive, or because it was too hurtful. It was a well kept secret, as secrets should be.

Junior rededicated himself to the Methodist church and to his wife. She began to wear the smile of a satisfied woman again without Virgil's help. Freida was elated and joyfully shocked with Junior's new amorous skills! (Perhaps, the men in the black yard shared some valuable tips.) Regardless, eighteen months after that fated morning escapade, Freida delivered a beautiful chocolate drop-eyed baby girl who was named after Junior's sainted mother, Trannie. So, Little Trannie Lloyd enjoyed an idyllic life in Red Hill. She was loved by her friends and her family, especially old Mr. Lloyd, her paternal grandfather, who permitted her to ride in the company truck bed between the protection of perpetual parallel stacks of lumber and the orange Igloo cooler. As loving as he was toward his granddaughter, he was just that unloving and unforgiving toward her mother even though he never really knew the truth or its sordid details. He had judged her long ago and she remained convicted. He only tolerated her because she was his only son's wife and the mother of his little angel, Trannie.

Junior and his father continued to work side by side, wisely avoiding mentioning Freida's name in any conversation they had, until old Mr. Lloyd died years later. After the funeral and a respectable amount of time had passed, a new partner, Foster, was named as the elder Lloyd's replacement. He was a friendly, skilled handyman, so Junior's work load eased somewhat. Little Trannie had loved her grandfather, but she was keenly aware of the narrowing of her grandfather's eyes when her mother came near. She was not cognizant of the cause of his resentment, but she knew it was real and intense; yet, despite his unloving attitude toward her mother, Trannie loved the old man dearly and mourned his death. She never asked her father about her grandfather's feelings toward her beloved mother until long after her Papa Lloyd was cold in the ground. When she did get brave enough to ask, he just brushed the child off and explained that Papa was just getting old. She readily accepted this lame explanation and inquired no more. As for Freida, she developed into the model wife and mother in Red Hill. She involved herself in the Home Demonstration Club, even serving as president twice. She was a class mother when Trannie started to school. She publically showed affection for her husband and that affection was publically reciprocated. As far as anyone knew, the tree remained planted in Red Hill and the fruit was not picked again.

Living in an isolated area like Red Hill in winter was always such a joyous time for children, but the poor road conditions and extended routes made for difficult circumstances for bus drivers. If there were any chance of snow, sleet, or freezing rain, the older children gathered excitedly near the steepest hills to pour washtubs of water over these tricky locations. The sneaky process rendered the slick hills and the surrounding dirt roads impassable for Bus 48 to venture its three-to-a-seat load anywhere on the route. If the road icing project was successful, the lost day of school was then spent sledding on linoleum, trudging in ill-fitting boots, (Conditions were so seldom icy that shoe sizes could not keep up between weather intervals.), and consuming large quantities of hot chocolate at Mrs. Cross's welcoming home.

Mrs. Cross, a white-haired grandmotherly type with the energy and zest of a teenager, loved children and thrived on providing and participating in fun activities. At Halloween, she fashioned them a magnificent haunted house in an eerie, vacant company house beside her own. She financed its construction and decoration with a few local donations and from her own resources. Hours were spent developing just the right ghoul or goblin. Sadly, the Braun corporate office in Bowling Green got wind of Mrs. Cross's creation and banned it due to a company clause-"misuse of a company dwelling". Naturally, the company executives left the unpleasant job of breaking that unpopular news to Mr. Beaux, who bore the brunt of both children's and adults' complaints on both ends-Bowling Green executives and Red Hill residents. But Trick-or-Treating was always delightful in Red Hill despite the demise of the haunted house. Homemade goodies were lovingly dropped in the plastic orange pumpkins stuck through the Red Hill doors; the presence of the tricksters was heralded with "TRICK OF TREAT" in this time of innocence and freedom from dangerous snacks when giggly children did not have to postpone their gobbling, and mandatory candy inspection by protective mothers was not urgent.

Even when winter melted into springtime, bus service could be sporadic and adventuresome. Because the daily route to school included even more rural areas besides Red Hill, a regular bus trip from

Red Hill to nearby Mount Gum stretched into anywhere from forty-five minutes to an hour, depending on the conditions of the poorly maintained roads. An unpredicted flash flood would consume a small wooden bridge near a secluded bus stop or saturate a low place in the dirt road, thus rendering that child and any other eager riders on his route stranded. The county bus driver would then select an alternate route, phoning the parents of the emergency change of plans; then, those parents could decide whether to drive the children to school or to just allow them to stay at home. Jansey's and Rabon's mother often drove them to Mount Gum and served as a taxi service for any other Red Hill children whose parents insisted they attend school.

Bus 48 and 27 shared the Red Hill and surrounding area route, although bus 48 went further south on the main highway while bus 27 traveled to the county line further north. One particular spring day, Bus 27 left Red Hill, stopped and picked up a few highway dwellers (never considered true Red Hill residents), and headed out Bunkum Road toward the high school. Mr. Wall, the patient and soft spoken bus driver, was highly skilled in maneuvering the yellow dragon onto primitive, rub board-like dirt roads while maintaining some semblance of order in the interior of the bus. The road, although still damp from the night's light rain, was not fully saturated, so Mr. Wall plunged through on his regular route. The standard transmission was performing well this morning, and Mr. Wall predicted that school drop off might even be a mite early.

Mr. Wall turned his long truck (as sometimes he called it when he was angry) with precision as he entered the last dirt cut-off before finishing his route on the smooth recently paved last stretch to Mount Gum. About two miles into the bumpy path, a shaky, but always reliable wooden bridge separated two red clay banks. As the bus approached and then mounted the slightly raised wooden planks, the bus driver felt the old bridge, which may have been softened and weakened by heavier rain than expected during the night hours, sway and groan like a land locked whale. He wisely and swiftly forced the steering wheel to the right in hope that the bus would at least lodge between the banks and avoid totally submersion in the rushing, swollen stream beneath. The

bus flopped like an oversized catfish, its top heavier than the girth, and
splatted when it fell onto the muddy bank. The force of that flop
slammed the windows on the right side into the spongy bank, produc-
ing a load sucking sound. Various pitches of screams directly related to
age and gender rose and mingled with fervent sobbing as the bus finally drew its last breath and accepted its natural grave. Mr. Wall hung
onto the metal rail behind his worn seat to steady himself as he made
ready to address the shaken crowd of youngsters. "Hey, hey, boys and
girls," he began loudly and confidently, although he was quite shaky
inside. "Look around you and see if the people around you and *you*, too,
are okay." He paused; no one actually spoke, but he spied several affirmative nods. As the sobs begin to dry up, the bus driver readdressed
the riders. "Here's the plan; listen up closely and no one will get hurt,"
he ordered gently as if he had rehearsed this speech and this moment
for years. "The stream is not that deep. I'm going to climb out my left
window, go over to the house over there," he pointed, "and git a ladder.
Then, I'm gonna come around and open the emergency exit and all
you little ones will exit first in single file. I'll be right there to help you
down the ladder one at a time and set you onto the dry bank on the
left. If'n there's a high school boy or two that would be willin' to help
me, it'll go a lot faster," Mr. Wall petitioned. Some shuffling and
mumbling commenced.

Mike, a senior and a mountain of a kid, boldly spoke first. He was
president of the Mount Gum Student Council, captain of the football team, and a son of the Rashes whose musical talent was known
throughout the area. "Mr. Wall?" The handsome young man asked
respectfully. "Let me help you get them to the other side on the bank,
and then you won't have to waste time going up and down the ladder.
You can just hand one to me, and I'm pretty sure if I put myself in
the middle of the stream between you and the bank, we'll go faster.
You did say the water was not deep, didn't you?" he asked for reassur-
ance. He was quite athletic, but he was not a strong swimmer. He
might be capable of saving himself, but he was not sure about saving
another. He began to make his way toward the back of the lopsided
vehicle.

"Sounds good, Mike," the relieved middle aged bus driver answered. "Well, let's get you little 'uns lined up in abc order, okay?" He felt reasonably sure that the bus had formed a firm suction into the mud bank and would not totter during the emergency exit. He spotted a wide eyed eighth grade girl named Mamie. "Mamie, you help line them up. Quickly, now! Let's go."Mamie was shy but reliable and didn't hesitate to accept her new role. Her father was a truck driver at Braun; she was used to caring for children while her father was away and her mother was left with four to get ready for school each morning.

As Mamie took on a schoolteacher role, herding the sniffling elementary kids in alphabetically order by last name, Mike rapidly positioned himself in the knee deep swirling current. Amazingly, in the emergency situation they were now in, the shuffling children ceased their shouts and bawling, choosing instead to obey Mamie as she patted each child on the shoulder when they positioned themselves correctly. Rapidly and methodically, the bus was almost vacated-at least the children were out and safe. Mr. Wall's riders sat, laughing and joking, on the damp bank as if recessing during a normal field trip on a beautiful spring day. "Okay, you teenagers, come on out on your own like you saw the little 'uns do; only, this time, I'll steady the ladder and Mike will guide you as you walk through the water to join the little 'uns," Mr. Wall announced, quite pleased with his handling of the potentially dangerous situation. And thankful for Mike stepping up to assist!

While this reluctant parade of teens began to exit, a rotund, smiling, elderly lady donning a homemade checkered apron tied around her wide waist waddled down the overburdened back steps of a tiny white house located within a few yards of the crash site. Between her stubby arms, she was uneasily balancing a large black enamel tray which was daintily decorated with painted flowers and colorful fruit between her stubby arms. The Japanese style tray was laden with sugar cookies. "Cookies?" a diminutive blonde girl asked as she still clung to Mamie's strong hand. Other children asked, hopefully, "Cookies? For us?" Most of the excited, yet polite children began to pick themselves up from the muddy band and to move toward a handcrafted pine picnic table where the cookies were headed. What luck, they thought.

"That's right, kiddos," the pleasant faced lady proudly validated. "I was a'bakin' them for the church social, but I reckon younces need them more right now that we fat adults at church. Why, I can whip up another batch later, anyhow. Little feller, you and that rat faced little girl right there," the woman pointed to two doe eyed children near the shade tree, "come here and help me take this tray. Now you get on each side of me and we'll park it on the picnic table. You walk slowly and watch where you're going," she warned. The children did as they were told; and, soon, the first batch of deliciously homemade cookies was in front of about fifty drooling mouths. The old woman continued. "My husband, Williard, made that table. Hit's strong. Some of you can sit on it if you balance each side so's it won't tump over." She turned her wide backside around and headed toward her house. "I've got you some drink, too," she added with a raspy chuckle. No one touched the tray, but everyone wanted a cookie. She spun around and chided, "Eat, children, eat!" That was all it took, but still the hungry group each took only one cookie a piece and one cup of lemonade while they showered thanks repeatedly on their unnamed hostess.

By this time, the last stranded rider had descended the ladder and had picked up his pace as he saw the tasty delights awaiting him on the bank. Mr. Wall and Mike escorted this final soul, even though he was a teenager, so he could join the strange little band of bus gypsies who now began to hover over the table laden with even more cookies—a seemingly endless supply—and several pitchers of lemonade. The grateful bus driver shook hands firmly with Mike as the two heroes marched through the water for the final trip, Mike carried the ladder back to the shed behind the small cottage. Both men breathed a collective sigh of relief.

"Well, Mis'...., we shore do appreciate your kindness. I 'ppreciate the use of yore ladder, too. We've got ourselves in a fix, but it could o' been worse. I 'spect I'll need to call the bus barn and the school to get some help. Before I do, though, I believe me and Mike need us a cookie for strength." Mr. Wall smiled and handed an oversized sugar cookie and a cup of lemonade to Mike as he grabbed each for himself, too, heading briskly for the house. "Excuse me, M'am, where is your phone?" He stopped halfway up the back steps and turned to face the students' angel of mercy. She was busily occupied with the children, but raised her white head to answer him.

"Yes, I'm Bessie Reece. Do you know my Willard?" Mrs. Reece asked.

"He's my husband and he truck-farms with our neighbor, Mr. Reynolds. You know, you look familiar to me, Mr. Bus Driver. Do you farm when you're not driving a bus?" Bessie puzzled over his identity as he patiently awaited the directions to the home phone. "Oh, yeah, you need the phone. Hit's a'hangin' on the wall in the hall. We got a private line; we ain't got no party line, so you can jest start dialing. There's a phone book on the shelf by the phone." She had remembered the initial question and finally answered it before turning her attention to the cookie eaters. She coaxed each child to have a second cookie and another glass of the sweet lemonade as casually as if she fed that many hungry strays in a daily basis. She appeared to be accustomed to mass quantities of food and mass consumption of it as well!

After Mr. Wall completed his phone calls, he stepped back outside and headed for the picnic table. He remembered her questions, too, and decided to respond accordingly. "Yes'm, I got a little hog farm down the road, and I tend to it when I ain't driving the county bus. I've seen yore husband at the Pend's Feed Store down toward the county line. Kids, grown, right?" he asked. The conversation between the two newly acquainted adults continued to pick up the pace as they racked up kinfolks and mutual friends. The more Mr. Wall interacted with this winsome lady the more the whole crowd relaxed and almost forgot what had brought them all together this spring morning. After all, this now amiable lawn party could have had devastating consequences quite differently from the present cookie feast in front of the two adults. Mentally reviewing the last hour after the conversation lulled, Mr. Wall's hand shook as he grabbed another cookie and gulped down a snuff glass of syrupy lemonade to stabilize his nerves. His gnarled, tanned hands were less shaky now, but he had had to steady them earlier when he was alone in the hall looking up phone numbers. Relax, he reminded himself; all is well, and it was.

The relief bus arrived about two hours after the accident, and the hesitant, but full-bellied students reloaded the foreign looking bus. Mr. Wall decided to accompany his precious riders, patting each one's back as they were safely deposited at the appropriate level school. He stood guard beside the borrowed bus, wiped his weary eyes and addressed the anxious crowd before it completely dispersed. "You've all been troopers; I'm proud of each and every one of you," he congratulated them as his voice cracked with emotion. The grateful riders gave him a round of applause and off they went to conquer the world, or at least Mt. Gum. The two drivers in the empty bus rode back to the bus barn; Mr. Wall cranked up his old but reliable blue Ford and headed to his hog farm to complete his morning chores. The accident and the rescue activities afterwards had put him painfully behind in his daily work. It was, regardless of the morning's events, just another work day. No special award, recognition, or citation was ever offered to the everyday hero whose quick thinking and smart action saved a whole bus load of children that day. Mrs. Reece was recognized in her Good Samaritan class at her church, but she, too, faded into anonymity in the community.

The bus accident was retold, relived, and heavily revised for not just days but years to come. Sadly, in the histrionics, more emphasis was placed on the accident itself than the strategic moves and heroic deeds of the simple county bus driver. Mamie, Mike, and Mrs. Reece knew the truth, and they honored Mr. Wall in their hearts with their respect and admiration for a job well done beyond what was expected from the county board of education. Only when the riders of Bus 27 grew up and became parents themselves did they fully realize how fortunate their little group was on the day the bus fell off Little Spring Bridge. Few grateful individuals returned to the common pig farmer to express their gratitude for such quick thinking and responding, but after all, a man of genuine integrity craved no assurance from the outside world that he had chosen wisely. Intrinsic affirmation was enough satisfaction. In addition to the unfairness, few grownups understood youth and its intense selfishness and its convenient forgetfulness better than the lowly, underpaid bus driver who had been charged with the huge responsibility for the lives who rode on rural overcrowded buses each day. He took it all in stride. After all, he knew kids and he loved them in spite of themselves.

After the whirlwind growth in Red Hill during the Roaring Twenties had stopped circling and the impending economic drought blew its vengeful wind against the clay banks, the community's well-respected general practitioner and the young crackerjack lawyer saw the handwriting on the wall and jerked their shingles down, relocating to nearby Colona, the site of a new pulpwood plant. Red Hill residents relied on the untrained medical help of their boss; or if the injury was more serious or work related, Dr. Davies was only twenty-five miles away. Dr. Gwin was even closer. No other physician or lawyer was interested in establishing a rural practice there.

Chiropractic medicine was considered a bastard child of "real" medicine. Few practitioners of the new science were able to maintain an income in their field of expertise. However, the Red Hill community of the 1960's appealed to Dr. Bice, a chiropractor from Sardis, so he set up a closet sized office in the vacant right side of Ada Barr's now defunct boarding house. On a sultry Friday afternoon, the shabbily dressed doctor began moving in cheap, flea-bitten office furniture and bizarre (to the residents) pieces of medical equipment, heavy and awkward to lift. Through the back of the old hotel, Dr. Bice threw up a makeshift ramp over the tall creosote staircase to ease the extreme weight of the pieces of his medical apparatus. He had employed (without pay) two scrawny helpers, who were later identified as his cousins, to help him move. By Monday morning, he and his bedraggled crew had raggedly furnished an office/waiting room and two treatment rooms.

In the front of Mrs. Barr's widest room was the reception area complete with two lime green plastic couches and eight canary yellow plastic chairs for his patients. A small wooden desk equipped with an Underwood manual typewriter, steno pad receipt book, edger, coffee can of fountain pens, and a wooden wall phone that required an operator to connect to another party were housed in the same room. The examining room consisted of an unusually heavy metal table with pedals and levers. There was a bright examining light, a small stool, and a few jars of murky, questionable liquid. In the other room, Dr. Bice had installed an x-ray machine which resembled some machine on an alien spaceship in a B movie. When the x-ray was not in use, the room would serve as a dressing room. A half-bath was placed in the same room, also.

Ada, who was more than a little interested in the moving process, shadowed Dr. Bice as he and his half-starved movers worked at a furious pace to get all the furnishings off the pack mule truck and into the vacant side of the then equivalent of today's bed and breakfast. Ada only downsized her hovering when Sunday came, and she dressed for Reverend Gaddy's Methodist service at 10. She was all too eager to divulge every minute detail to her ladies circle Sunday school class. Fortunately for Mrs. Barr, the Sunday school teacher was late, allowing Ada to hold court immediately.

"Why, the doc and those two pitiful waifs worked past midnight Friday and last night, banging and bumping across my hall," she half-complained and half-bragged as she shared the information before the class began. She continued her precise news report about the move as the fashionable ladies with wide brimmed pastel hats, matching kid gloves, and worn leather shoes leaned in closer to absorb each morsel, not to assure validity when the details were retold, but to ensure the best way to embellish the account as each church mother passed the news along to her peers, not unlike the game of Gossip played in the 1960's to fill up dead time at school.

Ada paused when the harried teacher arrived and established herself at the handmade podium. When the lesson was completed, Ada resumed her tale with renewed energy. "He *says* he's a real doctor. Went to Palm School in Georgia and got a certificate for graduating. I saw that myself. His picture looked just like him, so I guess it's true. The three men were finishing up that tiny bathroom when I left for church services. I didn't bother to invite them to church. I knew they were in their work clothes, and they were trying to meet a deadline," she presumed. She hushed as the Reverend called the noisy congregation to worship.

After morning worship services concluded, most curious parishioners' interest was piqued to see for themselves what was going on and how the dilapidated, abandoned structure was being transformed into a full scale doctor's office. Most Red Hill residents walked to the nondenominational church because its location was within a mile of almost all the houses there. So, it wasn't an imposition to stroll by Ada's place after services. Ada served as their unelected grand marshal.

During church, the ambitious little moving crew had cleaned up all the building materials, scraps, etc., loaded them in the bed of the truck, and even hung a hand painted sign in the front of the old boarding house: "Dr. Ellis Bice, Chiropractor. For Appointment, call county-8602. Drop-ins welcomed." The price was not included on the sign but Ada turned to the curious group behind her as she mounted the steps. "Len, one of the skinny cousins told me that there is not set price. He said every case was different, but one dollar was due at the time of your appointment. Then, if there are other charges such as an x-ray, the price would be more," she explained. From the demeanor of the church crowd, those terms seemed reasonable, but the label, "Quack" was mumbled throughout the standing group. Several members strained to see inside the building but refrained from asking Ada to unlock the latch to verify the details for themselves. They were hungry and ready for a Sunday afternoon nap on their last day of the weekend. Plus, out of spite, some of the ladies didn't want to give Ada the satisfaction of knowing that they were interested in her new boarder. The group of citizens trailed along down the road discussing the new residents and their strange style of "doctoring".

Chiropractic was, indeed, a relatively new form of medicine especially in the slower south, and because change in Red Hill was about as slow as Golden Eagle syrup leaving its jar to soak a buttermilk biscuit on a winter morning, Dr. Bice's office was not full of patients even after almost a week of hanging his shingle. He had overhead the snide comments about "Dr. Quack and Crack" as people walked to the black yard, making a shortcut through Ada's yard. He also knew that his innovative form of healing was not covered by Red Hill residents' insurance; it was all cash up-front, but still inexpensive in comparison to some co-payments. He still showed up for work every morning as if he had a waiting room brimming with eager patients. He knew the

speed of the rural south all too well. He prayed that perhaps at last he
would enjoy financial success or just financial stability.

Because the boarding house was so accessible, reasonable, and
available, Dr. Bice relocated his odd looking family to Mrs. Barr's
back rooms west of the doctor's quarters. His little brood included a
short, stout, wild-eyed spouse, two squirrel-faced daughters (preteen
and teenaged), and a flounder faced infant son possessing the same
dancing eyes as his mother. The spacious apartment was divided into
three large bedrooms, an open sitting room, a typically tiny kitchen,
and a small bathroom. Since the building belonged to Braun, and the
company only charged a dollar a room for rent, Dr. Bice's rent was
only ten dollars a month for the entire northwest wing of the dog
trot house. In turn for this favor from Braun, Mr. Beaux required that
Bice do some part-time mowing and sling-blading around the
church and the black yard to qualify him as a Braun employee and
thus, providing him legal eligibility for company housing.

In the front, widest room where Mr. Bice had established his of-
fice/waiting area, he hung his framed degree and a black and white
picture of his unattractive family. He was most proud of the wooden
wall mounted phone and the fact that he had his own phone number
even though he was on a party line and had to employ an operator
for any outgoing call. The rooms were spacious and seemed vacuous
now without patients. The dog trot architecture lent itself to Ada's
frequent progress checks during the day. Dr. Bice continued to busy
himself with minor repairs and restorations of the abandoned side of
the boarding house and with meeting his Braun requirements as well.
He also had to make time to train his daughter Ina who was to serve
as his personal secretary/receptionist/medical assistant. She, unlike
her obviously disturbed mother and odd little brother, showed signs
of intelligence as did her withdrawn younger sister, Rose. The doctor
didn't anticipate Ina having any adjustment problems, but he knew
how important her social skills would need to be as she was the patients' first contact in the unfamiliar office. If he were able to secure
some regular customers soon, the Bice family might survive in Red
Hill, his last resort.

Hanging out the white clothes on her clothes line, Ada, her neighbors knew, was available for updates on the office and the doctor as well. Talking in a loud speaker voice to Mrs. Pake (and to the other dozens of ladies cooling on their porches or hanging out their own wet clothes to dry), Ada repeated her Sunday's news report, "He says he's a doctor. Went to Palmer school and got a certificate on the wall. His name's under the picture, but it don't look much like him. People can change, though. Look at you, Mrs. Pake, why, you used to be as wiry as your husband, but you've tanked up through the years." The mortified woman sharply pivoted on the tips of her bleached Keds, tucked her fallen tail, and headed for home. Ada continued, addressing no one in particular and oblivious to her own insensitivity which led to her audience's flight. "You know, once them starved fellers left, that little war-orphan-looking wife of his and those possum faced girls finished up that bathroom before I even got out of church. It would be a cryin' shame not to have no clients after all that work. I didn't invite them to church, remember, 'cause it looked like they ain't got no Sunday-go-to-meeting clothes," Ada proclaimed and cranked up again like an unwanted engine disrupting a drive-in movie.

"Hey, Mrs.....Now, where'd that woman git off to?" Ada asked herself, and though she had no visible hearer, there was no shortage of listening ears from the ladies of Red Hill, still hungry for any morsel of gossip about the newcomers. "Jest look at that sign on the front of my boarding house. 'Dr. Ellis Bice, Chiropractic by appointment or walk-in. Call county 8602,'" she read for the community. "Len, one of the doctor's helpers and his own cousin told me that their cousin has a magic table that moves and drops when he examines you. I ain't never heard of such! Len told me that this wasn't Dr. Bice's first rodeo, and it wasn't his, either. Now, I found that curious and I'm not right sure what he meant, but it made me think that the fam'ly has moved a right smart," Ada finally felt a little foolish now that there was no verbal feedback from anyone, so she finished hanging out her laundry and marched back into her side of the house. Spin doctoring was her specialty.

The idle time without clients allowed Dr. Bice during his first week of practice in Red Hill to receive a mixed blessing; yes, he needed the money from patients, but he also needed additional time for Ina to help organize the office, filing cabinet, pamphlet shelves, and the tiny bathroom/dressing room. Ina, hereditarily cursed with her mother's rodent countenance, had dropped out of high school but had attended Averson-Draughn Business School and completed a business/medical receptionist course when the Bice family had lived in Sardis prior to relocating to Red Hill. She was a nervous, jerky little girl, but she had a spark in her brown mouse eyes that was different from the danger and instability so characteristic of her mother's darting eyes and her baby brother's vacant ones.

Ina was busying herself sticking blank name labels on manila folders the second week after opening the new office when a Neanderthal creature dressed in muddy, tattered overalls and a faded red and green flannel shirt silently appeared in the heavy oak door jab of the reception area. He purposely cleared his throat, but his vacant eyes stared out like a confused, wounded animal; Ina jumped off her swivel seat behind the desk like a jackrabbit being pursued by a coyote. The possibly potential patient, in Ina's terrified but hopeful eyes, removed his dusty, worn Bama cap and parted his weathered lips to speak as he ducked his oversized head to clear the door facing. She was ready to step into her new role.

Gaining courage as she thought about her disheartened father, she asked kindly, "May I help you, Sir? Do you need to see my—I mean—the doctor today?" The unusually shy teenager spoke surprisingly clearly and grammatically correctly, staring boldly into the anguished aqua eyes of the giant. Her father had dutifully coached her on the necessity of making this move to Red Hill their last and most financially successful one. By speaking properly and clearly and by treating each patient with respect and integrity,—he coached her—she would display a sense of authority and decorum. The doctor himself, as a youngster, had been strictly home schooled by his extremely zealous maternal grandparents, who eventually abandoned him at age ten for the mission field in Port Antonio, Jamaica. Ellis Bice was then placed by child welfare authorities into a wealthy foster home in Sardis; the elderly couple doted on Ellis and later furthered

his education financially and eventually funded his chiropractic training. Unfortunately for Ellis, the generous couple had died penniless,
having depleted all their savings to educate their foster son. Ina knew
this about her father, and, even at her tender age, she knew that the
Bices had financially exhausted both sets of relatives and what few
friends the couple had made through the lean years since Dr. Bice had
graduated from medical school. Her father was middle aged and desperate. She often wondered why he had married her unstable mother.
She wasn't beautiful and she wasn't sane. Yet, her weary father appeared
to be totally devoted to Belle Bice.

"Yessum!" the lumbering giant spoke with a tone radiating from
great pain. He grabbed his side and lowered his voice's decibel level
as the spasm momentarily released his body from its excruciating
grip. "I threw out my back plowing, and I thought the Quack, I
mean, the doc might loosen it up a mite a'fore I have to go to the
wood yard this evening. I got to try something', and I don't need no
pain medicine to dull me or I'll cut myself in two at work," he added.

"Well, Sir, you're in luck. Dr. Bice is free right now." (He had been
free since he hung his shingle.) Here, just sit right by my desk, and
we'll begin the paperwork," Ina suggested cheerfully and anxiously,
ready to sharpen her secretarial skills on this injured guinea pig. She
rose from her seat behind the desk, this time not from being startled,
and pulled the canary yellow patient's seat even with her desk and
directly facing her typewriter which already had a blank page in it.
She drew out a new pen from the Maxwell coffee can holder and
grabbed an official looking medical form from her open file drawer.
When she had completed her ever so efficient ritual, she glanced
back up at the 30ish aged man and motioned for him to take a seat;
she was confused when he continued to stand, so she reinforced her
intention for him to obey, "Please, have a seat, Sir." He grimaced and
grabbed his side, crumbling toward the ground.

The pain wracked sufferer refused to move, choosing rather to defend his reluctance. "Ma'm, I can't set down here nor anywheres else.
I'm a'hurtin' fierce. Can you jest let me lean on you and get me back
to yore daddy's examination room? Ain't that what they call it? That's

what a real doctor calls it, right?" He paused, looked down, and began again, "I'm sorry. I didn't mean to insult yore pappy," the voice rose and stopped suddenly as he was clutched by another spasm. "OOH!" he shouted loud enough for Ada to stretch her rubber neck around her own door to better size up the situation. The doc finally had a patient! And what a patient he was!

Ina, realizing she was more concerned about protocol than pain, rushed around her desk, calling for her daddy and forgetting professionalism, screaming, "Daddy, daddy, you have a patient in great pain. Can you help me get him to your room? I don't think I can lift him by myself." Ina's panic was evident in her raw, high pitched voice, which imitated a feral cat's meowing or an errant pupil scratching on an old slate chalkboard, equally unsettled and unwanted. Her few courses in school had not prepared her for this, she thought. Patients were supposed to sit down, to fill out papers, and to follow her lead to an examination room while she promptly posted the medical chart on the closed door and swished back to the security of her swivel chair behind the auspices of her desk. She had not been adequately trained for aiding a leviathan in agony on her first day—or any day! Yet, he was here and her dad had a chance.

Dr. Bice had been organizing and revamping his various charts and diagrams, pretending to be intensely engaged in his work; in actuality, he wanted to be near the office and away from the house, avoiding the chaos of the mountains of boxes still cluttering the living quarters. But at the sound of Ina's banshee cry, he quickly dropped the files and grabbed his white lab coat, hoping to appear more professional, while he widely paced his large feet through the hall and into his new waiting room.

"Here, Sir. I'm the doctor, Dr. Bice. Let's get you up on the table and see what we can do to relieve your pain before we do anything else. Ina, you steady the right side, and I'll take the left," Dr. Bice spoke kindly and firmly, reassuring the injured man of his own strength by steadying the man's arm around the white lab coat collar. Leaning toward the doctor and following Ina's hand, the two led him to the first examining room. The trio was drenched in sweat when they finally cleared the doorway, and they paused briefly before attempting the next potentially excruciating move to the examination table. "Now, if you can just let us gently turn you around, sir, we can help you up a little at a time to minimize your pain," the sympathetic doctor reassured the anguished patient. "Ina, help me with this." Ina and Dr. Bice turned the man's back toward the table and pulling him from under his deep armpits, they awkwardly slid his massive body up onto the thin table pad, adding the foot extension for additional support and length. He barely fit on the table.

"Oh, mercy! Somebody help me! I'm a'dyin'!" the injured man moaned as Ina instinctively rolled him over on his side, placing a flattened pillow between his thick knees. His pain appeared to ease up with that move. "Oh, Miss, that hoped me. I'm much obliged to ye. Doc, I don't think I'll be able to get myself up off this table when my appointment is over. His short, labored breaths slowed up, and he appeared to experience some relief. "I'm a'gonna be a invalid, Doc?" he asked, with premature surrender in his voice.

"Oh, no, no, Mr.-er-I didn't catch your name, Sir," started Dr. Bice. "You've met us already, but let me introduce us by name. I'm Bice, and my assistant is my daughter Ina," he continued to talk to divert the sufferer as he commenced to gently manipulate up and down the man's wide back to locate the source of his problem. Grunts and gasps presented the man from reciprocating with his identity. Finally, feeling a slight break, he raised his oversized head up to face his healer.

"I'm Joe Ross, a worker at Braun. But, I wasn't at work when I hurt myself. I was a'plowin' and my back went out on me. Can ye help me? I swanee, you done eased it up a right smart with that rubbin' down my spine and that piller between my knees. You know, I can't miss work. My momma needs me to make the living since my old man passed," he volunteered. Joe went silent, and the injured man flopped his head back down on the cheap pillow.

And on that first day of active business, Dr. Bice's career in Red Hill was successfully launched. Joe did, indeed, raise himself from the table and walk out on his own power with a slight limp and some stiffness. He shook Dr. Bice's hand, and pulled a wadded dollar bill from his pocket. The doctor beamed and assured Joe that all visits would only be $1. He sensed that Joe Ross might boost his business, and so, despite his dire need for cash flow, he let Joe be, as the supermarket business coined, the "lost leader".

Joe promptly appeared for his appointments every day for two weeks, and each time, Dr. Bice gently and accurately worked on the area around the swollen and inflamed disk until the pain had subsided and the infection had disappeared. Normally, a quiet worker, Joe proudly sang Dr. Bice's praises to anyone and everyone on the second shift who, in turn, repeated the miraculous and glorious report of Joe's improvement that continued without expensive medicine or dangerous surgery. Even though the men in the black yard kidded Joe good-naturedly about the "witch doctor", his restored flexibility in his back was undeniable and visible. At the end of those two weeks, Joe was virtually pain free. The boarding house office was almost immediately filled with anxious patients hoping for results like Joe's. The Bice's larder was becoming full. Life was good, as Red Hill residents liked to say. Maybe at last Dr. Bice had found his gold mine.

Red Hill was warming to the new family, especially Dr. Bice. He was even invited to the traditional Rash weekend musicals first, as just a passive listener until he showed up one Friday night with a bright red mandolin; soon, the doctor graduated from interested observer to regular performer in the accomplished band. To ease the doctor's financial woes even further, Mr. Beaux offered Belle Bice a part time job cleaning the Braun office and laboratory; but, oddly, Dr. Bice was unwilling to allow her to work, explaining nervously to Beaux that his children still needed a full time mother. Mr. Beaux, having heard of the family's financial difficulties prior to Red Hill, was surprised by the doctor's reaction, but not overly concerned or offended over his rejection of the opportunity to gainfully employ the doc's strange wife. After all, Mrs. Beaux worked for him but was able to leave at will if Rabon or Jansey needed her. He just figured Dr. Bice had his reasons, and they were possibly more complicated than just the need for adequate child care for Rose and Lee. The intuitive Beaux sensed some deep insecurity in the doctor's voice when the position was offered to Belle, so he did not press the issue. He perceived that the doctor's rodent-faced wife was probably a handful. He'd seen how her eyes unrhythmically darted when Ellis had occasionally brought the corpulent woman to the Rashes' musicals.

Now, although Dr. Bice was gaining in acceptance and even in popularity in Red Hill, his cock-eyed reclusive spouse stayed holed up in their apartment in the boarding house. It appeared to the Beauxs, along with fellow Red Hill residents, that Ellis Bice approved and even endorsed her isolation from the other ladies in town almost as if he were concealing her or shielding her from the possibility of embarrassing him or affecting his newfound success. Most ladies, even though they perceived Belle as odd, still wanted her as a part of their society even if it were merely to satisfy their own insatiable curiosity or just to enrich and extend their channels for community news.

Red Hill was a simple place filled with simple people, and at times, the ladies were more concerned with HDC, PTA, church socials, political rallies, reunion picnics, baby showers, wedding teas, and recipe tips than the impending doom in Viet Nam. Theirs was not an oppressive structure strictly guided by Amy Vanderbilt's etiquette handbook, but Belle's obvious reluctance to participate or even to show up for these activities was puzzling and offensive. She was publically and privately "cussed and discussed" around the close-knit community of ladies.

Mrs. Barr, the Bice's self-appointed landlord and home guard, decided to change the situation with Belle and to invade Belle's cloister. As a prominent member of the ladies activities and acting president of the HDC of Red Hill, she, one bright morning, confidently walked across the dogtrot hall and rapped on Mrs. Bice's apartment door. She aimed to invite Mrs. Bice to the afternoon meeting of the HDC which was scheduled at 2 pm that day in Ada's own home. She knew Belle had declined all invitations to any ladies' functions thus far, but she hoped that because Ada was her neighbor, Belle might relent. It was the perfect meeting to have a visitor; it was a little more relaxed on this day because today's abbreviated club agenda included light snacks, a short business meeting, no speaker from the county of state, and a simple charity activity-pruning the rose bushes that lined the ditch between the community center/nondenominational church and the boarding house after adjourning the meeting. Ada would introduce Belle as a potential nominee for the club who would elect or reject her at the next monthly meeting.

Ada Barr tapped lightly on her neighbor's door and spoke kindly, "Mrs. Bice, oh, Mrs. Bice? Belle? This is Ada, Ada Barr, your across-the-hall neighbor. May I come in and set for a spell with you if it's conven-ient? I promise I won't take much of your time. (No reply) I haven't been much of a neighbor just leavin' you over there to fend for yourself, have I?" Ada, stopped herself, embarrassed, realizing she had altered her nor-mal voice to a softer tone, slowing down the enunciation and creating the effect of playing a 45 rpm record on a 33 1/3 speed. It was similar to the communication style she generally reserved for her weekly visit with her mentally disabled brother who still lived at home with their aging mother who lived in nearly Bunkum. She amended her sedated and pos-sibly insulting tone to be sure she didn't sound condescending and continued. "I would like you to come to our HDC gatherin' today which just happens to be at my house. If you need to bring your baby, that is just fine; we're not going to be formal today, but we will surely have a good time, eatin' refreshments, swappin' recipes, and plannin' certain community projects. You know we only meet once a month. Our meetin's over in plenty of time for you to meet the school bus; I know you have a girl in school, too," she added with a pleading spin. Again, silence followed. Maybe I should have continued to use my simple voice, she questioned herself. She conceded defeat and began to step away from the door and to return to her side of the hall when the door knob squeaked and moved counterclockwise.

"Mis; Ada, I'm comin'," answered a distant voice, low and in a monotonous like the pitch similar to the friendly robot who starred in the hottest television space show. "The door's a mite hard to turn. Let me put little Lee in his pen first." Ada was relieved to at least get a response, although the lack of inflection or emotion in the woman's tone was not altogether encouraging. The huge pine door opened wider and Belle's head and grimy hand appeared around on her side of the frame. A short, stocky, dark-headed matron, whose average, chunky form could have blended in a crowd of shoppers without being noticed, smiled at Ada. In contrast and with quite a disturbing effect, the woman's unusually deep-set eyes which danced with random movement and her wharf rat appearance which almost unnerved Ada when she made eye-to-eye contact with the odd recluse, all contributed to a stereotypical image of a diabolical and evil character in an Edgar Allen Poe story. The continual eye darting was incongruent with the lethargic body which shared the same home. "Let's jest talk in the hall a spell, Mis' Ada. I can leave the door cracked so's I can still see and hear Lee if'n he was to make some racket," the peculiar woman suggested.

Ada stretched her neck taunt to get a glimpse of the living area of the Bice home. It was an absolute disaster: dirty and clean clothes intermingled and flopped onto a rose colored Early American couch; filthy, mismatched gasoline station plates and cups were left on the coffee stained table and even stacked on the wobbly piano stool. Wadded and soiled cloth diapers lay festering in a paint bucket in the center of a hideous multi-colored braided rug. An additional, unpleasant acrid smell attacked Ada's nostrils almost immediately after Belle widened the door. Ada, holding her breath, nodded her head affirmatively at Belle and hastily shifted to the right side of the door, hoping for a rescuing breeze from the open hall. Belle stepped out slightly toward the hall and trailing along with her was the sour odor of dirty socks and corn chip smelling athletic shoes.

"As I was saying, Mrs. Bice, I came to invite you to our Home Demonstration Club today at my house at 2. It would give you a chance to meet several of your neighbors at one time without having to leave the boarding house! We haven't seen much of you since you moved into Red Hill. Oh, and do you like living here?" Ada nervously chattered while Belle's head commenced to rotating from right to left as if it were attached with a swivel joint. Ada starred down at her dusty penny loafers to avoid glaring at the woman's bizarre head motion and unnerving, flashing eyes.

The younger woman slowed her pendulum head action, leaned forward, and peered at Ada, invading her personal space as she spoke in a rattled whisper. "You know, the doctor's practice is doing right well since Mr. Ross come in with his ailment, and Ellis was able to ease his pain, so that sure helps out; but as for makin' friends, well, I ain't never had no luck making friends in the places we've lit in the past. I reckon I'm jest a homebody. Now, Ina, she works fer her paw, and little Rose ain't never complained about nothin', so's I figger they done made some friends. Of course, a baby like Lee is happy if it gits nussed, has food, gits held, has a bed. He's my menopause baby, Mis' Ada, and he's spoilt rotten!" The strange new acquaintance exposed her own weirdness to the unsuspecting neighbor as Belle picked up the conversation. She embroidered her bizarre characterization with the intermittent production of deep grunting and teeth sucking as Belle seemed to interject for emphasis. (As if there were ever an appropriate time for such a sound!) When Belle finally composed herself, she leaned ever closer toward Ada's space. "Jest call me Belle like everybody does; that's my given name-my first name," she added with more animation and head jerking than before. Was she the new Sybil of Red Hill, Ada thought?

"So, Mrs..ah-Belle, you think you might be able to come today? We're having orange poke cake and coffee. You can bring Lee, or if he's napping, we can open both our doors to the hall so you can still hear him if he wakes up during the meeting. My parlor is right across from yours, you know. And if you want to move his pen into the hall or even over to my house, we can do that, too. I just think you'd enjoy our little group. The ladies are going to trim the roses around the church yard after the meeting, but, of course, if you have to leave early, that's okay, too," Ada explained cheerfully but her voice was still a little quivery after experiencing the constant movement of Belle's eyes and head. Maybe she had "neralgy", as her own mother had diagnosed persons with unexplained body movement.

"Well, Mis' Ada, let me step into the doctor's office and ask Ellis if he don't care if I go to yer little shindig. He don't like me fraternizing too much. Say, would you be willing to watch Lee a minute for me? You can come on in and set a spell if you was to find a place. I'm not much of a housekeeper since Lee came along," Belle admitted, and before Ada could agree, Belle vanished out the door, down the hall, and into her husband's office. Ada gingerly stepped into the scene of destruction that was before her. The powerful odor was more pronounced as she reluctantly pulled the door behind her. She wisely chose to kneel in front of the wooden playpen rather than to attempt to sit on the mounds of laundry which could have been ranked in various categories of wet, smelly, dry, clean, wrinkled, etc, but were jumbled together in a disorganized fashion. She turned her focus toward the little flounder faced prisoner incarcerated in his paint chipped cell. He appeared to be around four years old, although Ada wasn't certain because he was partially squatted on the far side of his pen. However, she did know that this child was too old and too large to be sentenced to such a small area; yet, he didn't seem to mind his confined space. The baby's strong looking back was turned toward Ada, and he began to navigate himself around by lightly holding on to the greasy rails. Surely he could walk! His filthy, fat hands finally made it around the railing until he was face to face with his reluctant babysitter. He released one grimy paw and offered it through the wooden rods to Ada who patted it gently. Upon focusing her eyes on Lee's pudgy hand, she saw that under the fingernails was black dirt-not new dirt-but dirt that accumulated over several days without having been cleaned out after bath time. It was packed in like rich, potting soil-compost! He grunted at Ada but did not speak outright.

"Hello, little feller. How is Mr. Lee today?" Ada, in her best primary school voice, asked. Lee puckered up to cry. "Oh, no, don't cry. Your mommy will be back in just a minute," she assured the puffy baby who had been unfairly cursed with his mother's same bizarre, dancing eyes which blocked any maternal affection Ada might have normally had. For a cruel instant, she felt the strong urge to abandon ship, to escape to safety, and to breathe clean air again, but she thought better as she knew the innocent child stood the possibility of harm with no caretaker to guide or to protect him from danger. She still was not inclined to cuddle Lee, not just because he was nasty-she'd seen and

touched nasty before in church cradle roll—but the eyes, the eyes
that flickered and dashed like bolts of lightning in one's unsuspecting
peripheral were responsible for her hesitancy. The inconstancy of his
focus plus the oddity of his mutant features sent sharp shivers down
Ada's backbone. He looked possessed! Once Ada acknowledged this,
she felt shame and prayed for forgiveness from her merciless judgment of a mere infant! Yet.....

"Good news!" Belle announced loudly, causing Ada to jump up
and drop Lee's hand. "The doctor, I mean, Ellis, said I could go if'n I
was to behave myself like a lady," Belle declared as though her husband's permission was surprising and rare. "Thank ye, ma'm, fer
a'watchin' Lee. I hope he didn't cause you no trouble. Ain't he sweet?
And he's so pretty, looks just like me, don't you think?" Belle asked as
she scooped her chunky baby up into her equally chunky arms. "He's
the only child I got that favors me; the girls is all Bice," she said with
an audible sigh. Ada, not wanting to lie about the remote possibility
of any beauty, nodded in agreement, and headed out the door, hastily
excusing her abrupt exit by recounting all the meeting preparations
that had to be completed before the hallowed meeting. She shut her
own door behind her and fearful that the Bice scent had saturated
her clean clothes and her freshly washed skin, she fought the irresist-
ible urge for an additional bath. She vigorously scrubbed her hands
and arms as a deterrent to the filth she had just encountered.

Two o'clock arrived and the HDC members, all twenty-four ladies, were assembled in Ada's parlor. Red Hill's chapter members of
the statewide club were seldom tardy or absent from the monthly
meeting even though the same ladies might not have that same
strong propensity for promptness at church services, school functions,
or other social obligations; this was a prime time for the homemakers
to catch up on community news and to share exciting recipes or efficient new household cleaning tips. A few minutes after two,
abandoning her hope for Belle's attendance and logically sensing that
the absence might be for the best, President Barr, dressed in a
homemade pale green shift of the latest fashion from Simplicity patterns, stood and addressed the awaiting group. "Good afternoon,

Ladies. The clock on the wall tells me that it's a few minutes past two, so we need to get started with our first fall meeting. Secretary George, will you call the roll and share the minutes from our last meeting? And, also, would you read any correspondence the club has received since our last meeting?" Ada asked Mrs. George kindly and then she took her seat near the front of the group. Mrs. George, dressed in a hot pink sundress, pink patent leather shoes, and her Woolsworth's pearls, gracefully and alluringly arose from her second row perch. She could feel the disapproving stares from her club sisters which were only mildly in check because of their southern heritage of proper breeding about ladylike behavior and also because she had prudently covered her bare shoulders with a hand knitted shrug. As the club secretary opened her register and began roll call, Mrs. Belle Bice stumbled through the door without knocking or tapping-totally unannounced. She was outfitted in all red-fire engine red-from her peanut shaped head to her feet rammed into improperly fitting shoes, resembling overstuffed lobster tails in a high end restaurant that didn't skimp on the filling. From the top to the bottom, she unsuccessfully modeled a red pillbox hat, red plastic pop beads, a red shirtwaist dress, and red plastic sandals without hosiery. Ada rose quickly to welcome her guest. "Oh, welcome, Mrs. Bice. Girls? Please make Mrs. Belle Bice welcome in our little club. You know, she's the doctor's wife. Belle, I'm so glad you could come. Where is little Lee? Do you need help movin' him closer to our door?" Mrs. Barr addressed Belle with her syrupy sweet tone that was *really* sincere even though it sounded too good to be true. Ada rapidly spoke in a valiant attempt to counteract the possible back lash from the pastel attired club ladies who immediately shifted their focus and critical fashion eye away from Mrs. George's scandalous sundress and toward the vermillion fireball who had just exploded inside the fastidiously ordered and serene parlor.

Belle tottered as she awkwardly steadied herself on her ill-fitting sandals. Her little toe had escaped its plastic confinement and was now snagged on Ada's braided rug. "Oh, hello, ladies. Thank you, thank you, Mis' Ada. But, there ain't no need in makin' no fuss for

Lee; my daughter Ina took him up to the office since they ain't' too busy right now. Hey! Now ,where do I set?" Belle looked up from unlocking her toe from the rug yarn, and continued speaking. "Who are you, Ma'm?" she asked Mrs. Cross. "This looks like as good a place as any right by this big, elderly woman," Belle declared to a shocked audience. Belle embarrassed herself unknowingly when she labeled the good natured Mrs. Cross as both fat and old. Mrs. Cross, a patient and graceful woman, kindly smiled, introduced herself, and patted the cane bottomed chair beside her, reassuring the newcomer who had just insulted her that her feelings were uninjured even though Belle had actually never petitioned for the kind woman's grace. Belle plopped her loose and uncoordinated form instead onto the more fragile needlepoint chair. "Whew!" she blew. Her upper torso had actually arrived at the station a second or two before the rest of her body caught up with it-a trait sometimes characteristic of those individuals who seldom wore dress shoes and lacked the balance necessary to pull them off.

Mrs. Barr stood again and regained the floor and the attention of the club. "Okay, Mrs. George, go ahead now with the roll," Ada reconvened, squelching the multiple stares and disapproving murmurs throughout the members. Mrs. George's sensual outfit, as she rose this time, paled now in interest and in gaudiness as she stood up to call the roll. The short business meeting was conducted after the roll call; the treasurer's report was rattled off by Mrs. Van, a recently added member. The club Collect was recited, and the old business was tabled until the next meeting. Mrs. Wick moved to adjourn the meeting, and a random voice in the crowd seconded that motion. The hostesses officially invited the members to the tea. Mrs. Barr had washed and arranged her best Royal Rose china, made her crystal glasses sparkling with a detergent and vinegar solution, and vigorously polished her best silverware in preparation for the refreshments. She had inherited all these elegant pieces of dinner décor from a wealthy spinster aunt-Aunt Gertrude. Aunt Gertrude, an attractive, and benevolent spinster, had scandalously relocated in New York City to train for the stage, and had left no heir except Ada; so the former Zeigfeld Folly showgirl (show name Debbi Dove) bequeathed the valuable table treasures to her only living relative, who was seldom afforded an opportunity to showcase the table treasures in the Red Hill setting. But today was the ideal time for Ada to shine among her peers.

"Mmmmm, Mis' Ada, that ther's a good cake! I ain't had no homemade cake since my momma-rest her soul-died," Belle commented loudly. In the south, bad grammar was common, was ignored, and was even accepted as correct. In some cases, by some of the residents, ladies included, regardless of well meaning language teachers throughout the grades, accurate speech was not a priority. It begat itself—generation after generation. Belle's errors were no more outstanding than any other Red Hill resident. Grammar was the least of her problems.

During the course of the refreshment time, one by one, the curious members, some more reluctantly than others, introduced themselves to Belle, who was, to most members, a little more aggressive with her hand shaking and bear hugging for the club's comfort zone. Mrs. Cross, totally dismissing Belle's earlier unflattering comment about her, spoke first after all the introductions were completed. "Belle, how are you likin' Red Hill? I know your husband's been gettin' on pretty good after Mr. Ross's visit and recovery was spread around the town." Mrs. Cross, unlike many others who whispered unfavorable comments under their breath about Belle, was genuinely interested in her and in all the residents of Red Hill. She truly loved mankind and her nonthreatening and cordial tone reflected a gracious heart. "We are so glad you joined us today. Tell us about yourself. We're anxious to get to know you," she encouraged. "I'll bet you have some stories to tell," she baited Belle innocently..

"Well, Mrs. Cross, I've never been what you call a socialite, but my husband's practice, hits a'takin' off like rocket fire, and that shore does make me like it a right smart more than if he was a'strugglin," she repeated what she had told Ada earlier. The club had quieted down when Belle and Mrs. Cross talked, half out of respect for the older member and half out of the desire to know more about the socially inept woman who might soon be a permanent part of their club.

Most of the ladies who had been patients were pleased with Dr.
Bice's unique healing practices, and they had certainly reveled in his
musical talents on the weekends at the Rashes' hootenannies. Several
of the club members mentioned one or both of these strengths to
Belle which gave Belle self confidence by proxy through the acceptance of her husband. Relaxing slightly in her new ladies only
environment, Belle longed to contribute to the community gossip
and to join in with the lively banter among the members. She wasn't
convinced that she was ready to dig out too many details of her and
Bice's life; that would be dismal and unflattering. Yet, still, she craved
attention, and right now, she was in the club's spotlight. She turned
her chair in a ninety degree angle so that she could see the majority
of the members in the parlor and dining area. With growing strength
in herself, she now felt fueled not only to engage in the conversation
but to actually dominate it with the bombshell she was planning to
drop on the unsuspecting members of the Red Hill HDC. Her
fickled irises grew darker and deeper in her bloated, mouse-like face.

"Y'all want to know more about old Belle? Well, let me tell youns
somethin' that you won't believe." Belle's eyes gyrated as she saw the
bevy of Maybelline decorated eyes turn her way. No one spoke, but
their silent attention granted Belle permission to overtake the floor,
and so she began her "tale told by an idiot". Belle continued. "You
know my younger girl, Rose?" Nods around the room. "She's twelve
now. And, well, she has done gone and got herself knocked up by a
feller in this here town! Yeah, she shore nuff went all the way with a
man over twice her dang age! That gurl must a'come into this world
with a evil lust in her. Now, I ain't tole her daddy yet. She's mighty
young, but I'm a'aiming to marry her off to the daddy so's the poor
little baby won't be no bastard. Ain't that what you call it?" I knowed
that's what you call a boy born out of wedlock. Is it the same fer
girls?" She dropped the bomb matter-of-factually and then seemed
more preoccupied with the bastard issue than the actual issue. Her
insanely flickering eyes scanned the room for the shock factor effect
she had hoped for; she was not displeased. She added, "Damn Joe
Ross!" and finally turned around.

During the 1950's and 1960's, a southern lady seldom even spoke the word "pregnant" even in an intimate conversation. Euphemisms such as "in the family way", looking for a little one", "the patter of little feet" or "the rabbit died" were sprinkled throughout their modest speech. Belle's own use of the term "knocked up" was unacceptable by the average person even when the "knocked up" woman was a married one. Usually, if an unfortunate soul did get the "cart before the horse", so to speak, her next stop was the first available church altar or the closest justice of the peace. If the pregnancy was visibly undetectable, an expedited and somewhat abbreviated wedding ceremony covered the transgression. If no attached relationship existed between the two procreators, the girl, if one of privilege, was whisked away to some distant private boarding school, later returning home without an offspring or a plausible explanation for her urgent flight. Yet, others, stupid, brave, or just innately evil, sought termination of the unwanted pregnancy by the skilled hands of the Cherokee midwife who lived near the swamp. Poor Rose's predicament was more scandalous than the usual ones; she was poor, pregnant, and unmarried. Once Belle finished her twisted tale, the club remained uncomfortably speechless. No one heard the clinking of Ada's Steif forks, the plinking of the Japanese china, or the sloshing of Waterford crystal. The lone sound in the stuffy parlor and dining room was the sinister and condemning ticking of the massive grandfather clock that ruled the foyer. It counted down in slow, rhythmic motion the inevitable and benevolent halt of the HDC fall meeting.

As usual, Ada Barr summed up inner courage and quick thinking amid the thick atmosphere of the room. "You know, ladies, I think that it just may be a little too warm to tackle those rosebushes today. Why don't we just adjourn the tea, and I'll phone you later in the week when it's supposed to cool off a bit." Ada's fitly spoken words allowed the squirming club a welcomed escape from the awkwardness of the moment. Ladies grabbed their gloves and hurriedly stacked their unfinished plates of goodies, depositing them on the nearest counter. Generally, the other assigned hostesses would have picked up the items individually from the members and then helped Ada tidy up after the meeting. But, not today! No, white flight was alive and well in the Red Hill HDC that day, and it had nothing to do with race relations. Only one soul beside Ada remained in the parlor after ten minutes had passed-the infamous Belle Bice.

Mis' Ada, I guess I run yore friends off, huh? I was a'tryin' too hard to fit in, I reckon. I have a hard time keeping pals, as I told ye. I knew that piece of news would stir 'em up, but I 'spect they weren't ready for it," Belle, still ignorant of the magnitude of her news, offered up as a weak apology. The juicy, scandalous fabricated details of her daughter's plight were already public as indicated by the busy party lines throughout Red Hill as soon as the members returned home-hot on the trail of the best story they had heard in a while.

Forced into a discourse of discomfort, Ada replied slowly, "Mrs. Bice, perhaps you should first have discussed Rose's..uh..uh.. condition with your husband before you splattered-I mean shared-such a delicate matter with total strangers. She's still a little girl, and now, your little girl has a big reputation. But be that as it may, the damage has been done, and, honestly, I've got supper to start. The bus will be here soon, and you will need to be getting home, I'm sure. Here, take the rest of the poke cake to your family. We'll just waste it." Ada was suddenly weary of the situation at hand and the woman in her face. Belle was like a canker sore that began to cause some pain initially and then, untreated, it expanded its disgusting borders eventually eating out a hunk in the sufferer's jaw. Ada was frustrated, angry, embarrassed, nauseated, and anxious all at one time. She, uncharacteristically, firmly shoved Belle toward the hall door and immediately shut her out into the hall without even a goodbye. Slumping back into the security of her home, Ada mindlessly melted into the nearest chair, totally dismissing the mess awaiting her in the cluttered kitchen.

As Ada had predicted, Belle's bombshell sailed like a paper airplane throughout the salivating community for days. Ada avoided answering her phone or even using it at all because she knew answering it would just disturb her even more. She asked herself daily: Why did I try to be neighborly? Why didn't I let sleeping dogs lie? Mrs. Cross, when Ada asked for a Cliff notes version of the circulating gossip, admitted that a few of the members held her, their club president, culpable for providing an open venue for Bice's soiled laundry. But how could she have predicted the vile nature of Belle's tale? Mrs. Cross gently patted her longtime friend's shoulders and reminded her that this would pass when something more interesting and more shocking occurred. After all, she told Ada, you were just being neighborly.

Subsequently, the neighborhood children who rode the Red Hill bus learned that their fellow bus rider, just a kid herself, was pregnant! Kids can be unfeeling and many asked Rose embarrassing questions such as: "Do you really have a bun in the oven? Are you knocked up? How can you have a baby? You ain't got no husband. When you get married, are you going to sleep in the baby's bed 'cause your husband robbed the cradle? You hear the pitter-patter of little feet?" Of course, the children had overheard their parents, neighbors, and the high school riders discuss the hot topic of Rose. They giggled and sang a scathing jingle: "Rose Bice, not so nice. She's as nasty of hound dog lice!" Rose slinked down even lower in her bus seat as she refused to defend her honor.

At the same time, many children and some adults wondered how anyone could be even remotely attracted to a twelve-year-old, ugly, scrawny, dirty little thing-even if the suitor was a childlike bachelor who still lived at home. And how could her crazy ass mother tell the whole HDC? Poor Rose sat on the bus seat that had the wheel hump, causing the seat to only accompany one rider, ensuring that she wouldn't share the space with a hysterically laughing child. But, then, on the other hand, who wanted to sit by a whore? Each day, it seemed to her pitying bus driver, Rose shrunk daily in size as she gained an equal measuring of red dirt on her grimy, skeletal, face. Mr. Wall reprimanded the bullying offenders when he could, but he was a man living in a time when one never felt comfortable talking personally to a female about the nature of her deep sorrow. He predicted that she would soon drop out of school, and he would be liberated from the guilt of not comforting her and of not addressing the problem at all.

In rural communities, school teachers, counselors, and principals became alarmed when they noticed certain ones of their students who looked neglected, unhappy, tormented, enraged, hungry, or who appeared to manifest changing and disturbing characteristics in their appearances and/or behaviors. DHR was not as active or as professionally equipped in the '60's as the federally supervised program is currently. Courts were backlogged with civil right injustices and other pressing social agendas at the time. Neglected children were usually just that-*neglected* by ineffective social programs which were failing due to lack of adequate funding or overwhelmed workers. Therefore, the professionals who came in contact with students on a daily basis stepped into the roles as protectors and investigators.

Miss Pearl, the guidance counselor at Mount Gum School, was one of those unique and highly valuable educators whose concern and curiosity stemmed from her deep love of and holy calling for young people. She was especially gifted in intuitively searching out those bright young stars whose potential illumination was blocked from shining fully by unfortunate and sometimes even perversely evil home environments. Rose was one of Miss Pearl's fading stars. The counselor had heard the awful account of the child's predicament which vexed her tremendously; but the horrific truth of the mother's raw, even boastful revelation of her daughter's "affliction" was even more disgusting to the stately educator with a big heart. When her school day ended, Miss Pearl's concerns and fears for little Rose accompanied her in her sporty green Impala like unwelcomed hitchhikers who clumsily climbed into the back seat as she pulled out of the Mount Gum parking lot, often after dark; and those persistent passengers became intruding, overnight guests in her efficiency apartment, crowding in on her mind during the wee hours of the morning when insomnia entertained and sharpened them.

Miss Pearl had her own suspicions about the credibility of Belle Bice's bawdy HDC account. Her instinctive doubts about the real truth were even further grounded after a casual visit with Ms. Water, the girls' physical education coach. Ms. Water, a masculine featured woman was a crackerjack at her job; her physical education students were challenged far beyond the usual kickball game techniques. She planned her lessons and tracked progress on large color coded posters duct taped to the gym walls. She also exercised an uncanny sense of a child's particular home life, perhaps by a nudging of a sixth sense or by reason of experienced observation.

THE TEACHER'S CLUTTERED office was adjacent to the dressing rooms. She welcomed her counselor friend in her comfortably messy cave for a cup of strong coffee. After casually questioning Ms. Water, Ms. Water, in sworn confidence, assured the counselor that Rose had not even experienced her first menstruation period. She herself had become aware of Rose's immaturity when the class had been required to watch a dull and outdated health film which dealt with human growth and development. Rose had raised her spindly little arm before the film had rolled and had asked Ms. Water the innocent question: "Coach Water, do boys menstruate? My mother tells my daddy he's 'on the rag' all the time? Is that what she means?" Ms. Water recounted the peals of laughter from the rest of the "seasoned" girls after Rose's naïve question. Furthermore, when the class was studying the human body, a two week session just recently added to the curriculum by the state of Alabama, Rose had submitted a few written questions on her evaluation response sheet that would indicate her overall lack of sexual knowledge as well. Miss Pearl asked Ms. Water when the study had been conducted; Ms. Water recollected that the study had been completed the sixth weeks prior Belle's newsflash. Ms. Water early on had conferred with Miss Pearl; they had previously discussed the possibility that Rose, when she was initially enrolled at Mount Gum, had manifested some unusual behavior that might point to abnormalities in the home. Rose had recently appeared on her radar, especially in the past few days. Both women were in agreement NOT to consult with the male principal about the taboo topic. Miss Pearl drained her cold coffee, thanked the coach, and stepped across the hall to her snug office; but even in the security of her closed environment, she was unable to shake Rose from her thoughts; she knew she had to act alone.

Almost on impulse, she dialed County 8602 and Ina Bice answered, immediately retrieving her father from the x-ray room. "Dr. Bice, I'm

Miss Lou Pearl, the guidance counselor at Mount Gum," she began. A squawking voice responded and questioned her. She answered the parrot sounding voice, quickly reassuring the doctor. "No, no, Doctor. Rose's work is excellent; she is making a fine transition to our school. I'm just concerned about her recent behavior." More squawking. More reassuring. "Oh, no, she's very respectful in all of her classes, but she seems somewhat withdrawn and sad lately. Even as tiny as your daughter already is, she appears to be losing even more weight. She hasn't even been well enough to dress out in PE, according to her PE coach, Miss Water,"Miss Pearl continued. "I just think it might be a good idea for you, Mrs. Bice, and Rose to meet in my office when it's convenient for you three so we can help Rose get back on track. You know, Dr. Bice, I think your daughter has a bright future ahead of her if she can keep her grades up and gain her confidence back." Affirmative squawking. "Good, good, then, I'll see you both tomorrow at 1," she concluded the conversation, thanking the doctor for his interest. He actually hung up before their formal goodbyes, but Miss Pearl did not sense anger in the doctor's voice; it sounded more like embarrassment. He had readily agreed to the conference and had even volunteered to close his office on the afternoon of the next day so Ina could care for Lee. The only hint of reluctance, Miss Pearl could detect, was when she had suggested the inclusion of Mrs. Bice for the scheduled meeting. Dr. Bice hadn't openly opposed his wife's attendance, but she could detect a bottoming out of the doctor's voice inflection at the mention of Belle's name like the lowering of pitch in an ambulance's siren as it speeds away from an accident scene.

When Miss Pearl gathered her files to review for the night, she was suddenly stricken with waves of nausea and the developing of a thick knot in her stomach when she realized that Rose's fragile mental state might not allow her to endure a conference with both her parents and a teacher. It was too late to change that, now, she thought. The wearied counselor dropped her brown leather briefcase onto the floor. What could I do? She thought for just a moment; her answer came as quickly as her question had. First, she would include Rose in the meeting, and then, she would "suddenly" assign Rose some simple task in the office while the meeting continued without her. Ah, yes, the annual in school basketball game was scheduled for the next day; Rose could help the school secretary, Mrs. Judith (Mis' Judy) Thompson by collecting the teachers' money envelopes for admission into the game, return them to the office, and even help count the money if more stalling time was necessary. Why, if the meeting were to run even lengthier than expected, Rose could herd the nonattendees to their study halls. Yes! This plan will work! Her nausea eased and the knot began to shrink. Rose was certainly clever enough to assist Mis' Judy with these tasks and any more she could conjure. The relieved counselor grabbed her keys off the oversized metal hook by her and picked up her well worn briefcase. As she headed out of her office, Judith Thompson, stepped right in front of her, blocking her exit. Lou Pearl suspected that the garrulous woman had most likely eavesdropped on her last phone conversation with the Bices. She was notorious for eavesdropping all around the sprawling school building. Her business was gossip and she was an expert businesswoman!

Mis' Judy was privy to almost any occurrence around or concerning Mount Gum or Red Hill, reaching out like an octopus tenacle snatching its prey. Her many appendages were wrapped tightly around her news sources in churches, schools, clubs, communities, and politics. She culled no one who had a morsel to placate her insatiable appetite for "current affairs". Miss Pearl was acutely aware of her nosey, but loyal secretary's love of local scandal. She would know the identity of Rose's lover, the father of her child. Miss Pearl decided to question the walking society columnist for rural Alabama. "Mis' Judy, could you step into my office for just a minute before I head to the house? I need your advice about something." Miss Pearl asked the startled woman who realized she'd been caught in the act of unsolicited listening. She was somewhat fearful of Lou because the counselor was so open and honest with anyone who entered her office, and she had no tolerance for petty gossip. Despite her misgivings, Mis' Judy walked toward the minimalistic office.

"Sit down, Mrs. Thompson," Miss Pearl professionally requested. "Do you, personally, have any knowledge of the situation of which little

Rose Bice supposedly finds herself? Judy nodded, relaxing slightly as she recognized that she was not under fire for snooping. The relentless counselor continued to scavenge like a determined old mongrel searching laboriously for a bone long hidden and long forgotten. "I figured you did because it seems that the child's mother used no discretion in the heralding out her sorrow," she spilled for a moment, but the flowery words were lost on Judy. She only dealt with the facts, or at least HER account of the facts. "Tomorrow, at one, I have scheduled a conference with Rose's parents. And, no, I'm not going to include our boss man!" she assured her secretary who already had her wide mouth posed to ask that exact question. "I reassured Dr. Bice that we were well pleased with Rose's school work and her impeccable manners, but that lately, she had manifested behavior that indicated her unhappiness and despondency." Lou Pearl saw the wrinkled brows of her secretary, but proceeded, promising herself to simplify her vocabulary a bit for Judith. "Judy, she's a little girl; that's all she is-a child. Twelve? Right? Right? A seventh grader?" Judy, again, nodded, prudently remaining silent. She restrained her strong desire to control the conversation and to embellish the story, but she also served as a compliant employee; her superior had the floor right now. Her own moment of fame was pending.

"Judy, what would you think if I told you that I don't have a clue about who the father of this baby is? Would you consider me uninformed, detached, and distracted by my mounds of paperwork? Would discovering that tidbit of information be helpful to me in dealing with this most delicate situation tomorrow in that meeting? And finally and furthermost, have YOU heard any specific names of possible fathers being tossed around in the community?" The determined counselor now pushed the imploding woman. Miss Pearl wanted desperately to say "tossed around in your gossip mill", but she knew her goal was to keep Judy contented like a bloated cow so she could milk her for all the information she could before the meeting. She reminded herself, too, that this female harbinger was most likely the key to unlocking the identity of the mystery father, so she mentally coached herself to avoid her great desire to attack Judy's character. Keep focused on the issue at hand, she recited in her head.

After all, except for her obnoxious love of gossip, Mis' Judy was a stellar school secretary. Miss Pearl sat back down in her swivel chair even though she was way past ready to go home. She began to mentally count seconds in her head; Judith Thompson, she knew, would not and could not resist entering into this arena with both of her flat, sized eleven feet—even if the arena was a virtual cesspool!

Judith Thompson, an alumnus of Alverson Drawn Business School like Rose's sister, Ina, was a tall pear-shaped middle aged matron with flabby thighs which produced a slapping sound when they were awkwardly deposed from the three-legged stool she generally occupied behind the tall school counter. She, now standing in the threshold of Miss Pearl's office, pushed her larger than life frame into Miss Pearl's personal space. "Well, since you asked me, one of the church quilters at the guild at Lexington Church told me the other day when I delivered them some free thread that Belle-I mean-Mrs. Bice was practically shouting the father's name down at the Bethsaida post office while she was getting Mrs. Dell to fill out a money order for Sears and Roebuck. That was sometime last week, I think. The money order was for a Playtex Living Bra, I think Mrs. Dell said," she unnecessarily added. Miss Judy, her brows released, was in her element now, providing information for the needy and holding court for the attentive. Judith wanted to pace herself, feeding Miss Pearl tiny bits of information to whet her appetite for the main course, but she acknowledged that Lou Pearl was not like her; she wasn't interested in the build-up. She was unimpressed with the "they say" or the "I've heard" which often times characterized gossip with no substance or identifiable source—no exact antecedent to the pronoun "they". Miss Pearl was specifically interested in the name of the father, nothing more or nothing less. Leaning in further toward the counselor, Judith inadvertently partnered with Miss Pearl in a distorted tango dance—Miss Pearl leaned away as Mis' Judy leaned in. Judy positioned herself for the kill while Miss Pearl chose a position that afforded her space.

"Miss Pearl, you won't believe who that crazy Bice woman claims as the father to her own baby's baby." Her moment had arrived. Judith drew in a deep pneumatic cough and revealed the crown jewels. "Why, she says it's old Joe Ross, that clod hopper who lives in Red Hill and works in the black yard. Supposedly, he was Dr. Bice's first paying customer at his new office at Mrs. Barr's boarding house, and he sang the doctor's praises for weeks afterward, the silly fool," she pronounced with pride. "The dullard still lives with his momma, and he must be about three times Rose's age!" Mrs. Thompson abandoned her baiting technique; this information was too valuable to mete out. She had to blurt it out before she popped a straining pearl button on her unflattering shirtwaist dress. She smiled, pleased with her presentation and her ability to contribute to the counselor's success tomorrow. She was the seat of knowledge at the moment.

Miss Pearl, obvious to Judy, was certainly taken aback-Judy's favorite reaction to her twist on powerful gossip. The counselor leapt from her comfortable seat and began pacing rapidly and methodically around her animated secretary; then, she just fell back against her worn desk chair without speaking. Judy's excitement was suddenly tempered and her triumphant smile diminished when she realized how very sad the whole story truly was. 'OH, Judy, this situation could also be trouble for Joe and a law suit to boot if it's really true," Miss Pearl surmised. Judith nodded her head in agreement. DNA testing for paternity was years away, so one could only wait until a child's birth to determine a baby's physical or mental likeness to his/her possible father; even then, that subjective method was neither scientific nor credible. The distraught counselor continued to shake her head in disbelief. "Don't you just ache all over for little Rose?" Lou Pearl asked Judy, as she glared over half-spectacles straight into Judy's soul with her rhetorical question. Even Judy had a heart even though it might, at times, have been smothered in her pursuit and love of community babble.

"Is Mr. Ross aware of the accusation against him?" asked Miss Pearl. The counselor and the secretary as well remembered the oversized, mentally challenged Ross boy from his early years as a student. He was a prime target for bullying, but his overgrown body had shielded him somewhat from defensive actions other than empty threats, powerless confrontations, and mild name calling. There was a silly schoolyard song that Judy recalled: "JOE ROSS, HIS MIND'S A LOSS. HIS BODY'S A HOSS". Even that taunt had lost its strength as Joe continued to grow in height and girth, physically defending himself from playground aggression. As Miss Pearl mused about the man-child, she also recalled years ago when, in an uncomfortable conference, she had to gently suggest to Joe's broken down mother, who looked years older than her actual birthday candles indicated, that Joe might better experience life success as a manual laborer on the pole yard or as a gardener's helper on a modest farm than in the classroom where he was constantly discouraged when he received his red marked, dismal papers. His potential for excellence in academics was dim. Joe had already exceeded the age limit required for public education at the time of this memorable conference. He was twenty-two years old with a lower elementary school capacity to comprehend and to learn. Helen Ross, Joe's mother, both Judith and Miss Pearl remembered, had burst into hot, fresh tears when she openly acknowledged her only son's limited learning ability while, at the same time, adamantly blaming herself for the problem. According to Helen Ross, Dr. Davies had strongly encouraged her to permit the medical procedure that would remove Joe's adenoids and tonsils. He had felt that Joe's swollen and infected adenoids were crowding his skull and affecting his brain growth; she had stubbornly and ignorantly refused to sign for the surgery. True or not medically, the fact remained that Joe Ross would never finish high school, but his physical strength and his good nature would afford him employment—a strong back and a weak mind. After turning in his unused textbooks, Joe withdrew from Mount Gum and immediately found work on Braun's black yard. He remained a loyal, faithful employee for the rest of his working years. Academia was over for old Joe.

In addition to his work on the lumber yard, Joe farmed alongside his neighbors and his mother who patiently taught and remediated the weak minded boy in the effective techniques of gardening and even in the field of simple repair work. He was a willing worker, and both he and his loving mother grew beautiful plants and luscious vegetables. As old Josh, the crane operator put it, "That boy may be a fool, but he don't act a fool. He's gone a lot further than some so-called smart folks." That statement, in Red Hill, was considered a compliment.

Shaken from her nostalgic reverie by Judith's deep, husky cough that sounded like an engine tearing up, Lou Pearl thanked Judy and dismissed her without revealing her plans or sharing any serious obser-vations she might have had about tomorrow's conference. Judith was slightly miffed; she, in her self-righteous opinion, had earned the right to one juicy morsel since she had willingly provided her superior with a valuable entre'. But, she grudgingly exited the already crowded space and dutifully returned to the front office to continue her mission of personally manipulating the school as she saw fit. Besides, it was way past quitting time. She pivoted sharply on her right foot like a march-ing band member heading to his/her designated place in a Friday night half-time formation. Backing out of Miss Pearl's office, as Judith poised her hand on Miss Pearl's door to pull the wobbly doorknob, she felt an unknown presence in *her* office space. A chill shivered down her crooked spine, (southerners call that feeling "a rabbit jumping over your grave"), as she hesitantly turned to face it.

Dr. Bice, his disjointed, jaunting wife, and little mouse-faced Rose stood in the dark of the office, signing in on the yellow ledger pad for visitors on the counter. This was worse than a specter, Mis' Judy thought as she sucked in a deep breath. "Excuse me, M'am? We have an appointment to see the counselor here. I believe her name is Miss Pearl. I know our appointment was tomorrow at 1, but we just decid-ed to come a little early." Miss Judy was, for once, speechless so Dr. Bice continued. "You see, our baby Lee was a little fussy, and Ina- that's my other daughter-was freed up to watch him since office hours were about over. She ain't too handy with him when he's col-icky, but I gave him an adjustment, and he was a'calmin down some when we decided to come on this afternoon. I don't know how long that calmness will last," the amiable doctor added. "Thank you. Is the counselor-Miss Pearl-still here? I see the buses have left. We met Mr. Wall and got Rose off his bus before he got to Red Hill." Belle Bice, a demon-eyed woman, was dressed in the same red get-up she had modeled at the HDC meeting that ill-fated day. She seemed jumpy and anxious. She shifted her sizeable weight from one puffy foot to the other as if she were being attacked by fire ants one leg at a time. Rose never raised her tiny head while her father had chattered away. She fiddled with a dingy, half-sewn ribbon that dangled carelessly from her slim waist. Mis' Judy was reminded of carnival personnel when she absorbed the appearance of the little family.

Judith, always the efficient secretary, collected herself and maneuvered her disproportionate hips toward her side of the counter. "Yes, you must be Dr. Bice," she smiled and stuck her hand over the countertop and toward the doctor. "I'll just step in Miss Pearl's office and see if she can see you this afternoon. I believe she is still here. You all just take those seats in the corner by the glass window, and I'll be right back." Judith employed her acute skills of hospitality even when she was pushed, rushed, and still irritated over the late intruders. Nevertheless, she walked methodically toward Miss Pearl's door, gently tapping on it. "Miss Pearl? Would you be able to meet with the Bices this afternoon? They are already here and are waiting in my office," she added. She awaited an answer from the other side of the door, but instead, the door swung open and Miss Pearl stuck her slender, graceful form through the door way and marched straight past Judith and directly toward the Bices. She, like Judith, wore a plastic smile to mask irritation.

"Well, hello, folks! I haven't met you, but I have talked to you, Doctor, on the phone earlier today. I am Lou Pearl. Now, I know our Rose. So, I'm going to guess you're Rose's mother, Belle. Am I correct?" she asked, as she slipped her keys back into her pocket. "Thank you for being so interested in Rose that you would just come on today," she assured the family as she shook hands with Ellis and Belle. She *had* really wanted to go home after she and Judith had talked about Rose's problem, but at least, maybe she could tackle this situation now and perhaps enjoy a full night's rest when she did get to her apartment.

"Please," she directed the troop, "let's have our meeting in the principal's office where we can have a little more room. My office is so small, and it's cluttered with the incoming test results. Principal Herber is gone for the day, or he may be on the football field helping the coaches line the field for the big game tomorrow night. Are y'all coming? You know, it's just the Spring Jamboree, but it's a good time to see what kind of team we have to work with next fall," she rattled on to lighten the mood while simultaneously dreading the heaviness of the topic to follow. Her valiant effort to engage the parents in cordial conversation was admirable, but not altogether successful like the idea of a flammable zeppelin for mass transit. Miss Pearl could sense that the socially inept family was as confused about a football jamboree as most average Americans today are about the details of nuclear energy, but she was determined to continue her futile attempt to keep the conversation going, or at least attempt to connect to the Bices. The weird trio followed Miss Pearl as she whooshed around the mimeograph machine and toward Mr. Herber's locked door. Her chattiness about weather, school activities, and community news continued steadily as the air, in equally steady rebellion, thickened with the silence of incomprehension and anger.

THE SHREWD COUNTRY counselor did not choose Herber's office because of the spaciousness or its additional comfort; she choose it because of its reinforced inner walls which the principal had demanded from the school board prior to even considering accepting the administrator's job, the urgency possibly stemming from lingering fears he harbored from his uncertain and dangerous childhood in war torn Europe. For Miss Pearl, the walls would impede, if not completely block, Mis' Judy's ability to eavesdrop on this most delicate matter involving most indelicate people. The crestfallen secretary slumped her shoulders, accepting defeat and mentally acknowledging the counselor's strategy for what it was-insurance against snooping. She plopped down, deflated in front of her old Underwood manual and commenced typing furiously in an effort to vent her anger and disappointment. Dr. Bice pulled the heavy door behind him and any chance of Mis' Judy absorbing fresh gossip faded.

"Would you like some coffee or water?" Miss Pearl asked. "I'm sorry. That's all we have to offer you this late in the day." The three shook their heads like bobble head dolls. "Very well, then. If you change your mind, let me know. I'll have Mis' Judy—no—I'll get it for you myself," she added, overly cautious in her effort to block the nosey woman's ability to radar in on any of the forthcoming conversation. She thought to herself. It's getting late. Enough with the delays. Time to "shuck the corn", as her farming father would declare when she, as a child, procrastinated her chores in the wee hours of the morning before school.

"I've been informed by some leaders in the community that your daughter Rose is—uh—mmm—in the family way, so to speak. Is that correct, Mrs. Bice?" Miss Pearl stammered as she bit the bullet and turned to the matriarch of the family. For a woman who had always been a public speaker, she was struggling for the right words to say and how to say them gently.

Belle Bice, who had been complacently relaxed in the overstuffed office chair, leaped from her seat as if responding to a pistol shot fired to signal the start of a foot race. Her front, upper torso rocked unsteadily over the rim of the antique desk, causing her stubby body to sway until the bottom half caught up with the top half, a common motion to those unsure of their footing. As Belle swayed back and forth to maintain her balance, Miss Pearl backed away toward the window to guard her personal space as she had done with Mis' Judy earlier in the afternoon. Again, these two danced as unsuitable and untalented tango partners in an awkward backbend. Once partially stable, Belle began ranting in a high pitched voice capable of injuring a dog's hearing and destroying a human's comfort zone. "My baby Rose has been tainted, and old Joe Ross has got to pay. He didn't jest come back to Ellis for treatment; he came back for more than that from my innocent flower! We're a gonna schedule a shotgun weddin' no later than tomorrow whilst yunses'll be lickin' yore wounds over the whuppin' them football players is gonna git. The sooner we make this legal, the better it will be. This here baby needs a last name that's different from his momma's. Joe's gotta ante up fer what he done. It

ain't yore business nor this school's business what I do about my children!" She bellowed wildly, her rat eyes darting from one side of her
head to the other in a sickly cut time rhythm. As she looked as if she
were about to crank up her venom again, she was firmly pushed back
into her chair by her husband's forearm. The normally gentle doctor
glared at his irate worse half.

"Sit down, Belle, dang it! Miss Pearl ain't even concerned about
that mess. She's talking about what *she* can do to help keep Rose in
school and in good health while she's carrying this bastard. You
know, Miss Pearl, half the community knew this before my own wife
told me about it." Dr. Bice was disgusted but continued his treatise,
ineffectually chided his maddened spouse. "Belle, you just shut your
flapping mouth and let this educated, logical woman speak," he ordered. Belle's pinched face swelled and reddened like a puffer fish in
peril. During her parents' histrionics, Rose continued to hold her
head down as she mindlessly braided and unbraided her tattered ribbons on her ragged dress. She avoided the eye contact that her
mother had certainly demanded from the other occupants of the
suddenly smothering cubicle. The air now was more than just heavy;
it was as oppressive as a lead coat.

Miss Pearl characteristically snatched a shallow breath and
pressed on, finding nothing in her formal educational training to
guide her through the next step of this hellish intervention. "Well,
Mrs. Bice, those are disturbing developments; but as Dr. Bice suggested, let's stick to the facts as they are now in relation to the overall
educational health of your daughter here. "I supposed I must ask this
necessary question. I'm sorry. How far along in her pregnancy is she?
We will need to, first, adjust her physical education plan to continue
to provide adequate exercise without causing harm to Rose or extra
stress of the unborn child. Her academic teachers can work around
any doctor's appointments scheduled so that Rose will not get behind
in her studies. After reviewing her permanent record, Dr. and Mrs.
Bice, Rose has enjoyed academic success this her first year at Mount
Gŭm. She has made the honor roll each grading period. That's certainly says a lot about you as parents and Rose as a motivated young

lady." Miss Pearl knew that if she complimented the parents and their child, she could manage the most caustic parent conference. Rose looked up for the first time and shared a faint smile with her counselor, quickly dropping her head once again to its familiar position. "Has Rose been officially examined by a medical doctor, or, can you, Dr. Bice, determine her due date with a chiropractic analysis?" She directed her questions to Dr. Bice as he appeared to be the saner of the two adults. The wise woman desperately wanted to avoid any further outbursts from crazy Belle if possible.

"Well." Dr Bice scratched his now flaming cheeks as he fumbled for an appropriate response. "Her mother says she hasn't had her monthly for about two months." It was extremely difficult for a male, and most especially hard for a father, whose daughter was only an arm's length away, to talk about "female problems", as most men labeled anything remotely characteristically female ailments. Mrs. Bice, slightly calmer than before, nodded affirmatively when her husband looked at her for verification of the date. "Yep, I reckon, it's about two months," he surmised. "And to answer your other question, no, she hasn't been examined by a physician; I certainly wouldn't feel comfortable or qualified to examine her from-uh—that standpoint, Ma'm." He was relieved to shut the highly uncomfortable and loathsome discussion down for at least a minute or two. To totally switch subjects he asked, "Now, how long will Rose be able to come to school? I know there are laws forbidding obviously pregnant girls from attending during their full term. And will Rose have a tutor for her regular classes?" He was a man of logic, it appeared, except in his miserable choice of a wife.

Miss Pearl grabbed a notepad, made a few notes, and spoke again. "Rose, for the present, will have light physical activity in physical education classes until a doctor can determine more specifically where she stands as far as her condition goes. I'll inform Coach Water that she can select exercises for Rose that are not too strenuous. She will also be allowed extra breaks for rest and water or even a snack if necessary. Is this agreeable to you so far, Dr. and Mrs. Bice?" She didn't slow up for a verbal agreement; the doctor had nodded, so that would have to serve as a peaceful affirmation to her set plan. The suddenly exhausted, simple school counselor proceeded with caution, but was encouraged by the silent Belle. "Her teachers, I'm sure, will gladly work with Rose during a time during the school day that suits them and Belle. They will also provide additional home practice on various skills. So, if we are all on the same page with the school plan, I believe we are through here. It's getting dark, and I know we all want our dinner on time, don't we? Do you have any further questions? Any comments?" Miss Pearl held her breath during the last question, fearing Belle's reaction. Rose slowly and deliberately raised her spindly arm as her parents looked on disapprovingly. Lou Pearl suddenly remembered that her initial plan of removing Rose from the conference had failed due to her parents' day early arrival. She kindly addressed the pitiful war-orphan looking child. "Yes, Rose? Honey, ask me anything you want." At this point in the day, she felt that whatever Rose asked couldn't be any more uncomfortable than what had been said already.

"Miss Pearl, can you and me talk a minute or two-alone?" Rose spoke barely audible and exhibiting some fear, probably fear of Belle's reaction. The child needs a confidant, thought the counselor. She needs to ask me something that she doesn't want to ask in front of her explosive mother.

"Just about my school work and my classes," Rose added as if to insure against future repercussions from Belle. After all, Belle had exploded like an unexpected firecracker on a nonholiday at the beginning of the meeting; she could repeat her performance if her anger was triggered by some word or facial expression that put her on the defense. "You know, Miss Pearl, I might need a tutor if I get behind," she clarified her purpose for privacy with her school counselor. Miss Pearl sensed that Rose was lying, but she smiled at her, patting her skinny shoulders. It appeared that Belle and Ellis Bice bought into their daughter's obvious deception as truth.

"Sure, dear. And thank you, Dr. and Mrs. Bice. Please don't hesitate to call me so we can help Rose as a team. I know we all share the same goal-to care for and to educate our Rose." Miss Pearl wisely ignored the issue of possible father identification as she shook hands vigorously with both Bices. Mrs. Bice squeezed her hand back a little too long, a little too firmly, and a little too sweaty as if she were looking for female validation. However, both parents seemed more comfortable after Rose clarified her reason for a one-on-one with her educator. Miss Pearl continued to herd the Bices along toward the door to the open office space. "You folks are welcomed to wait in the front where you came in. There's a couch and some chairs over there. Make yourselves at home. I'm sure Rose and I will finish up before too long. How about that coffee or water now?" The couple smiled and bobbed their heads together like Siamese twins. Miss Pearl whispered in Judith's ears. "Give them anything they want." She fumbled in her leather purse, rattling a huge ring of keys that she found in the side pocket. "Here are the keys to the vending machines in the teachers' lounge. Just take orders and keep these weirdoes filled up until we get through in my office. I don't want another scene like we had in Herber's office," she offered. Judith smiled and found a small plastic tray to help her transport the junk food from the lounge down the hall to the crazies in her office. She rattled off a long list of food and drink choices to the already salivating couple. Judith was also encouraged that she might still worm out some details from the unsuspecting couple, but she also heard Miss Pearl's comment in relation to the mood of the recently concluded meeting. Obviously, there was a potential for a meltdown; so, she would have to shovel gently to mine out facts without digging up land mines. The parents looked wrung out, but surprisingly at ease in the foreign environment of the public school.

While the Bices were left in Judith's protected custody, Miss Pearl headed toward her office. "Sit down, sweetie," Miss Pearl coaxed. "Have a Coke on me. It won't hurt you," she reassured the shy child. She then selected the familiar green bottle from her apartment sized refrigerator and handed it to Rose. "I believe I'll join you; it's been a-a-a-an interesting day, to say the least, hasn't it?" Miss Pearl sensed Rose's building anxiety and wanted to help settle the child's nerves. She took a long pull from her soft drink, wriggling a resting place for it among scattered answer sheets and test booklets. "Enjoy, and when you're a little more refreshed, we'll talk," the motherly counselor suggested. "I'm here for you and I'll honestly answer any question you ask. If I don't know the answer, we'll look for it together," Miss Pearl scanned her free hand across the many reference sources she had collected through the years which lay dusty and torn behind her desk. The diminutive mother-to-be turned the six ounce bottle up like a baby's bottle, grasping it with both hands and guzzling its contents like a starving infant. Then she rested the drained pop container on the black and white tiled floor beside her chair. After that energy was expended, she appeared to breathe a little easier. She had been rehydrated, re-caffeinated, and re-sugared.

Miss Pearl settled into her familiar office chair and began to speak. "How do you really feel, Rose? Are you sick to your stomach? Do you crave certain unusual food combinations like some ladies in your condition? You can be honest and free. It's just the two of us. Speak openly. Now, if you do get a little queasy, I always keep some crackers and Cokes for you and other students as well. Remember: Mount Gum, the whole faculty, and staff are rooting for you. We want you to continue your education as long as you can. Now, as your father mentioned, there are written rules about attendance in the last trimester of pregnancy, and I don't agree with the policy," she explained. "The Board of Education prohibits a pregnant student to attend classes in a public school once her condition is obvious to other people. When you get to that point, and that appears a long time away," she stopped and sized up the thin frame seated before her, "I'll see to it that you have a homebound tutor assigned to you cost free to help you keep up with your courses until the baby is born and you're up to returning to school." Miss Pearl had spoken calmly to avoid causing additional pressure on the child mommy, and now, Lou paused to sip her drink, allowing Rose to respond. When she didn't speak, but chose instead to re-suck the last drop from her empty Coke bottle, Lou estimated, "As small as you are, you probably won't show early, and you also probably won't get big, I believe. Why, you might be able to continue coming to school until almost the delivery date!" the single, barren counselor encouraged Rose, but, of course, she had no personal knowledge of the situation, which somewhat discredited the validity of her positive prediction.

"No, Ma'm. I-I-I'm not sick at all," stuttered Rose when she finally talked. "I'm feeling just fine," she spoke barely above a whisper. Then, she cleared her throat, sat up straight in the office chair while she started to display confidence in the decision to open up to the kindly counselor. "Miss Pearl, can I tell you something? I know I can, but I'm not sure that I should, but this situation is getting too strange and too big for me to handle or hide." The older woman, listening intently, leaned forward to catch Rose's every word. She mistakenly interpreted Rose's statement to refer to her future physical growth, although she had already commented on Rose's tiny size not even showing a bump in the front.

"Sure you can, Rose. I'm here to listen and to help." Miss Pearl wondered if Rose was on the verge of revealing the father's name and/or the circumstances surrounding the premature copulation. She recalled Miss Water's observation about Rose and realized the distinct possibility that there was neither a father nor a coupling. She was not interested in the drama aspect of the revelation; she was absorbed in the apparent desperation of the baby-carrying-a-baby. She recalled what Judith had rattled off about Joe and wondered now if the old bitty had really known the truth. "Go ahead, honey. Shoot." She reclined even deeper into her well-worn office chair as she anticipated answers to some of her questions but not totally anticipating what happened next.

"Miss Pearl," Rose took a deep breath and began. "I ain't pregnant at all! I ain't even got my monthly for the first time. I don't know what's got into Mama, and to add to my misery, she has told everybody that Mr. Joe Ross is the father! I never even spoke to the man before. He's as old as the hills. What am I going to do? He never came to Daddy's office to see me; most of the time during Daddy's appointments, I'm at school anyway. I hear the talk on the bus; I see neighbors whisper behind their songbooks and funeral fans when I walk up the aisles at church. You know we joined at Red Hill, don't you?" Miss Pearl nodded and kept focused on the speaker. "I ain't been with *any* man. At the commissary, yesterday, when I went to get a banana flip for my sweet tooth, I heard Mrs. Bell say that she thought that my mother's reason for doing this to me was to blackmail old Widow Ross. Do *you* think Mrs. Bell was right?" Rose had spewed out the story as if she were equipped and controlled by a pressure cooker gauge which had been inadvertently bumped, dislodging it and forcing the powerful steam to escape. Once the power had been released, she was spent and her little rodent face rested in the palms of her pale, blue veined hands which were clasped together as if in anguished prayer. Her desire for more talk had abandoned her, and her body was as deflated as a cheap grocery store balloon only a few hours after purchasing it. So, Belle Bice *had* made this whole sordid mess up! Pearl checked her immediate rage over such a sorry excuse for a mother. What mother would voluntarily sacrifice her child to this hell? A mother from hell, she suspected!

Generally composed and confident of her own self, Miss Pearl was now unsure of the appropriate path to take. She took one last nurse from her soft drink in a lame attempt to stall for a fitting, wise gem to magically appear in her muddled head, wondrously alleviating the sad but ridiculous situation. A high intensity drama completely fabricated by an unstable mother—one that tragically unfolded in the Mount Gum's cramped school office—had her reeling.

Miss Pearl *was* a trained counselor, yet, how could she adequately guide this shattered child? She had, upon graduation from a private, religious, girls' college, anticipated her job as consisting of simple scatterings of life counseling sessions sprinkled among mostly scheduling decisions, testing data, and aiding in college applications and scholarship opportunities. Is that why she had sought this position, or was it really for the uncomfortable responsibility of rescuing young souls like Rose? Couldn't there be a midpoint on the counseling continuum between the two extremes—the perfunctory and the melodramatic? Between William Faulkner's "grotesques" and average everyday normal folk? Individuals like Belle Bice, who were visually and emotionally disturbing denizens whose stereotypes appeared in almost every rural community in the South, were peopling her office right now. Yet, there were equal groups of "normal" people in the community. How can I help this child who belonged to the "grotesque" Mrs. Bice? She pleaded to anyone and no one. Granny Bowen, Miss Pearl's substitute mother, a withered, wrinkled sage who spit her Bull-of-the-Woods tobacco in a peach half can, would, if she had still been alive, have explained away freaky behavior like Belle's in this way: "She ain't right, baby. She jest ain't right. She ain't never gonna be right." The old woman knew about life, her charge admitted in the confines of her school office. Granny B. would have had a practical solution to this impractical problem, but her educated foster child certainly did not.

"So, what am I going to do? I ain't ready for no honeymoon," Rose wailed with fresh tears. "I think I'll just run away from here and never come back. I'll miss Daddy and Ina and little Lee and...of course, I'll miss you and school and.....but I'm sick of mother's lies and accusations." Rose's dark mouse eyes blackened but never danced like her mother's as the poor child searched deep into herself for any fragment of respect or sympathy for her mother. "I know she's worried about money; we've been run out of town everywhere we've lived because she has always pulled some kind of stunt. In the last place we lived, she stole some pretty rings from the neighbor and tried to blame it on the preacher's wife next door. The place before that, in Remington, Mother flirted with the butcher, and when he wasn't interested in her that way, she locked him in the meat freezer. Thank God, he had a stick to trip the lock. Who knows what she'll do next? And Daddy? He can't do nothin' with her. His bark is worse than his bite. He always tells us not to upset mother, not to hurt mother, not to disobey mother. I'm sick of it all. Miss Pearl, do you think she can really get money from the Rosses with this new plan of hers? She wants to hoodwink them out of it by using me as the live bait! They ain't rich; they ain't even smart enough to make much money. Ain't nobody got no money in Red Hill, or they'd live somewhere else!" she defiantly declared. Rose slapped her back into the chair, breathing out as if it were her last air pocket. But then, the tiny child began to glower with energy as she sat up in the chair.

Strangely, Rose seemed to draw almost superhuman strength in expressing herself about the horrible realization that she had unwittingly served as her mother's pawn for ill-gotten gain from unsuspecting people who were just as poverty-stricken as she was. The newly acquired power fueled her leap straight up from her chair as she spoke through hysterical sobbing. "Miss Pearl, it makes me a-a-a prostitute like Miss Mabel at Sardis! I'm no better than that painted up old whore!" The mere mention of Mabel Overton's name in a casual crowd caused even her most secretive, loyal customers to blush and to excuse themselves from the shameful conversation. Miss Pearl moved out from her desk and gently patted the weeping girl as her tiny shoulders heaved up and down. Rose was a total opposite of the vulgar Mabel who would turn a trick for a new refrigerator or a set of tires even though, in essence, Belle was employing Mabel's technique on the Ross family.

"Oh, no, Rose, you're not like Mabel; you're innocent of all this mess. Don't beat yourself down. Let's talk about a plan for you. Honey, have you even discussed your concerns and the rumors that you feel are circling about you and Mr. Ross with your father? Or, was all his information from Mrs. Bice?" The counselor asked Rose, who removed her hands from her streaked face and indicated a no to the question. "I wonder what would happen if you were to undergo a complete physical examination with accurate results which would support your claims while at the same time it would discredit your mother's false ones." Miss Pearl stopped, wondering if she had stepped across the line between caring and meddling. But it was too late now for backing up, and Rose, for the first time during the discussion, looked up and shared an unexpected grin with her counselor. She quickly worked hard to harness her emotions and to cease her pitiful, body shaking snubbing to fit herself to comment.

"Oh, Ma'm, that would be the answer, wouldn't it? Would you please ask Momma and Daddy if I could see a doctor? I will be glad to do it. My regular doctor is Dr. Davies the company doctor. He could tell Mama that I am still just a-a-virgin. Oh, please, please, can you make that happen?" she pleaded as she grabbed desperately to the older woman's grey cardigan sleeve, clinging like a drowning man who attaches himself to an assisting lifeguard but who eventually dooms and drowns them both through his own panic. Miss Pearl peeled off Rose's stiff fingers one by one until she was free from the child's grip. She straightened her stretched sweater and patted Rose's trembling hand.

"Well, Rose, what I *can* do is to suggest to your parents that they schedule you a full physical examination to better determine your condition. That way, I can tell them, the school can better adjust your activities to match your needs. Now, I don't believe I'll be very successful if I try to convince your parents, especially your mother, that there is any possibility of judgment error on their/her part. But, perhaps, she would agree to this exam if we continue to assume that you are, in fact, impregnated," Miss Pearl strategized. She struggled to select her words carefully as she considered the culpability of the school and her own personal entanglement with this sticky situation that involved more of the personal side than of the professional side of a counselor's job. As she paused, she noticed that Rose had stopped weeping and snubbing, remarkably recovering, actually smiling, and even lightly clapping her tiny hands in relief, just joyous to be given a potential for escape. The bright girl knew she was not guilty of anything other than being born of a lunatic-a crime committed every day by many an innocent child. Rose's roller coaster emotions, if tracked on a medical chart, would resemble that of a heart attack sufferer in the middle of the actual heart attack.

ROSE STOOD UP confidently, and Miss Pearl followed her lead into the Mount Gum main office. The Bices were still comfortably perched on two vinyl stools now, leaning over the office counter and enjoying the ample refreshments Judy had provided through the legal burglary of the various vending machines. Belle broke her gaze from Judith and looked up, pausing in midsentence of some wandering yarn that halfway satisfied and entertained Mis' Judy's desire for gossip. She smiled into the tear-streaked rat face of her mirror image daughter who did not, thankfully, mirror her mother's insanity. (After all, every good Southern church goer knows that God *did* promise he wouldn't give us more than we could bear. And, the Lord knew another Belle Bice *would* prove to be much more than the world could stand!)

Lou Pearl cleared her throat and commenced to sell her own rational plan to irrational clients. "Now, I'm so sorry for the delay, folks, but Rose and I needed to do some further planning on her school schedule for when her time comes. If you'll follow me back to the principal's office, we'll conclude our conference and then everyone can go home." The three Bices ambled back, with Rose trailing behind, toward the original meeting place. Miss Pearl began talking before arriving inside the room; she was both physically and emotionally exhausted at this late hour. "I think, with your permission, of course, that Rose should just rest out here with Mrs. Thompson. I believe we adults can conduct our business quicker." She raised her voice slightly at the end of the last statement to indicate a question or an uncertainty of acceptance from the Bices, but they did not question her authority. They took seats in the office while Miss Pearl turned back to close the door. While closing it, she whispered something in Rose's ear. "Don't tell Mis' Judy anything unless you want it splattered all over Red Hill by morning. Volunteer to help her carry her boxes to the car, or to empty the trash, or to do any menial task to keep yourself busy and to keep her out of your business!" With that, Rose scampered away, and the door was slammed a little too hard.

Stepping back behind the principal's desk behind Dr. Bice, Miss Pearl noticed that Belle's demeanor had improved; she was unusually calm in attitude and deliberate in her gait. Maybe the good doctor had chastised her for her maniacal outburst, or maybe he slipped her a sedative; she was happy either way! Outside the sound proof office, hoping for a snippit of gossip, Mis' Judy sprang off her stool toward the pencil sharpener located by the principal's door, but her hope was not to be; silence reigned in the empty school as she returned to her office roost. She had nothing to share with her sewing circle tonight. Even when she had captured Belle alone while Doctor Bice was preoccupied with his whittling, she had gained no additional news. Belle had only offered a delusional stroll through memory lane by recounting her high school years when she was, according to her, a popular budding beauty. Inside the crowded office, Miss Pearl, still smarting from her last confrontation with Belle, began again, now more prepared for the scene.

"Dr. and Mrs. Bice? I think you would both agree that every expectant mother, regardless of the circumstances surrounding the situation, must have prenatal care to ensure the good health of the mother and the unborn child." Again, nods from both, almost as if rehearsed. No signs of the confrontation tidal waves so far, she thought, so she continued to follow her plan. "I would like to suggest that, at your convenience, you call Dr. Davies' office-he is your personal medical physician, right?" Miss Pearl's confidence was boosted by the couple's compliant passivity when once again, each parent nodded. "And schedule Rose for an overall physical examination right away. That will help us all in our preparations for what's to come," she closed, feeling assured of her success with the two muted parents.

As sudden as a summer storm blackens a brilliantly sunny day, Belle's countenance darkened and her John Q. Lewis eyebrows knitted tightly above her beady eyes as she realized that a thorough examination would unravel her diabolical plan and would expose her as a liar and a cheat. Repeating her earlier dramatic debut, she bounced up on her overstuffed heels like the first participant in a balloon bursting relay. "Absolutely not! I don't need no witch doctor of Braun's to tell me my baby's pregnant. The only thing we's a schedulin' is a weddin' to Mr. Joe Ross, Rose's suitor." Belle shouted, ranting and shaking her fist above Mr. Herber's cluttered desk. "I know how to care fer a expectant mother and I can care for a youngun', too. I done had three of my own. You are buttin' in where you ain't wanted, Miss Educated!" Miss Pearl's precious hopes were dashed as rapidly as they had been raised in what seemed like years ago when she and Rose were sharing her safe haven across the hall. "Dr. Bice will be handy helping me care for our girl in her time of need," the wild-eyed woman offered. She grabbed her husband's faded jacket sleeve and tugged on it violently. "C'mon, Doc, we's a'takin' Rose and headin' to the house. You won't hear from us again no more until after this weddin' or maybe not ever again! This is personal family bidness, and I don't need no uppity school counselor to tell me or my husband what to do," the deranged and enraged woman declared while huffing and puffing like the big, bad wolf. Lou Pearl's mouth was wide open, and Dr. Bice left his head down, studying his muddy brogans. And with that, Belle stalked out of the office, still hanging onto her husband's sleeve, jerked up totally startled Rose from the stool, and forced her reluctant little group through the double doors. Mis' Judy looked shocked and confused as she saw the family leave in a furious tear toward their jalopy. Miss Pearl, pale and exhausted, lingered at the mimeograph machine as it rhythmically continued spitting out purple copies while it grunted with age; she could identify with this colorful, technological dinosaur.

Miss Pearl, for once, let her guard down and desperately grabbed her secretary's smooth hand, leaning in to whisper even though Mount Gum was vacant. "Oh, Judith, that went terribly wrong. I tried to convince that foolish woman to take the child to Davies; then, he would tell her that Rose was, as you say, 'intact'. The child isn't pregnant; she isn't even menstruating, and she is still a virgin. She confessed that to me in my office." Miss Pearl shared the news into the tale-bearing woman's anxious ear as she abandoned the dire consequences of bleeding such delicate information to a gossip vampire, but she just needed to air her own feeling of hopelessness. Who cared now anyway? Rose's and Joe's disastrous marriage was on the horizon. Lou had failed Rose who was now tenaciously dangling between a life and a life sentence. "It's out of my hands now!" she conceded. Her porcelain skin wrinkled in deep lines around her sad eyes as the last gleam of unforgiving sun showcased her sagging face. Despite Judith's realization of being rewarded her greatest desire-juicy, fresh news-, she failed to derive any pleasure in the hollow victory that anguished her friend and destroyed her student in the process. She firmly squeezed the distraught counselor's hand and gently patted her shoulder with the free hand. Lou and Judy fought back hot tears of sorrow. For once, gossip lost its glitter for Judy.

And so, Joe D. Ross's elderly mother, Helen, soon heard from Mrs. Cross, who tried to cushion the blow of such scandalous nature, that Joe, her mentally challenged only son was the purported father of Rose Bice's baby. Mrs. Cross had softly knocked on Helen's door and had gently shared the unpleasant news to her neighbor before Helen overheard it at the commissary. After the old widow wept for about thirty agonizing minutes, she wiped her eyes on her cross stitched apron and reluctantly raised her weather-beaten face up from its wrinkled turkey neck docking station, peering back through her bloodshot, hooded eyes into the sympathetic eyes of her dearest friend. Raspy, her voice began, "You know, honey, that Joe D. won't know how to be a daddy to that little girl's baby. Why, he won't know the first thing about how to be her husband, either. He's a'headin' to Paradise through the fool's hole, thankey, Lord. But, what's right is right," she concluded. Helen was not delusional about her son's inability to function on his own.

"Tell Mrs. Bice and Dr. Bice that the boy and I will pay them a visit this evenin' to set up the arrangements for the hitchin'. Assure them that they won't need to load no shotgun, either. Joe D. will do it if'n I tell him that's what he has to do. I think when they are married, they should just live with me; I have plenty of room, and if it's agreeable with Mr. Beaux, I'll split the rent between me and Joe to help out. I might could help that little thing to be a good wife, help my boy to be a decent husband, and help both of them to be loving parents. I ain't perfect, but I got the time and the notion to do it 'cause they gonna need lots of help in life, I 'spect." She spoke, resigned to her assigned role in this twisted drama. Her friend patted the age spotted hand and held on to it as Helen continued. "Please, please, set this up fer me. I'm just too tired for all this, and I ain't got a phone yet," she requested, knowing her loving neighbor would promise to handle the logistics of the meeting. And she did. Fulfilling sacred promises was a valuable character trait highly respected and admired by Red Hill residents. Mrs. Cross would do this for Helen, and that fact afforded the old woman a little peace in the middle of a storm.

Somehow, the "fool" *did* understand his role and even embraced his duty when his mother sat him down and explained in detail everything she felt he could grasp; and as the wedding week progressed, he happily anticipated the simple ceremony that would take place in the hall between the doctor's office and Ada's quarters. Conversely, Rose, totally disheartened, refused to eat and took no joy in modeling the tan, muslin shift her mother had designed and hastily sewn for the upcoming wedding. The gown was a far cry from the white Chantilly lace sheath Rose had envisioned wearing one day, but then, Joe was not the dashing man of her dreams depicted on the front cover the most recent Bride's magazine; instead, her future husband was a clod hopping simpleton who still lived with his aged and doting mother. But, she knew it was unfair to blame Joe D.; he was as innocent as she. He was being used by Rose's own money-grabbing mother, and she herself was being sold as a bill of goods to him. What a miserable wedding this will be, she thought! And what an even more miserable life I'm going to have!

"Look on the bright side, Rose," her sister, Ina, had insisted. "At least you won't be holed up in this depressing boarding house, putting up with our crazy mother and babysitting Lee whenever Mother sets out on one of her unpredictable journeys. And," she added, cheerfully, "I've overheard some of Dad's patients say that Mrs. Ross is a real kind lady, a good cook, and a good housekeeper. You won't get that good treatment at Belle's," she called her mother's first name without respect. "My early morning patient, Mrs. Sully, said the ladies in the Style Shop heard Mrs. Ross comment about having you as a daughter-in-law. She said she was looking forward to having another girl in the house. I'll bet you won't live in filth like we do here, either. I can come and visit you whenever I want," she continued, attempting to comfort her depressed little sister. She knew the whole story was a farce; her sister was not pregnant, and she hated her mother for this deceit. She was a witness to the fact that Joe D. Ross had never even spoken to Rose, and he certainly hadn't had sex with her! She also knew, though, that it was futile to reason with an unreasonable, insane person like her mother. That's how Belle had been able to get her way every time. Ina felt defeated inside but continued to lift up her baby sister's spirits anyway.

"But, Ina, the bottom line is that I'm not what mother says I am, not with Joe not with any man! And, you, more than anyone, you know I haven't even started yet, so how could I be pregnant?" Rose argued, but quickly dropped the urgency of her pleading when her mother gaily paraded into Bice's office. Nothing could dissuade her mother, and her father refused to balk at Belle's edits. He actually never had argued with her about her way; he never would, she supposed. Yet, he was the logical one of the couple. Or was it really logical to allow an unstable person to call the shots in the family? Ellis's passivity in the whole matter was enough for both Rose and Ina to be disgusted with the ridiculous union of their own parents and the whole institution of marriage. The only institution needed here was a mental one for her parents, Rose thought.

Across the way and sequestered in her lonely school office, Miss Pearl, despondent, glared out the small, grimy window in her door. She couldn't get Rose off her mind. Despite Belle's initial demand for an immediate wedding date, she was, at least, persuaded by Ada Barr to schedule it the Saturday following the conference. The generous counselor had gotten wind of the Red Hill ladies' plan to prepare a respectable reception to be held across the hall from the office in Ada's house, so she had privately donated some money to Mrs. Barr, who, along with Mrs. George, and Mrs. Cross had graciously organized, decorated, and cooked for the morose celebration of the unholy alliance of Rose and Joe. The unselfish ladies had discovered the source of their cash flow, and Ada had called Lou, inviting the counselor to the brief ceremony and abbreviated reception afterwards and assuring her that her support was needed as a sparse group was expected. There, the hostess admitted, would be few brave souls in attendance; even though gossip was valued in the community, this event was just too disheartening to be validated by the usually participatory Red Hill crowd. Miss Pearl thanked the woman, refusing to commit either way.

Suddenly, Miss Pearl thought of a long shot! What if she did attend and also did invite a DHR employee to the wedding as a "guest" who might be willing to conduct an informal, yet unauthorized observation, and maybe would consider following up any abnormalities with a later investigation? She could take her car, pick up the worker, and they could both come as friends. She did know Melanie, a social worker who had visited the school and who was a fellow Methodist. The new, young and single hire was often on call on the weekends. No one would suspect any other motive than just the obvious-to support a young person in the county school system. In addition, she had recently shared a meal with one of the single, male directors in the Human Resource department. Maybe he would be willing to let Melanie accompany her to a wedding of a minor to insure that lawful procedure had been followed. She had done a few favors for him; she could cash in on them if necessary. It was a last ditch effort, but it was still worth a shot to rescue Rose. She looked on her Rolodex to find Melanie's office number; she phoned quickly in hopes of a midnight hour shining knight, but the girl's phone rang and rang without stopping. She slammed down the phone and realized that she was desperate because of her own personal guilt for letting Rose down. Extreme emotional exhaustion fell hard on her like the blue velvet stage curtain dropped on Mount Gum's wooden stage after a poor theater performance. The discouraged woman finally surrendered to defeat, left the school without completing the SAC paperwork, and headed to her secluded lake house for the remainder of the weekend with the knowledge that little Rose would soon be Mrs. Ross in a few hours. God bless that child, she prayed silently, as stinging tears laced her thick eyelashes and blurred her vision as she drove away from the school and toward the main highway.

Meanwhile, the wedding morning was shaping up to be, ironically, a beautiful one. The sun was warm and bright and the air lacked its usual oppressive Alabama humidity. Mrs. Barr had already gathered the few spring flowers she had growing in her yard and arranged them into milk glass vases throughout her parlor and dining room. Artistically, she had woven them throughout the damp, dreary hall and around the office threshold, perking up the unlikely event venue.

The gracious neighbor had purposely saved back one fragile red rose for the bride's bouquet. The atmosphere, however, smacked more of an unexpected funeral than of a joyous wedding, but the three gracious hostesses still gave close attention to the natural decorations and the tasty food, perhaps in an effort to blur the sadness that loomed in the boarding house and in the shattered heart of this young soon-to-be-bride.

Rose, still in her filthy bedroom across the hall, looked pitifully shabby in her handmade dress which hung off her razor sharp shoulders like an ill-fitting and premature shroud. She had neglected to style her wispy hair or even to apply the slightest of makeup to her thin, white face, thus forcing the direct focus of the crowd on her charcteristic mouse eyes-the imitations of Belle's, minus the insanity factor. Her hysterically and unnaturally ecstatic mother, oblivious to the actual mood of the dismal occasion, was too busy parading around the entire boarding house like an arrogant, wayward child to lend any useful assistance in dressing her daughter for the big day. So, Rose felt there was no point in paying attention to her own looks. Who cared anyway? Her death sentence had been delivered, and she was not in line for pardoning.

She had begun to loath her deranged mother for staging and directing this mockery of a marriage. Ina had absolutely refused to participate in the spectacle even after Belle begged her to serve as Rose's only attendant. She could not put her stamp of approval on this madness, so she chose to man the office in her father's absence as he presided over the ceremony; she would answer the phone, make appointments, and catch up on the mountains of paperwork that had landed on her already chaotic desk due to her father's recently acquired fame and popularity. And to think, Joe D. Ross, her future brother-in-law, had greatly contributed to that notoriety by publicizing his own personal testimony after his first chiropractic visit! Belle scowled at Ina's firm decision, but in the end, she was too enamored with the wedding hype to pursue further argument with her strong-willed daughter. Besides, *she* could serve as her daughter's attendant. The idea entranced the self-serving woman.

Even though it was actually *Rose's* wedding day, Belle's focus was totally on Belle and her matchmaking success. Denying her obvious repulsive appearance, Belle flaunted her overgenerous curves by force feeding them into a neon yellow sheath which reminded one of an off brand can of biscuits just waiting to explode from its confines with a twist and a whop! She had, once again, selected ill-fitting pumps that pushed on her corpulent feet, causing them to swell over the tops like lunchroom yeast rolls on a stainless steel pan, but without the aesthetic appeal.

Belle had fashioned a crudely sewn chicken manure brown dress suit and wildly stitched tan dress shirt for her pork-faced little son, Lee. She had added a homemade red satin bowtie to decorate the boy's rolled neck. He was too young to sense the serious undertones of his sissy's ceremony, but he was, nevertheless, eager to attack Mrs. Ada's wedding cake, which had been promised to him by his mother if he was a "good boy", a promise which was a strong contributing factor to his more than usual compliance and to his endurance of the hideous wardrobe he frequently tugged at in a futile attempt to give his puffy little form some additional space.

As the forlorn troupe made its way in front of the ivy covered doorway, in the meantime, the few guests were wandering into Mrs. Barr's sitting room. During a pregnant pause between whispering in the audience, loud footsteps intruded. The creaky screened door, decorated with beige and red tissue flowers opened to reveal the clumsy groom and his meek mother who followed behind her dullard son and immediately plopped down on the first comfortable chair available by the door. Joe, the foolish man of the hour, wore the grin of the Village Idiot as he lumbered near his child bride who was leaning on the door facing of her father's office. The doors of the hall were propped open to accommodate the spectators seated in the parlor and dining room. Joe was wearing a freshly laundered Dickey work set; his stiff label was topped off with a new red rosebud that Mrs. George had stripped from her scraggly bush. Truly, the groom was the only jovial spirit in the makeshift wedding chapel except for his future mother-in-law.

"My children and our guests, let's get on with this," Dr. Bice started his monologue in a matter-of-fact tone. "I've got patients to attend to after this." The doctor swallowed and continued his address without the aid of the Holy Bible or even a prayer book. "Now, before we commence, let me assure you that I am licensed because I'm a Justice of the Peace as well as a doctor. I filled out a form in a magazine I found in my office, I mailed it, and the certificate came back to me this morning," he explained defensively to the uninterested audience. He breathed slowly and added, "The state of Alabama recognizes the couple's application for the marriage license even though they won't receive the official copy from Montgomery until later. Belle called someone in the office down there and told them it was urgent that the marriage take place quickly, so they accepted her explanation and gave her the go-ahead to get this done. Also, me and the Missus gave our blessing to the union even though Rose is a little young," he volunteered, blushing, to a totally detached congregation. No one openly questioned his authority or his hasty justification. In rural areas like Red Hill, there was a tendency on the part of less educated people to blindly accept the actions of professionals in the field of legal and medical matters even without actual proof of the facts. That certainly did not mean that there weren't doubters in the group. The hostesses had subtly flashed knowing grimaces across the room to each other. But, overall, the sense of impending doom fell like an Italian mourning veil over the group, paralyzing their desire or ability to rebel as the vulgar rite began.

Mrs. George, with the pressure of her thumbs, gently folded the odd couple toward the center of the archway in front of the faux preacher. Then, without delay and with the realization that there was no maid of honor present, she, dressed as usual in her favorite, provocative style, took Mrs. Bice, whom she assumed now served was her daughter's attendant, by her fluffy shoulders and squared her up beside her pitiful daughter. Belle was the sole witness-a witness of the most unfair union that had ever appeared in front of Red Hill residents. But then, in just as quick a move as before, Mrs. George and Mrs. Cross together hoisted Mrs. Helen Ross from her doily covered winged chair, assuring the old matron that her stand would be brief like the ceremony to follow, and positioned her beside her grinning, imbecilic son's right side. The two ladies then glared at Dr. Bice to return to his pronouncement, but it was not to be. At that point, Lee wobbled up to the middle of the wedding couple, but then backed himself up to find his mother who picked up the heavy child and automatically began unbuttoning her tight dress at the top to openly nurse her oversized and over aged son during the ceremony! Mrs. Cross quickly slid two straight-backed chairs up for each of the mothers, an action which aggravated Belle but pleased the Widow Ross who already showed signs of leg weakness. The absurd sound of Lee's sickening, rhythmic pull on Belle's saggy breasts broke the silence and should have disgusted anyone within hearing distance. However, astonishingly, the emotionally neuropathic audience barely acknowledged the child's ludicrous action and instead, chose rather to focus on the few family members and even fewer empathetic neighbors who had slipped in late and seated themselves on the shiny, white, painted church pews that Mr. Barr had moved inside to accommodate the guests. The bizarre was now the accepted and even the expected in this marital freak show.

Strangely, there were no traditional vows repeated, just two audible "I do's" from the couple after some undecipherable mumbling from Dr. Bice whose head stayed shoved into his chest during the rest of the ceremony. There were no wedding rings, so there was not a need for that traditional symbolic explanation. There was no music- no organist, no pianist, no soloist-, and there was no real wedding kiss (just a childlike peck from the groom to his baby bride); and in Rose's opinion, there was no hope. The ceremony lasted approximately five minutes, and within a minute after that, Lee, suddenly aware that the wedding was over lost interest in his mother's withered, unappealing breast and was bee-lining it for the wedding cake and the other refreshments of yellow punch, ham sandwiches, and mints. After all, he had been a "good boy". His noisemaker had been otherwise corked and improperly occupied with inappropriate nourishment during the wedding.

Dr. Bice, skipping the reception, kissed his teary-eyed daughter, shook his new son-in-law's hand, and headed back to his noisy office which was rapidly filling up with anxious patients. When Ina was certain the nauseating farce were over, she vacated her desk in front of the confused patients and rushed over to hug her married sister, whispering in her ear as the other guests were shaking hands and eagerly forming a line for Ada's treats. "Remember; you're free from the old witch we call 'Momma'!" Rose squeezed her back fiercely and signaled a weak "V" for victory sign, finally shuffling back into the ragged receiving line and dutifully shaking sweaty hands and hugging dirt ringed necks.

During the meet and greet session, all the while, Belle wore the twisted smile of a dishonest and deranged champion. She greeted each guest, proudly declaring, "MY girl is a married lady now. Ain't no use fer nobody to say nothin' about her condition. I done got her a husband and a father to my grandchild. This baby is all legal as of today!" Most guests just ignored Belle like a small pimple that was annoying but not worth squeezing as they shuffled wordlessly through the receiving line and into the reception area.

Around an hour after the ceremony, the doleful but full guests began to disperse and exit through the side porch. The new couple and Mrs. Ross remained alone in the parlor as the hostesses were removing and storing the tired decorations while Ina trudged back across the hall to her desk. Belle took the overfilled and drowsy Lee home for an early nap, unnecessarily nursing the sleepy boy on the way; the other ladies went home to prepare lunch for the rest of their family who had not chosen to attend the marital train wreck. The industrious hostesses busily retrieved empty and half-empty cups, wadded napkins, and forks laden with heavy cream icing as they gathered up trash from the littered parlor and dining room. Leftover flowers were recycled into newly arranged bouquets for the elder Mrs. Ross, Rose, and some of their shut-in neighbors who could use a little joy in their lives. The three ladies agreed that additional flowers given to Belle would neither sweeten her up nor magically restore her to sound mental health.

Joe spoke first as Rose stared out the sparkling window of the parlor. "Well, little bride, I gotta go back to work to make up for my lost hour, but I done et enuff at this here fanfare to last me 'til tonight anyways. Now, Rose, you jest rest and take care of our baby," he ordered as he lightly and gently pecked his twelve-year-old spouse's pale cheeks and boldly patted her bony bottom. Rose impulsively grabbed his huge hand and jerked it away from her hip, an embarrassing move that caused Joe's face to burn hot with shame; he thought that was what he was supposed to do after the wedding, according to his friends at the black yard. Upset, he literally ran out the back screen door of Ada's porch, down the rickety stairs, and back to his safe place on the wood yard—even though running at his size was not his specialty nor was it an athletic show. No one left in the empty parlor challenged his prudent decision to choose work over honeymooning; it mercifully granted Rose a short delay before assuming her wifely duties. Mrs. Barr and Mrs. George held back tears as they hugged the child bride, surrounding her entire body from front to back with their loving bodies and promising her visits and help anytime she needed them. Mrs. Cross was too distraught to encourage the little girl right now; she hid in the kitchen and pretended to sweep. When Rose gathered her bouquet and turned her back on the ladies, they waited until they were certain she was out of hearing distance before they joined their grieving friend in the kitchen-all three wept without restraint as they washed, rinsed, and dried the dishes. They wept, not for themselves but for Rose.

Daughter-in-law and mother-in-law both recognized this undesired union as a hideous joke on them and the slow-witted Joe D., who was ignorant yet blissful with his new role assignment. The older woman cringed as she imagined the base comments offered up on the pole yard to her little boy. And Rose, poor Rose, the older woman thought, was probably in for shock after shock as reality would soon cruelly claim her innocence. The two lady Rosses headed down the front stairs to the damp yard. A few yards were crossed before the silence was broken.

The elder Mrs. Ross split the silent air between the two new relatives. "Honey, come on home with me now 'cause I'm a'gonna help you to be a wife and a mother, but first, I'm a'gonna finish raising you 'cause you ain't fully turned out yet." She lowered her already husky voice and narrowed her blue eyes. "Yore mammy ain't got the brains the Lord gave a billy goat. I'm sorry, baby, but it's the gospel truth. If I'm a'lyin' then I'm a'dyin'. Yeah, you need somebody to hope you, and I'm jest the one to do it," she assured Rose, patting her hand and smiling. Rose, surprised at the old lady's candor, obediently fell into step with her new mentor, and the two hoofed it on down the sun drenched path to their mutual home. Rose relaxed a little after hearing Mrs. Ross's affirmation of what she already knew and had experienced—Belle Bice was insane. She even allowed herself to skip along beside Helen as the warmth of the spring sun tempered her sorrow. Maybe Ina was right after all; maybe Mrs. Helen was okay.

Life at Red Hill perked along like a reliable coffee pot, familiar and consistent. To the outside world and even to Mother Ross, the new couple housed under her roof got along mighty well. She had been pleasantly pleased at what a quick study Rose was in the arts of everyday chores such as cooking, cleaning, washing, ironing, gardening, and serving. Rose's new family reaped the benefits of the Widow Ross's patient instruction in daily work which had begun the first evening she spent in the house. Perhaps, the elder woman assumed, the majority of the chores in the Bice home had fallen in Rose's spindly lap since crazy Belle, as both she and Belle started calling her, preferred caring for Lee only and not much else. Mrs. Ross the elder found herself re-energized since her sweet little daughter (as she called her) came to live with her and Joe. Even under such strained circumstances, Rose flourished and grew healthier both mentally and physically; the baby issue was not addressed by any of the three. When Joe mentioned it, the girls never commented, so he finally dropped the subject. He knew he wasn't familiar with woman folk's ways; he thought this might be a normal reaction to pregnancy.

It was true that Rose and Joe talked very little, but then, Joe had never been capable of deep conversation. Instead, the three of them shared the evening meal, cleared the dishes together, and then, hastily reconvened to the closet sized den to enjoy their favorite television programs while they picked out pecans or sorted clothes. It was quite unusual for a Red Hill resident in the early '60's to even own a television, but the dearly departed Mr. Joe D. Ross, Sr. was reticent at first about buying an "idiot box", as he called it, laughing; yet, Helen's good-natured husband seldom missed his regular favorites after working all day on the pole yard. He had even purchased the largest screen available at the time from the local Western Auto store. After Mr. Ross's death, his surviving family members continued to enjoy the fruit of his progressive thinking in the new emerging world of technology. The Rosses were passively entertained without having to actively entertain.

About two months after the wedding, Mr. Cross, an extremely timid and introverted railroad worker, shared with his wife, Bea, an interesting tidbit of information about the Ross couple: Joe had confessed to him in private that he had not "lain" with his preteen bride! He told the older man that he had been patient because he knew that women in the family way were not always frisky, but his younger coworker on the black yard had insisted that it was time for him to claim his rightful prize. Mr. Cross asked Joe if his father had ever talked to him about marriage and women. Joe admitted that he could barely remember his father explaining to him about the "birds and the beast" (he called it); he said his old man had explained the moodiness of a distant female cousin at a family reunion when the very pregnant woman spurned her husband's advances in the back room of the cabin where Joe had accidently wandered. The elder Mr. Ross, it seemed, gave just enough information about the facts of life to confuse the already confused Joe Junior.

Mr. Cross, confused, told his wife that he really wondered if the simpleton, as the father of Rose's child, had actually forgotten how to have sex. At that point in the intimate conversation, Bea reassured her husband, "Honey, it don't take no IQ to do that! It comes naturally; ain't no teachin' nor rememberin' necessary!" She squeezed her loving husband's upper thigh and laughed lustily. He, reddened, agreed with his witty, commonsense wife, but was still perplexed as how to help the boy, as he thought of him. "Why don't I jest have a word with Wider Ross? You know, she trusts me especially adder I come to her privately about Joe's predicament, and she's told me time and again that she 'preciated all that me, Ada, and Mrs. George done fer Joe and Rose. Now, you don't mention this to no one-either on the pole yard or even to Joe," she added unnecessarily to her reserved husband. She patted his jittery knee. "Baby, I'll handle this. You jest make us a livin'", she promised. He knew that she would.

Mrs. Cross had heard the well-circulated rumor which probably had originated from Mis' Judy's flapping gums. Supposedly, Rose was not only NOT pregnant, but she was not even capable of a pregnancy even if she'd been exposed. Bea had a plan; she rested her head on her fluffy sunshine smelling pillow beside her snoring husband. She was confident of the success of the next morning's activities. She offered a quick prayer and soon joined her husband's log sawing, forming a loud duet.

As soon as Bea had hustled her husband off to catch the train to the stockyard to Verle, she hastily stacked their breakfast dishes, smoothed her stark white hair, and with her apron still tied loosely around her ample waist, she aimed for the Ross place. Widow Ross was in the back yard hanging out her worn, but freshly washed percale sheets. Perfect timing, Bea thought. "Oh, Mother Ross, what a fine warshin' you put out this early morning! Is yore little daughter here? Doesn't she help you with your warshin'? I heard from your close neighbor, Eva, that Rose was a'comin on nicely since she-uh-moved in with you and Joe." Bea spoke cheerfully and quickly, leaving little space for feedback from the older woman. Nosey as the inquiry seemed, it was not uncommon for close neighbors to pry into another neighbor's business if that person had previously established a mutual, trusting relationship, and Bea had certainly done that through the years. The listener still had a choice; answer the questions or ignore them. The friendship between the two speakers was generally strong enough to withstand either option.

"Yes'm, Bea. She does help me a right smart. I'm a'learnin' her somethin' new ever day and she learns quick, too, but I just sent her down to the commissary with a long list of supplies that we need.

She loves to walk and pull that old red wagon jest like a child," she paused. "Well, you know she IS a child, ain't she?" Mrs. Ross added thoughtfully. "Poor little thang," she uttered into the blindingly white laundry flapping in the early morning breeze.

"Yessum, she is jest a child, I reckon, and that's why I come down here to talk to you this morning," Bea proceeded with caution, kindness, sensitivity, and most of all, sincere love for her elderly neighbor. Mrs. Ross's furrowed face reddened at the delicate nature of what she suspected next in the conversation; she loved Bea, though, and she knew her intentions were honorable and just. But, just the word "pregnant" was enough to make her cringe. Why, Helen Ross's own mother was too embarrassed to explain the facts of life to her teenage daughter. So Victorian was she that when Helen started her first period, she immediately and silently diagnosed her own imminent death from hemorrhaging! Only when an older sister came home from trade school and asked Helen what was causing her to mope around the house did Helen learn about "Aunt Flo", as her cosmopolitan sister coined it. Feminine products back then were scarce, but her patient sister brought some basic supplies for her naïve sibling and tutored her in personal hygiene in relation to this new development in Helen's health and care. Now, even as an adult and dealing openly with pregnancy, sex, and other taboo subjects, the delicateness was just mortifying the old woman.

Helen put down her wicker laundry basket, and both women sat together on the red glider under the big oak tree in the back of the house. Bea calmly but firmly recounted her husband's tale. Helen wept and wiped her tired, baggy eyes with the hand embroidered handkerchief she kept in her bosom. "Bea, what can we do?" she asked, truly seeking advice from her dear friend who had the guts to bring the subject up to her. "I can't talk to Joe about those night things," she declared. "Would Mr. Cross tell him what is going on?" she stopped abruptly, catching her breath and continuing. "Oh, never mind that now. It's that girl we gotta help. It's Rose. What can we do to help HER? I never thought Joe would—mmmmm-know as much as he let on to yore husband. I did see once when I went into their bedroom to get another quilt for my bed, Joe was turned towarg the wall, and Rose was barely hangin' onto her side of the bed, and she still had on a gown and a housecoat. I didn't put too much stock in it at the time. She's so puny; I figgered she was just cold. But, I also noticed she don't act like no expectant mother, and she ain't getting no bigger neither. I guess I didn't want to know what was goin' on, or what was NOT goin' on," the older woman admitted sorrowfully. "I've growed to love that little ole thang, Bea," she finished, wiping her forehead with her apron pocket.

"Helen, dear, I've been a'studyin' 'bout this matter since yesterdee, and I think you and me can help little Rose right by ourselves," Bea confidently introduced the plan. Helen opened her wrinkled mouth to speak, but Bea rushed in to reveal the first step of her solution. "How's about me and you take Rose over to see Dr. Davies to make sure she's feeling like fulfilling her role as Joe's wife? She might be anemic or somethin' since she's so young to be married and expectin'. We can tell that hateful, nosey bulldog of a receptionist he hired, and she'll tear her toenails off to get us in jest so's she can find out what's really goin' on," she chuckled to Helen who perked up. It was true; Dr. Davies' receptionist felt that she had been called by God to pro- tect "her" doctor from the stupid requests of his lowly patients. Ms. Clements, a sour divorcee', spoke to the Red Hill residents in such a condescending manner that even the other nurses in the office were ashamed of her actions. Dr. Davies was just too overwhelmed with sick people to even be aware of her hatred of mankind. However, the one catch was that old Ms. Clements *did* treasure a good tale and any compliments about her granddaughter, though, and Bea knew these topics were the old battle axe's Achilles' heel. It was worth a try, she thought.

"You know," Helen grinned, knocking ten years off her age, "I have wondered about Rose myself. She's a mite peaked and low; she's thin as a black racer, too. Hey, have you got yore car? You know, time's a-wasting." Bea was relieved at how quickly Helen accepted the benevolent plan of deception and redemption. Bea had been so confident of her plan that she had previously phoned the doctor's office before leaving her home and lavishly buttered up the Bulldog by complimenting her only granddaughter's new Girl Scout badge and faithfully promising Ms. Clements that both she and Mrs. George would surely purchase cookies from the little darling when the sales started next month.

"Sure thing," Bea assured Helen. "I jest got my old car fixed and it's full of gas and ready to go. Mr. Cross won't be in for lunch today because he's running some errands with Mr. Beaux in town. He said he and Mr. Beaux would stop by Dairy Queen and get a barbeque for lunch-Mr. Beaux's treat! You know that man shore can eat, can't he? Here, Helen, let me help you finish hangin' out the rest of your warsh, and you go over to Mrs. George's and borrow her phone. Call Mrs. Bell down at the store. Tell her to hold Rose there. Tell her we'll pick her up since she's got too many groceries to tote in that old wagon. We won't even stop at yore house; I'll park in the shade at the doc's office so's yore milk, eggs, and the like won't go blue-john in the heat," Bea commanded. Both women shifted into high gear, and in about ten minutes, the three of them were puttering down the road in the saucy red Falcon.

At first, Rose was a little confused and somewhat nervous over the unplanned doctor trip, but she trusted the two ladies who had been so kind to her. After all, she had a diversion! She was getting out of Red Hill, and she might even get to eat in town today. She loved Mrs. Ross and was grateful for her kindness and her life lessons, but she was still a child who never got to be a child-never to play, never to run, never to skip, or never to savor any other childish activities that twelve-year-old girls enjoy. Anything was better, though, than living in that filthy boarding house with her mother and the still nursing Lee! Ina's visits, fortunately, occurred more often as their mother grew more bizarre with every passing day. Her unhappy older sister reminded Rose every time she visited the Ross house just how good Rose had it, and Rose couldn't disagree with her when she heard through the Red Hill grapevine the ridiculous stunts her mother now pulled frequently in public.

Bea Cross sensed Rose's apprehension, and softly addressed her unspoken fears as they puttered down the road toward the two mile sign. "Honey, me and your momma-in-law's been a'thinkin' 'bout how pale you been lookin' lately. You know how hard it is to git an appointment to see Dr. Davies? Well, he had a cancellation, so we jest decided to load you up and get you checked out. This was as good a day as any. You know he won't hurt you, baby. And, maybe, we'll have time to stop at the Diary Queen. You know Mr. Smit makes a mighty fine thick malt. You need some fattening up, and we are already fat, ain't we, Helen?" she laughed as she steered the Falcon onto the main highway to town. The child bride shared a shy grin with her navigators, relaxed slightly, and rested her head back on the head rest, as she dozed off.

Upon arriving at the yellow brick and tan painted office building, Mrs. Cross dropped the other two passengers off at the expensive oak and beveled glass entrance which looked completely out of place against the tacky, cheaply constructed exterior. Then, as Bea had promised Helen, she expertly backed her little red compact into a completely shaded parking place across from the office. Helen and Rose waited on Bea outside the hand crafted door, and the three women walked in together confidently. Rose signed in, and the Bulldog, whose ego had already been primed and stroked, was actually cordial when she pointed out three vacant, neon colored office chairs near the front office. The dreaded Ms. Clements even smiled at Rose as she handed the receptionist the clipboard and pen. Rose, finding a recent copy of Teen magazine, seated herself safely in the middle of her two supporters who had helped her with the necessary forms.

"Mrs. Ross-uh-Mrs. Joe Ross-uh-Rose?" stammered a cheery young nurse who held the door back for Rose. "Would you come with me, please?" Rose put down her magazine and looked expectantly at her devoted escorts, but they just nodded and motioning her to go on into the hall toward the examining rooms. The friendly nurse anticipated Rose's unspoken question. "Honey, they'll have to stay out here in the waiting room. The rooms only have one chair, and the standard procedure for routine examinations only allow the patient, the doctor, and the assisting nurse, who is me," she explained with a sincere but syrupy southern voice. She smiled warmly and compassionately as she tapped Rose's shoulder to direct her through the stark white corridor. Oddly enough, Rose was not in the least ruffled. She knew that the two ladies outside waiting for her cared for her like normal mothers do, totally different from her own mother's self-serving attitude toward her.

In addition, the nurse who held her newly inked chart gave her an unexpected and strange sense of peace and a sense of maturity as well. With all this genuine female support, Rose willingly followed the nurse and obediently sat down on the white sheeted exam table. As the nurse closed the door behind her, she gave Rose specific instructions. "The doctor will see you soon. Go ahead and strip down, sweetie. That means everything that you have on. Just put on that hospital gown, tie the strings in the back if you can, or tap on the door, and I'll help secure the ribbons for you. You can stack your clothes over there in that white tray." The health professional grabbed a file folder and headed out the door, shutting it noiselessly behind her.

As modest as young Rose was, she followed the given directions to the letter. She shed her cotton frocks and "step-ins" (as her grandmother Bice called panties), slipped on the flimsy hospital gown, awkwardly tied the ribbons, and perched herself on the very end of the examining table. She let her worn shoes drop to the black and white subway tiled floor, but realized that her feet were filthy from the morning walk to the store. She sprung back up, now barefooted, and found a washcloth near the stainless steel sink. Wiping her dirty feet with the dampened cloth, she then tiptoed back to her perch, tossing the used washcloth into a white metal can marked "soiled laundry". She quickly re-checked her almost naked body and found no other offensive smudges or odors, so she took a deep breath and waited for her familiar physician. She innocently thought of this visit as an adventure. She recalled the last time she saw Dr. Davies when she had hurt her knee. He had a gentle voice and a kind manner about him.

The usual waiting time at Doc's office was generally around an hour or more due to the occasional work accident or other community injuries that required immediate attention. However, Rose had barely gathered her oversized gown around her bird legs when the stocky, affable doctor tapped on the door. "Rose? Are you ready for me to come in, or do you need some extra time?" Dr. Davies asked gently from the hall. Even amid the busyness of his office, he had heard of Rose's plight, and he remembered who she was and who her crazy mother was, too. Belle Bice was a nut case for sure, he thought. Dr. Davies had also treated her dim-witted groom, who had been injured on the job due to his own carelessness and stupidity. Lord, what a pair—the infant and the imbecile! He was filled with pity when he thought back to only a few months before when Rose had fallen from her rusty bike and gashed her scrawny leg. He had cleaned the wound, stitched it, and ordered a tetanus shot for her. Such a little thing to be considered anybody's wife, especially someone like Joe who wasn't even capable of living alone. When he cracked the door and actually saw Rose again, so young and so vulnerable, sitting once again in his office, he sighed and wondered how much of the rumor was true. A future mother? Lord, Lord, heaven help us all, he prayed mentally. He pushed open the door and plastered a smile on his worried face.

"Well, well, young lady. You've come a long way from that bicycle wreck, haven't you? Let me see how that old cut looks," he began lightly to keep the mood non-threatening. Rose turned her leg up for the doctor to see the scar. "Not bad, not bad," he pronounced. "Is it true that you're a married lady now, Rose? You're a right smart younger than most new brides, aren't you? I hope you are still attending school. Mis' Judy told me that you're a good student. Yes, you need to get your education. Who knows? You might be examining me one day!" he said as he pulled on his stethoscope. Rose avoided the doctor's glance because she had quit attending school.

"Dr. Davies, my momma made me marry up with Mr. Ross because she thought his old momma might die and leave me some money. It ain't right," she protested in a wail. "I went ahead and quit school because I'm supposed to be in the family way, but that's a lie!" she shouted. Dr. Davies rubbed her narrow shoulders and put his index finger to his lips in an effort to quiet her down before the embarrassing exam. The attending nurse attempted to hide her shock, concentrating on her patient's well being and avoiding eye contact with both Rose and her boss.

"Just lay back on the pillow, Rose. Relax. I wouldn't hurt you for the world, but I need to see how you're doing and what's going on inside you. If you are pregnant, then we need to find out why you're not already the size of a pumpkin by now. We can talk after the exam is over," the doctor reassured his young patient. Rose tensed up but kept respectfully silent.

Before Rose had a chance to continue pleading her case, the accuracy of her claim was quickly validated by Davies after he completed the internal examination. After only a few delicate touches and virtually no painful probing, Old Doc knew three facts: Rose was not pregnant; Rose was not even menstruating yet; and Rose was still a virgin! What was wrong with her idiotic mother? He was so angry that he, without thinking, jerked off his rubber gloves and slammed them into the metal trash bin. Rose, startled at the loud, metal clang, sat upright and then fell back again against the cold sheet. The incensed man inhaled and exhaled slowly while his back was turned from Rose in an unsuccessful effort to steady his emotions before facing the simple fawn unfairly splayed out on his table. He opened his mouth to speak, but Rose again raised herself up from the pillow; and with her beady mouse eyes, she desperately searched for confirmation of her innocence in the obviously troubled eyes of her beloved practitioner. "Rose, honey," he led off before she did, but he paused when he saw the deep sorrow mixed with anger on her face. He grabbled for this next line, but unexpectedly, Rose patted his hand and brightened up as she readjusted her body on the uncomfortable table. He knew! He knew! She thought she saw validation in between his anger and his pity for her. Now, *she* was ready to talk.

"So, now, you know. YOU believe me, don't you? Can you help me? Can I be free again? she asked pleadingly. "Before you answer me, let me say this," she continued. "Now, don't get me wrong," she confessed. "I do love Mrs. Helen, and living with her and even with Joe is a heck of a lot better than living with my loony mother in my own house, but I don't want Joe Ross for a husband. I don't want

ANYONE for my husband. I want to finish school at Mount Gum, and then, I'm leaving, and I ain't never looking back, neither!" Rose spoke convincingly as she sat half-nude on the edge of the table. The doctor was astounded by her bald honesty and strong determination after having been beaten down by her mother and prematurely given an internal exam by someone she loved and trusted. He admired the spunky little girl with the rat eyes.

"Yes, Rose," he answered as he took her skeletal hand in his. "I think I can help you now that you've had a legitimate exam, not just someone's wild accusation with ulterior motives." He was so proud of her for her inner strength she was exhibiting even in the sterile, unfriendly environment of his office. "Nurse Jan, would you please step outside and allow me to consult with my patient alone about a private matter?" he requested and was permitted to do just that, even though a second party's presence was already federally mandated during an exam to witness the doctor's correct, professional protocol and to protect him against law suits. Rural people trusted and depended on (right or wrong) their doctors and their procedures. Seldom ever did a disgruntled patient pursue legal action. As the suspicious nurse exited, Dr. Davies rearranged Rose's hospital gown in a more modest fashion and drew up a stool nearer to her. He placed his smooth hands on her twig arms.

"I believe, Rose, that because your marriage has not yet been consummated, and because you're still under the legal age for marriage, although your mother signed for your father to marry you and Joe, your marriage is eligible for an annulment! The young girl was puzzled. "In other words, your marriage is null and void." She still frowned with confusion. "Rose, your marriage is not legal or binding," the doctor explained. "Even Joe D. could contest its legality because deceit was employed by your mother to convince him to marry you in the first place because you're not really pregnant!" Rose was listening intently, taking the news in gradually. The doctor stopped himself from continuing, realizing that his patient had only received a partial seventh grade education which may have not fully prepared her for the legal jargon he was throwing to her. Mentally reviewing, he re-

worded his findings. "Honey, because you've never had sexual relations with Mr. Ross, or with any man, the law does not recognize
your marriage as legal. That means you have a very strong possibility
of becoming free again! Let me make a few phone calls, and I promise I'll get back in touch with you in just a few days. I understand
from my receptionist that you have two Red Hill lady residents with
you today. Rather than have any venom spread all around the community, just tell Bea and Helen that I'm investigating some issues
pertaining to your situation, and that I have promised that I'll get
back with you as soon as I have some answers. If either one of them
have any further questions, tell them to call me at home; they have
my number. I don't want this discussed in this office or outside it either," he sternly cautioned. The concerned doctor also wrote his
phone number down on a prescription pad, ripped off the sheet,
handing it to Rose as he dismissed Rose to dress and to return to the
waiting room. He continued his specific instructions. "You just go
back home and keep our conversation to yourself. I'll either come by
or call Bea-I know she has a phone," he reassured the relieved child.
"Things are going to get better for you, I promise." He reached his
hand out to help her to her feet. "I am committed to seeing you get
justice," he pledged and then left the room, leaving behind the faint,
woodsy scent of his aftershave.

Rose took care redressing herself and tidying up the room. She
walked on past Bea and Helen and bounced toward the car as if she
were floating on a fluffy cloud. Respecting her privacy, although dying
to know the doctor's findings, neither woman picked her for information. They just followed her out to the car. Bea and Helen had
accurately predicted that the equitable company doctor would take his
newly discovered truths and run with them. Bea cranked the Falcon,
and the trio headed for Red Hill after a short lunch break at the Diary
Queen. Bea, still sipping her chocolate malt, dropped the two Mrs.
Rosses off at their home, and returned to her own place, hoping to
avoid Belle, who generally began her wandering in the street about this
time of the day when Bea was headed to the post office. She was resolute in letting the doctor handle the problem from here on out. Hers

and Helen's job was done; she was elated to pass the torch to someone else who actually had the power to change things.

Dr. Davies, refusing to put Rose's problem on the back burner, recalled the semi-retired crackerjack lawyer Willis Moore who had once practiced law in Red Hill when the town still had hopes of booming. Perhaps, he could identify a sound plan for Rose's emancipation. Ironically, Davies had written Willis's new telephone number and his address on an old wadded church bulletin in his coat pocket last week after running into the old barrister at the commissary where Attorney Moore still had shopping privileges. Mr. Beaux continued to honor the elderly statesman's steadfast loyalty to Braun in the past by allowing him to take advantage of company prices even though Willis had removed his shingle at least twenty years ago and long before Beaux was even hired. Beaux's predecessor, Mr. Lang, had jokingly recounted several colorful yarns that showcased Moore's astute strategies in the courtroom—a Matlock of sorts.

Dr. Davies excused himself to his personal office, and got out the church bulletin. "Willis Moore, Attorney-at-Law. This is Effie, his secretary. How can I help you today?" a pleasant, but quivery female voice answered the phone after the very first ring. The doctor figured that Effie was Willis's wife, but he wasn't sure. He seemed to remember Willis downsizing his staff when he moved into town, so the secretary was probably also his wife, scaling down cost by keeping it in the family.

"Good morning, Mis' Effie. I hope you are well. This is Sam Davies calling. Does Willis have a minute he can spare? I really need some legal advice on a very sensitive subject," he explained in a cheery voice. Without answering his questions, Effie put the doctor's call on hold but quickly clicked back to his line; this time it was Willis who spoke. "Willis? This is Sam-Sam Davies. Do you know anything about the Bice/Ross gossip going around?" Dr. Davies went on to explain Rose and Joe's sticky situation, and the brilliant lawyer confirmed his conclusions—the marriage was illegal on several levels. Dr. Davies sat back in the worn leather recliner and continued," So, Willis, what can I do to help this child get to *be* a child again?" he suggested, laughing to himself into the receiver. The lawyer suggested that Sam slip out of his office immediately using the fire escape and meet him at his city office just down the street from the clinic. Not saying a word to his staff, Sam grabbed his coat and hat and headed for his friend's recently remodeled office. He sensed that Willis knew the case already. The old lawyer picked up the conversation where Sam had left it when the two were talking on the phone. Effie ushered him in and then made herself scarce.

"Doc, old friend, this is a simple case; you don't owe me a red cent. The unfairness of this just makes me physically sick. Just to think that a mother would inflict this sentence on her own innocent child just to squeeze a little cash from an old widow and her mentally handicapped son who probably has little more than a workman's pension. I tell you what; a fair bargain for my services, Sam, would be a nice quart jar of your wife's famous apple butter like she brought over when mother passed away. I'll never forget those hot, cathead biscuits slathered in creamery butter and that melt-in-your-mouth apple butter she brought over the first morning after mother died before anyone even knew about our loss! What a saint! That would be sufficient payment for me and for Effie," he gently bargained.

Willis, a large man with a healthy appetite, was almost salivating at his own description of Mrs. Davies' culinary treats. Quickly switching back to the subject, he criticized, "I just hate the fact that the Bice woman stirred up this pot of trouble because of her greed. Does Bossman know about what's going on in his incorporated little town? Being a company man, he wouldn't want all this turmoil in Red Hill," the older man sized up. "Anyway, back to my answer. The only requirement necessary is that the couple jointly signs this form swearing to any one or all of the following statements: fraudulent intent on the part of said Belle Bice to blackmail money from Joe D. Ross, an incompetent man; no consummation of said marriage between Rose Bice and Joe D. Ross; illegal marriage of an under aged minor to an adult according to Alabama code 143; and/or proof of deceit in the claim of pregnancy of the under aged female. All of these conditions nullify the marriage as recognized by Alabama Law."

Willis concluded. He continued, indignant, "And, to top that off, Dr. Bice is NOT an ordained minister; he has never even applied for a Justice of the Peace license, either! How 'bout them apples?" the aggravated lawyer asked.

Willis Moore pulled out his top file and triumphantly handed over the necessary forms to his grateful friend. Sam vigorously pumped Willis's oversized hand as he ordered his busy wife to place the form in a new file folder for protection. Dr. Davies hurriedly left the office, slipping in the same way he had left. Furious, Ms. Clements had already dismissed the patients and had gone to lunch, closing the main office until one. Dr. Davies crashed in his leather chair, taking a minute to review the lawyer's written instructions. Convening court was not necessary for their case. The couples' signatures signed in front of a witness and notarized by Effie back in the office would suffice for proper legal annulment. Rose's release from incarceration was near!

Suddenly, Sam Davies, who never even took a lunch break, made a snap decision to head toward Red Hill to speak to Rose and Joe during Joe's lunch hour. As he drove up the crooked highway in his black Studebaker convertible, he reflected on the many patients he had treated in the small community. Most of the cases were ones involving superficial wounds, but poor Rose's injuries were internal and would not be so easy to ease. However, as he headed toward the two-mile sign, he was confident that giving a twelve-year-old girl her life back was a strong start to recovery. But, would the courts force her to return to the insane asylum she called home where the maniacal matriarch still reigned? Perish the thought! First things first, he reminded himself as he pulled up to the Rosses' neatly trimmed yard.

Rose heard the soft purr of the Studebaker's engine, and she ran to the front porch to see who was driving the expensive car. Surprised and gratified that it was Dr. Davies, she smiled and stepped barefooted off the porch to meet her new hero as he released the unusual door of his sports car. "Hello there, Rose. I'm sorry I didn't call, but I got the information I needed for your case much earlier than I expected, so I decided that I would take a chance of meeting you and

Joe both together. Is he on his lunch hour?" he asked. About that time, Joe came to the screen door. "And the elder Mrs. Ross? Is she here, too? I know she is concerned about you, so it's fine with me if she stays during our little talk, but it's strictly your decision, Rose," he spoke quickly as he and Rose entered the screen door Joe had opened wide for them. Joe was confused at the reason for the odd visit, but Rose was shocked and excited that the doctor had results so soon after her visit. Was she going to be released?

"Mother Ross? Joe? Dr. Davies is here to talk to us; don't you worry 'bout them dishes right now. I'll clean them up after Joe leaves for work, Mother," Rose assured Helen. "The doctor has come all the way out here from town on his lunch hour, so we don't want to waste his time, do we?" she asked the mother and son. "We can pack you up a sandwich before you leave, or I can fix you one right now. We had some good souse meat and some pineapple to go on it for lunch, and we had some left, too," she suggested. Rose nervously chatted while the doctor removed his jacket and claimed a seat at the kitchen table, shaking hands with Joe, who was just downing the last of his sweet tea. Sam winked at Widow Ross and tipped his fedora respectfully before removing it and pitching it squarely on the plastic lace tablecloth in front of him. Helen Ross anticipated the doctor's speech as much as Rose. She turned her ladder backed chair in closer toward the doctor's seat. She didn't want to miss a word. The doctor began to speak as he took breaks between bites of his sandwich and gulps of his syrupy sweet tea, washing down the large pieces.

"Friends, I know you are good honest people," he introduced the coming news gradually. "Joe, I also know you felt that you did the right thing by Rose because you agreed to marry her and move her into your mother's house. Now, Rose has shared with me just how kindly you have treated her since she arrived, and she told me herself that she is happier and more content with her new family than she ever was with her birth family; but there are some facts that you don't know and that you have the right to know about this whole marriage business," he continued to speak plainly even though he was naturally gifted in his rhetoric. He purposely simplified his speech and his vocabulary choices to make himself better understood by Joe, who had great difficulty understanding the most elementary concepts. "You see, Joe, Rose is still a virgin; she's never *been* with a man, *lain* with a man, not even *you*," he chose the archaic word *lain* because Joe would probably recognize that word, as it was a common Biblical term for copulation. Joe looked down at his empty dinner plate, embarrassed to hear such and to know that the doctor knew about his and Rose's farce of a marriage. The persistent doctor pushed on, deliberately, yet gently, delivering the uncomfortable message. "Rose is not only a virgin, Joe; she's not even—uh—a woman yet, if you know what I mean. She hasn't had a period-ever!" He emphasized EVER as he paused to allow for any confusion on Joe's part. "Joe, son, I know that you are not the father of Rose's baby because there is no baby, never was a baby. You and Rose have not made a baby, so you do not legally have a marital relationship." Dr. Davies lifted Joe's drooping head with his soft palm and faced the disappointed man's teary eyes. "I recommend an annulment-a document-which will legally declare your marriage null and void. In other words, it will be as if the marriage never even happened, according to the laws that define what legal marriage is. Let's allow Rose to grow into the fine woman she will be one day. And then, when she is older, she can decide if or who she marries. She's still a child. She should be riding a bike or laughing with girlfriends at school," he spoke as he shook his head with disgust at Belle's mess. He had to remind himself to stay composed and agreeable; but merely verbalizing the words about this ridiculous and unnecessary situation angered him, and he raised his voice above his usual bedside tone, turning to Rose who bravely maintained eye contact with him without shame. "I'm sorry, Rose, but your mother was not of sound mind when she forced her own daughter into this nightmare, and I'm sorry for the hurt it has caused you, Joe, and you, Helen. I apologize for discussing this in mixed company, but I can't, as a medical professional who swore to the Hypocratic Oath and as Rose's personal physician, allow this sham to go on destroying you three. Helen, I know it's your boy who has also been caught in this evil mire; but, I've always known you to be a reasonable woman who

wants the best for her child, just as all normal mothers do. You know
continuing this charade isn't best for anyone involved, especially you
who knows your son's strengths and weaknesses better than we do,"
he concluded as the three Rosses absorbed the loaded message. No
one spoke. What was there to say? After an uncomfortable five
minutes, Helen arose, steadying herself by holding the railing of the
dinette chair.

She moved and spoke in slow motion as if underwater. "Dr. Davies, when I was a student at Mount Gum school a long, long time
ago, I studied about Patrick Henry, who said that he 'smelled a rat'
when he had sensed a lie. And I, too, smell a rat, and the rat is Belle
Bice! I'm sad to lose Rose as a precious daughter, but I reckon I'll jest
be content with keepin' her as a friend, won't you, Son? I don't want
to never disrespect a mother, but how could yore momma drop so
low as to use her baby girl to come up in the world if'n I was to wink
out and leave what piddlin' I had saved for my son? It's a good thang
that the Good Book promises, 'Vengeance is mine, saith the Lord!'
But, you know, me and Bea done suspected this when we hauled
Rose into town for a checkup. I'm just glad that it's almost over," she
added, exhausted. The doctor stood up and the others formed a circle
around him as Joe and Rose stood up, too. Rose looked like a starving
prisoner of war who had just been liberated and had taken in her first
breath of freedom; while, on the other hand, Helen was clothed in
sadness, yet she was also just as relieved as Rose that the two were
not longer living a painful lie. Joe just dropped his head again and
twiddled his thumbs; words escaped him, but then, they always had.

"Now, my friend, Willis Moore, has given me a form for you to
sign. Helen and I can witness your signatures, and I'll getMrs. Moore
there in the office to notarize the paper. Your signatures will clear this
up once and for all," the doctor paused and then rushed to speak.
"Rose, instead of bothering Mrs. Moore, just run get Mrs. Winder.
Tell her it's very important that she close the post office and come to
the Ross house," he ordered Rose, who raced out the door to fetch
the local notary public rather than even wait to notarize it in town. In
a flash, she and Mrs. Winder were back, having both hopped in the

lady's car after locking the building. "Joe, here's a line for your signature; take your time and make it neat," the doctor urged the slow thinking man child. After Joe laboriously signed his whole name, he automatically handed the pen to Rose, who also signed it, but with rapid speed and a huge smile on her thin face. The two witnesses signed and Mrs. Winder notarized the document. "Now, are there any questions, Joe or Rose?" the doctor asked, hoping to wrap up this ordeal. Joe D. Ross remained quiet; Rose did the same. However, Rose had the advantage because she had the capacity to understand and she had the desire to be free; Joe had neither. Mrs. Winder returned to work, a little addled, but confident of her actions.

Joe slowly raised his head and began to speak. "Doc, I never knowed I would ever have a wife or a baby, but it was fun to pretend for a little while. Rose, I hope I ain't hurt ye. We can still be friends, okay? And you can come down here and play cards with me and momma sometime, right? And maybe, you could cook me some vittles like you did arter Momma teached you how," he requested innocently. Rose walked over to Joe, grabbed his chapped hands, and stretched as far as she could to reach his red cheek where she squarely planted a kiss. Then the Lilliputian in the midst of giants ran to Helen, hugging her tightly and promising to visit after things settled down. Leaving the comforts of the Ross house, Rose walked alone, head held high, toward the Bastille she called home. She was too exhilarated to speak to the confused neighbors veiled inside their rusty screened porches.

By the next morning, Red Hill residents already had the full scoop of the story, but overall, the feeling of victory for Rose overpowered their pity for Helen and Joe. Factor in the exposure of Belle Bice's diabolical plan, the whole town was buzzing with various observations. Mis' Judy, gathered her ammunition from her garden club meeting and updated Miss Pearl, as well as many other willing and unwilling listeners. Miss Pearl automatically alerted DHR about Rose's story and her potential harm as she returned to a hostile environment, or at least a hostile one from Belle, whose rants and tears could be heard throughout the clay hills and damp hollows of Red Hill for several days following Dr. Davies' discovery. Unfortunately, the understaffed department assigned a novice case worker to assess the atmosphere of the Bice home; she vicariously assessed the status over the phone with Belle and never actually set foot on the Bice property to see for herself the damage an insane mother has on her pitiful children. The significantly unhealthy effect on the family who failed to thrive in that home was ignored, the case study files eventually falling through the bureaucratic cracks either due to apathy, ignorance, or overwork. The other two children functioned on a day-to-day basis and appeared to be "normal" (whatever that is) at school and at church according to the neighbors who were informally and unprofessionally questioned by the DHR representative who stopped at the commissary one afternoon, camping out on the porch as customers trickled in to stock up on supplies and groceries. Regardless, the case was quickly closed, and the pitiful matter was soon dropped. Dr. Bice's popularity waned in the community as his once bustling office was now dusty and barren; his standing invitation from the musical Rashes to join them in the weekly concerts was withdrawn. He had lied about being a licensed Justice of the Peace, but even more damaging to his character was the fact that Ellis Bice was not the Biblical head of his household; he could not or would not restrain his wife, and he refused to stand up for his children. Those facts, to Red Hill residents, did not afford him the respect he had once enjoyed from them.

Toward the end of fall after the cotton came in, the community watched dispassionately from their front porches as the Bice family once again loaded up their meager furnishings on a relative's old truck and headed for Vivette, Alabama, which was located about thirty miles northwest toward the Mississippi/Alabama border. Only Ina Bice remained behind; for, she had landed a receptionist job in Dr. Davies' office, finally replacing the Bulldog upon the long anticipated event of her greatly celebrated retirement. She rented a town garage apartment from Ms. Clements who grew to love the girl and eventually introduced her to her brother's son-a doctor. She was going to make it despite her poor upbringing!

Later on in the harsh winter of the next year, Mrs. Barr received word from Rose that she had fled Vivette to live with a distant cousin in Middle Tennessee who was willing and financially capable of bankrolling Rose's education at a well-respected private Christian high school nearby. Rose told Mrs. Barr she had never been happier and her grades were excellent in her new school, admitting, somewhat regretfully, that neither her mother nor father had ever contacted her once she left their home. Cheerfully, she switched subjects and repeatedly praised Bea and Helen as well as Dr. Davies for helping "set me free", she stated. Respectfully, Rose asked Ada about Mrs. Ross's health; Bea was secretly listening in on the party line and answered for her, assuring Rose that Mrs. Ross was well and Joe was lonely, but surviving her absence. Rose sent them all her love and good wishes. Ada ventured bravely to ask about Rose's baby brother. Lee was now eligible to begin elementary school in Vivette where Rose bragged both to Ada and Bea about his academic success; however, she admitted that his social skills were weak probably due to their mother's insanity and her insistence to continue nursing in public while the boy waited for the bus each morning. Rose giggled as she recounted a bizarre story concerning Lee sharing a dead crow with the unsuspecting class for his Show-and-Tell offering; then the chatty girl followed that tale with one even more disturbing: Lee had selected to display a pint jar of his own fresh vomit as his contribution to the school's annual science fair. When Ada asked Rose about the teacher's reaction to such a sight, Rose only laughed and said the old principal just commented to the disgusted judges: "Peculiar young man. Yes, indeed. Peculiar young man, but creative." Then, he dropped the jar into a nearby garbage can, ordering the janitor to permanently remove it from the building. Rose, sadly, didn't indicate to Ada that she thought her brother's antics were unusual or unsanitary. Yes, the Bices, including Rose, were odd, but Ada remained hopeful about Rose's future, and she shared that hope with Helen when she visited her later after Rose's unexpected phone call.

As for Dr. Bice, an unwilling but milque-toast pawn in the perverted chess game Belle orchestrated, he continued chiropractic healing quite lucratively once again; however, he stubbornly refused to wear the protective gloves and vest specially made to protect the body from dangerous rays from his prized x-ray machine. This foolish refusal through the years exposed the doctor to cancer causing rays which eventually claimed his left hand and quickly metastasized, spreading the cancer throughout his exposed body. He further rejected his medical doctor's insistence on chemo to stop the ever growing and mutating horror, so he was soon beyond any further help. His wracked body was not even suitable for embalming due to the radiation still present in his diseased body. He was given a pauper's funeral and was buried in an unmarked grave in the overgrown section of the paupers' cemetery, according to a former patient of Bice's who had married Ada's cousin in Vivette. Mrs. Barr, mercifully, did not inquire about the infamous Mrs. Belle Bice, and the cousin volunteered no additional information. Neither had Rose when Ada had spoken to her over a year ago; in fact, it was said that she never spoke about her mother or to her mother from the day she ran away from Vivette.

As for jilted old Joe, he continued to share his mother's tidy house and work faithfully in the black yard. He, on occasions, would recount the story, lamenting the loss of his "little woman", as he called Rose; but his co-workers only responded with an affirmative grunt or a sympathetic pat on his wide shoulders; they refused to rekindle his sorrow or to hopelessly stoke the impossible passion of his love for the almost forgotten Rose. If a newly hired recruit, only partially aware of Joe's history, joined the close crew, and commenced to publically mock or ridicule Joe's stupidity, Joe's self-appointed protectors put that green horn in his place. The men did not dispute the story, but they never shared it with outsiders who just couldn't understand his pain. Red Hill defended its own.

As always, life moved on in Red Hill, slow and thick as molasses, and the Bice name eventually faded from the memories of its residents. However, occasionally, when a betrothed couple was considered a mismatch by the ladies who shared a porch swing as they drank sweating pitchers of iced tea, one of them would comment; "That sounds like a bad case of Bice, don't it?" Usually the mention of the name would evoke a chuckle and, afterwards, a frown from the older women who would then repeat the epic tale to the younger ladies; then the morose, but nevertheless entertaining story experienced rebirth and renewal of fresh embellishment with each added detail. But, like their men, these women also thwarted any criticism an outsider might have of poor Joe or his kindly mother, Helen.

Mr. Beaux's genuine concern for the welfare of his employees and Braun's fairness about wages, safety, benefits, and housing privileges made Red Hill attractive to the average skilled or unskilled worker. It seemed that the sagging economy around them only served to trigger and jumpstart the success of the wood plant as it caused an increase in the town's population. Extra crews were hired to fulfill the new accounts Beaux had acquired thorough diligence, bargaining, and aggressive sales techniques. The quickest and heaviest boost came when Beaux landed several overseas orders. New settlers ready to work piled into the isolated swampland. Two extended families relocated their whole tribes to Red Hill-the Stones and the Grants who had intermarried and lived compound style for many generations. The older Grant branch had produced sons, and each brother had married one of the four Stone daughters, quickly fathering an assortment of offspring. Each of the newly formed families was granted the more spacious company houses; but, the larger houses in Red Hill that were readily available featured no indoor plumbing. The pressure treated houses were vacant during the early years when Beaux's men were busily installing running water in most of Red Hill's other dwellings, so the frugal boss saved money by not remodeling the empty buildings and updating the occupied ones. However, these two clans were so relieved to find steady employment together that they assured their new, easy going boss of their plumbing abilities. In time, they themselves would install sinks, tubs, etc. once they got settled into their homes and new jobs. Anyway, the eldest Stone admitted that none of his family had ever had indoor plumbing, so they were used to hauling well water to their houses; he added that Red Hill's water was clean, close, and plentiful for the Grants and Stones to share for now. "After all, Braun work beats sharecropping anytime, Mr. Braun," the eldest Mrs. Grant had declared after settling her multitude into the little community.

The fertile families increased Red Hill's population by approximately twenty-five people with more babies expected as the younger couples continued their commitment to replenish the earth with amazing speed and number. Mrs. Cross and Mrs. Ross, who had transported homemade chicken pies and gallons of sweet tea in a red wagon in an effort to be "neighborly" to the new residents, relayed the news to the gossip hungry HDC members that Mrs. T. Grant proudly declared her clan's religious stand on birth control when Ada had innocently commented on the massive size of the two blended families. "Grants and Stones don't use no birth control; we have 'em like God gives 'em to us-often and strong," the tall Grant matriarch announced to the two embarrassed do-gooders. The prune-faced Mrs. Grant continued to deepened the redness of the ladies' pale cheeks as she went into excessive detail. "Yep, we believe that the bed is undefiled. Our men is fed and satisfied. That ain't creepin' around lookin' fer alley cats when they got a fine, seal-point, Siamese at home waitin' for 'em'," the withered woman figuratively worded. She ended with a witchy laugh which, oddly enough, was flippant but not really base even though it was spoken with her characteristically sadistic rattle which was attributed to years of tobacco usage. Mrs. Cross and Mrs. Barr immediately tried to erase from their minds the mental image of these two hillybilly families practicing their beliefs about procreation. Besides, the Grants nor the Stones were camera friendly. The mortified ladies grabbed their empty vessels and left hurriedly. The outspoken country clans brought an odd dimension to the complexity of Red Hill's population.

One of the Grant brothers, Seville, proved to be an exceptionally skilled truck driver, one who merited one of the highest paying jobs at Braun-a truck driver. Mr. Beaux was flabbergasted at Seville Grant's ability to endure incredibly long distances fueled by very little sleep or adequate food. And, upon his return from one of the long hauls, after a short snooze, he would anxiously, but politely hound the office personnel for yet another assignment. Perhaps the noisy seven children and his overworked, loving wife, Margie, kept him constantly working just to provide a steady income for his ever-growing multitude; or, perhaps, he longed for a temporary escape on the open road from the little ones-stair steps in age and constant in motion. Regardless of his motive, Beaux was pleased with his new trucker. And Seville was equally thrilled with his more-than-fair wages.

Barely a year after settling into the incorporated town, Margie Grant discovered—and she'd had some experience in her observations—herself pregnant again. However, this time, she was shocked and confused; Dr. Davies had performed a tubal ligation on her after she delivered her last child, Robert, child number seven, right after the Grants and Stones had relocated their compound to Red Hill. She decided that this time she would not bother the doctor; she had not always had doctors present at earlier births and had not always taken advantage of prenatal care, so, since she was somewhat wary of Dr. Davies' skills after this slip-up, she dismissed the idea of professional health care. She felt confident enough to care for herself, heavily leaning on the common sense actions she had observed from previous medical care-taking vitamins, drinking milk, avoiding soft drinks and coffee, eating healthily, and munching crackers for her ever-present nausea. As the months passed, her eighth pregnancy continued without incident, following her usual pattern until just a few weeks before the due date she had determined, her water broke while she was hanging out the white clothes on a humid morning. Seville was unavailable, out on the road to Natchez, and he wasn't expected back in town for at least two days, or perhaps, even a week; the town had suffered heavy damage from a violent tornado, so snapped and fallen utility poles had to be replaced before electricity could be restored to the residents there. She ordered her eldest and brightest son, Jeremy, to run to the commissary and ask Mrs. Bell if she or Mrs. Beaux could take her to the hospital since she had either miscalculated her due date or the unborn had a problem. "Now, Jeremy, slow yore speech down, so's the woman can 'cipher out yore message. You know how tongue-tied you git when you git in a hurry. Tell her it's an emergency. Then you come right back here and tell me what she said. You can git a tea cake from the cookie jar if you do what mamma asked, okay?" Margie spoke haltingly between the horrific contractions. Jeremy scampered off in a cloud of red dust.

"Mis' Bell, Mis' Bell, my-my-," the frightened, breathless lad stopped to catch his breath and remembered his mother's warning. He forced himself to slow down so he wouldn't stutter too much and he then cranked back up. "Momma is about to have the baby, and it ain't been enuff time to ha-ha-hatch it yet! Can you come help her? I'm skeered she gonna die; she's hollered awful loud." He waited for an answer as Mrs. Bell opened an Orange Crush and handed it to the boy, urging him to drink up. She grabbed the black phone receiver and called Mr. Beaux who immediately granted permission for not only Mae Bell, but his own wife to leave work and take Margie to Dr. Davies. He called the doctor and alerted him to the situation; Sam, sharing his frustration with Beaux about Margie's obviously poor choice, nevertheless, faithfully promised to meet the three women at the Drew City Hospital. In the meantime, Mrs. Beaux's pale yellow Pontiac whistled down the rough road between the main office and the commissary as she blew her horn and her baby sister literally ran down the steps of the store; both the worried women headed toward Margie's rambling house at the end of the Ross Road. In no time, the women, along with Jeremy's help, had awkwardly loaded up the miserable Margie and had lain her flat on a white sheet in the back seat of the Bonneville. Mae held the screaming woman's head in her lap, occasionally mopping her sweaty face with a dampened washcloth.

About twenty bumpy minutes later, the makeshift ambulance wheeled in on two tires at Drew City ER. Dr.Davies was suited up in his scrubs and waiting for action inside the automatic, sliding glass doors. Mrs. Bell, in the back seat of the car, still cradled the squirming mother's head and neck. "Get a stretcher out her, Luther! She can't get in that wheelchair in her advanced condition!" Doc yelled at the ancient orderly who hurried dropped the folded wheelchair to the pavement. Another orderly handed the shaken aid one end of a gurney as they both headed out toward the car. Sam then turned his immediate attention to Margie, addressing her in a loving, but scolding tone, "Margie, you haven't even been in for *one* checkup, have you? Why, I didn't even know you were pregnant. Wait a minute! You weren't *supposed* to get that way ever again! Mmmm..." the doctor dropped the conversation and refocused on his patient's care. Priorities. Dr. Davies never got used to the ignorance of some of his rural patients who now had access to better affordable health care than ever! Yet, they continued to trust natural remedies, wild, uncertain herbs, and untested, risky practices of witch doctors like the swamp midwife or Mabel, a common prostitute. Some of their methods might actually be safe and effective, but ultimately, if there was a problem, he was called in to fix it. Nevertheless, he never turned away the patients who suffered from botched procedures or harmful medicines, and he didn't today either. He also dismissed his disappointment in Margie's choices as his thoughts were split open with her agonizing screams.

Margie, in distress, was immediately sedated and prepped for possible surgery while she was still in the bustling ER. Tomplin P. Grant was born by Cesarean without any difficulties entering the world. Tomplin, named after a close family member and whose odd name was later shortened to Tomp, was a strong healthy eight pounder. It appeared that Margie miscalculated her due date because Tomp was definitely not undersized or underdeveloped. Dr. Davies quickly passed off the thriving, crying newborn to a nearby nurse while he attended to Margie, who was his main concern now. During a post delivery exam, the doctor detected excessive scarring which probably contributed to the failed tube tying (layman's term for medical procedure) being completely effective. After explaining his current medical plan for Margie to Mae and Eula while they paced back and forth in the crowded waiting room, he hastily scrubbed up for the additional surgery which would hopefully prevent further infection and further children! He felt remorse for chastising her apathy toward professional prenatal care; and this time, he made sure there would be no more muffins baking in her already worn out oven. Margie's recovery from the Cesarean plus the additional removal of massive scar tissue and a tubal cleanup would slow down her healing process significantly. He shared this information with the ladies; but, in the long run, Dr. Davies assured them, it would improve her quality of life by diminishing pain, breakthrough bleeding, and the potential for infection. Unfortunately, she would also require additional assistance at home from someone who could pick up her heavy work load at home. Davies shook hands with Eula and Mae, thanking them for their concern. Margie would be confined to the hospital for at least a week before he would be willing to release her. The sisters had not even cleared the parking lot before they began to strategize the care of the children and the house while Margie was hospitalized. Knowing the condition of the house and the meagerness of its supplies, Eula pulled into the discount store on the edge of town to purchase the necessities and to select some soothing lotion, cream, etc. for Margie when she returned home.

During Margie's absence, the surrounding neighbors and family members farmed out the Grant children, brought home cooked meals to Seville when he wasn't on the road, and kept the sprawling house tidy in preparation for Margie's inevitable return. Mounds of dirty laundry were washed, dried, ironed, and stored every day by the individuals who kept the children and looked after Seville's needs. After about a week, the "new" mother and Tomp were released and issued clean bills of health, but Margie still needed help with heavy housekeeping and other chores that required lifting. Again, the loving crews stepped in to ensure that the Grant army ran as smoothly as possible under the current conditions. Margie's was not a home; it was an institution, large and demanding. The exhausted helpers were truly in awe of this woman's daily work load.

A month had passed since Tomp's delivery and Eula Beaux, and as part of her new daily routine now that Margie was "lyin' in", as it was called by the old timers, stopped by on her way to her short lunch break to deliver some ham sandwiches, chips, store bought cookies, bananas, and fruit drinks. She had prepared her own family's lunch, left it in the refrigerator, and was only going to drop off the food and leave in the thirty minutes allotted for Braun employees. By this time in her recovery process, Margie had gradually added minimal household chores to her day even though she was still swollen and tender in her abdomen area. Mrs. Beaux noticed on this day, though, as she unloaded the lunch items to the extended mission style pine table, that Margie was still wrapped in the rumpled sheets of her high posted bed. She called out as she walked up the dark hall. "Margie, are you feeling okay today? Do I need to take the laundry with me and get started on it?" The usual mountain of filthy laundry was uncharacteristically stationed at the footboard of the Grant bed. It was normally already sorted and bagged when Mrs. Jackson picked it up in the afternoons. She had volunteered to manage the household's laundry at her own house; she had a new agitator washer and even had a dryer—both considered luxury items for most Red Hill housewives. She could process those clothes much quicker and more efficiently with her new machines. Margie only had a wringer and a clothes line for her laundry tools.

The concerned neighbor entered the pale lady's darkened and cramped bedroom, which was not much larger than a closet in comparison to the rest of the rooms in the huge house. "Honey, what's the matter? Can I get you something to eat? I brought some sandwiches? Or maybe a banana would give you some strength?" Margie only responded with a slight grunt. As Eula Beaux stepped closer to the woman's bedside, she touched her hand to the suffering woman's burning forehead. "Oh, Margie, you've got a fever. You must have an infection of a sort. I probably need to call Sam. Do you have an aspirin? We could start cooling you down first before I call him." She knew Margie had no phone; Eula would have to wait until she got home or back to work before she could contact the doctor. The Grant/Stone compound was not equipped with much of anything other than the basics Braun provided. Margie gave no response to the question; she had no more strength to even grunt. Eula spied a clean diaper from the nightstand and dipped it in a glass of water that set on the nightstand. When she leaned in to mop Margie's fevered face, a faint smell of rotting flesh drew Eula's head back. She likened this horrid odor to one she had experienced when she and Mae had cleaned out an old meat locker when they both lived in Morris. Was there some spoiled food accidentally left in the bedroom, she wondered. That was certainly a possibility with some many little mouths to feed and a sick mother to boot.

She excused herself to search for some aspirin, but she actually needed some fresh air to replace the fetid air still swirling in her nostrils.
Standing on the riddled screened porch, Eula recovered from her nausea
and while digging in her coat pockets for a handkerchief, she discovered
a small tin box of aspirins. She savored one last pleasant breath, scooped
out a clean dipper of well water, and headed back to the sickroom. "Here,
Margie. Take these two aspirins with a fresh dipper of water. That will
help lower your fever until I get a'hold of the doctor," she offered.

Margie motioned for Eula to come in a little closer to her. Margie
lifted her head up as Eula bent her tall body over as Margie requested. The sick woman labored to speak, and when she did, the sound
came out raspy and faint. "Mrs. Beaux, I think it's the place where
Doc cut me to git Tomp out. It ain't my insides; they's healing jest
fine. I hate to ask ye sumthin' lack this, but would you please raise up
my gown and look at it? I can't see it myself. And, I don't need no
doctor. I wouldn't mind if you was to call him and ask him fer a name
of a cream to put on it, but I don't want no more doctors lookin' at me
fer a long time, if'n I can help it," she wheezed as she immediately fell
back on her dingy pillow.

Eula had been a witness to many unpleasant sights in her lifetime:
gunshot wounds, lumber yard accidents, her grandmother's death in
Eula's own bed, the Small boys' car accident, and the homebirth of
Rabon years ago. She still shuttered over her terrorizing duty of
dressing various deceased relatives' cold, stiff bodies in preparation for
their funerals; intense poverty blocked the use of an undertaker, so
the wakes were almost always in the home. As an eight-year-old
child, she had been assigned the job of putting her grandmother's
stockings on her atrophied legs before the adults placed her in her
hand carved pine coffin, a fact she remembered until her death eighty
years afterwards. However, none of those repulsive scenes prepared
her for the actual sight and powerful smell that burned her blue eyes
and permeated the lining of her nostrils even deeper while slowly she
moved toward Margie's side to evaluate the gash.

As she gently lifted the poor woman's thin Shadowline gown,
which was unnaturally attached to the dried yellowish fluid oozing

from the swollen, red scar, the abominable stench from the obviously infected wound attacked Eula's equilibrium, sending her reeling across the room toward the open window; the shock forced her to drop the wet gown, thus returning it to the putrid pond of pus that surrounded the length of the scar. Gaining her balance and common sense, she recalled her mother's home remedy for almost any open wound she had suspected as being infectious, and Eula raced to the kitchen where she grabbed a foot tub, scrubbing it thoroughly, and filling it with hot water from the white, porcelain kettle which sat on the wood stove. She hurriedly snatched a sliver of Octagon soap from the shelf above and prayed that the water would cool some in transit to the sick room. She used the other end of the same diaper, dipping it in the soapy pan and gently patting Margie's exposed stomach. Rolling up the soaked gown, and holding her breath to avoid vomiting right there in front of her patient, the makeshift nurse swabbed out the wound as quickly as she could. She returned to the back of the house, taking the pan and cloth with her to wash them out after she stepped to the back porch to regurgitate before reentering the abhorrent smelling bedroom. She faithfully repeated the cleaning procedure (including the porch vomiting) four times before she was satisfied with the wound's cleanliness. She was unable to carry on any light conversation while she worked, which might have served to lighten the mood, for fear that her own projectile vomit might prevail and slap the headboard of Margie's own bed like the flapping tale of a freshly caught bream against the bottom of a fishing boat. She sensed that Margie interpreted the silence and appreciated the relief that the washing temporarily rendered. She sighed bravely and pantomimed, "Thank you." Eula patted Margie's clammy arm and nodded her head in acknowledgement.

So, without outward dread, Eula Beaux carried out the loathsome duty this day and for six days afterwards coming twice daily during her lunch and again immediately after the quitting whistle blew. She arrived in a rush, but she always spared the time to issue Jackson lemon snaps to the grimy little ones playing under the enormous limbs of a partially dead oak tree. She had on that first day phoned

Dr. Davies to describe the horrifying condition of Margie's unhealed wound, but the doctor assured her that indeed her mother's folk medicine was an accurate prescription for the infection; regardless, he also made a house call and gave Margie a sample tube of ointment and an antibiotic shot to expedite the healing process. "Eula," he scratched his head as he pulled her aside in the hall during his visit to the Grants' house, "of all people to help Margie! The boss's wife? I admire you for your humble service," he spoke honestly as he surprisingly reached around her with a bear-hug. Yes, Red Hill looked after Red Hill, regardless of one's origins or position in society. Eula remembered her own humble upbringing, oblivious of her comparatively rapid rise in society for as long as she lived.

Margie soon regained her vim and vigor, but she never forgot the tall, blonde lady whose lemon colored whistling Pontiac pulled into her grass deprived yard twice a day to provide food, to share an unlikely but genuine friendship, and most astonishing, to bravely and willingly clean the vilest of wounds without complaint. Long after Margie's recuperation, Mrs. Beaux continued visiting regularly, bringing the children homemade sugar cookies, greeting each dirty face with a sloppy kiss and a strong hug, and presenting a fine pattern of a "true Christian lady", as Margie described her elegant nurse. She sensed that this same thoughtful woman, too, perhaps, during some night's pillow talk, had convinced her husband that Seville Grant was needed at home because soon his driving schedule allowed him short, frequent hauls with an occasional weekend haul to replace his former grueling traveling schedule. Yes, life was better in Red Hill for the Grants. They were accepted and even loved, despite being considered by the outside world as "the unlovely". The daughter of half-starved sharecroppers was completely aware and unashamed of her "unlovely" heritage, too.

Because the commissary provided the news hungry community with a meeting place like Europe's town squares do for their citizens, many exaggerated stories were spawned and swapped back and forth among the Braun employees who lounged on the rough hewn creosoted front porch. Single workers, and even the married ones who craved a little male bonding time during their lunch breaks gobbled their hog's head cheese, liver loaf, sardines, and various other popular lunch items hurriedly to set aside a little time for an interesting yarn or two. One of the most captivating story tellers in Red Hill was middle aged foreman Skipper Grover. Skip was an enormous man with an enormous voice to match. When he laughed, it shook his entire massive body; when he teared up, it was infectious although no man would admit it as he silently wept into his perspiration stained hanky. The men could sense when a story was forthcoming. Skip deliberately picked his Chicklet-shaped teeth after polishing off his traditional sandwich—a ten cent slice of bologna, a dime slice of sharp hoop cheese, and a healthy slathering of Duke's mayonnaise, which had been applied with a spatula, a thick ring of onion, and all between two slices of white sandwich bread made locally. Chuck Bell customized each sandwich prior to the blowing of the lunch whistle according to the specifications hand written on a tally card and received with the midmorning snack order delivered by the newest hire. With the hearty sandwich in his ample belly, Skip wiped his hands on his rumpled overalls, leaned against the porch column, crossed his brogan covered ankles, and settled in to a more comfortable position; the men followed suit as they were surely about to be entertained. "Did you ever hear about…" he always began. The awaiting listeners quickly disposed of their trash and scampered for the nearest post for a prop. Skip absentmindedly scratched under his safety hat and rubbed his already wide mouth (two tics), chuckling to himself as he mentally arranged the plot; he inhaled slowly and deliberately for effect before he spoke.

"Do y'all recollect that old foreman we called 'Ponyboy'? He useta operate the old red crane that's settin' at tracks now." Skip asked, knowing his audience would only mumble in agreement to avoid interrupting the upcoming yarn. "Well, then you'll recall his silly daughter who took a shine to Midget Mike, the pole peeler who worked for the company around the same time?" he scanned the audience for any response and also to ensure no greenhorns were present in the circle-they would require more explanation than he was usually willing to share; they, in turn, were more afraid to show this mountain of a man their ignorance by asking anything, just hoping one of the other less intimidating men would fill them in later. "Well, despite Mr. Beaux's warning to Pony to keep that fool away from the equipment and machinery around the tracks, she would slip out of their house-it was the shack that Shad lives in now-and high step it onto the pole yard right up to the peeling shed! It was just her and her daddy living there; Pony's old lady had run off with the Mayfields when they skipped Red Hill. Anyhow, back to my story, that crazy girl was like the Tasmanian Devil in the Saturday cartoons; she blazed a trail of destruction wherever she went!" He passed and gazed toward the yard, probably visualizing the foolish girl slipping across the road to the peeler shed. He refocused and snapped back into character. "She even started to practice her cooking skills to impress Midge 'cause Mike's mother's cookin' was p-o-i-s-o-n," he smacked his sun-parched lips at the memory of the lady. (Poison in the rural south meant extra delicious, thus a compliment of the highest level.) 'You know, she was sweet on me before she married Mike Sr.," Skip added nonchalantly. The audience also knew that the affection was reciprocated and that it had, for many years, flourished regardless of marriage vows, births, and guarded whispers. The clandestine meetings between Mike's mother and Skipper were routinely scheduled in Uncle James's tool shed. (What was it about that place?) "Yep," he commented wistfully," she surely could whip up a fine meal from almost nothing. Why, she had to after she married that n'ere-do-well husband of hers. Ain't no Free ever been worth their salt, and Mike Sr. was no exception," he frowned with detectable resentment in his voice. Folks said that Skipper and this rural chef were in love, but Skip's sainted mother disapproved; so, out of respect for her, he just settled for part time romance.

Skip swapped his ankles and recrossed them, resuming the rural drama. "That loon went down to the commissary and picked up a yeller cake mix box, slammed it on the counter, and glared at ole Chuck. Well, you know Chuck; he asked her if she needed any other ingredients for her baking. She and Pony had traded down there for years, and Bell knew she was light a load," Skip explained to his temporary congregation of believers. "That ole gal just shook her head and marched out the front door, without saying a word or even getting a poke! Now, the fact that she didn't speak weren't no surprise to Bell 'cause he knew she couldn't talk plain. He also knew that her daddy would pay his ticket without a question; she'd done this before because she didn't carry no change, didn't have no job, and didn't have no credit on her own. So, Chuck obliged and filed the ticket under her Ponyboy's account."

Skip stretched his long arms behind his head, using them for an uncomfortable cushion and continued his story. Customers came and left without noticing the men, but his listeners were captivated with their orator. The only thing that would dislodge them was the plant whistle. "The next morning, bright and early, Mrs. Bell spied Pony's baby girl scuttling across the loose gravel like a confused, malformed snow skier, lacking in both grace and skill. She slammed open the screen door, shaking the Sunbeam sign until it shook off its hinges!" The storyteller scanned his audience and found them with confused looks all around, so he broke the story's rhythm to analyze the problem.

Ah, he thought. An old problem. Skip had slipped into a more advanced speech pattern which included comparisons and other literary devices; he had slipped away from the vernacular of his peers and reverted to his actual natural manner of speech. Unknown to Red Hill residents, except for his lover, Mike's mother, Skip was, in reality, a highly intelligent and educated man. However, when he became entranced in his own storytelling, he reverted to the correct, accurate grammar which included the use of metaphors and similes to form a mental picture in the minds of his listeners. His troubled, alcoholic, Vanderbilt educated father thoroughly took on the responsibility of homeschooling his only son for the first twelve years of his life before that same devastated and devoted son discovered his father's limp body swinging by the neck from the rafters of the dilapidated barn on their unkempt and unattended farm. Suddenly, Skipper Grover was an orphan at fourteen and on his own with no relatives around him; however, in his faint memories of his absentee mother, he remembered her reminiscing about her family in Red Hill. Equipped with only his father's academic teaching and very little, if any, practical training, the frightened young man, with his father barely in the grave, bargained with a nearby farmer to sell the property and its meager holding for a fair price. Next, he cranked up the old Ford he negotiated to keep and headed south toward his mother's mysterious hometown.

In Red Hill, Skipper Grover, at fourteen years old, interviewed well, and was awarded an engineer aid with Braun. He rented a three room house and kept to himself. He avoided the truancy officer and continued to work fulltime until, when he reached a legal working age of sixteen, he was promoted to full cylinder engineer. As he became more confident and made friends on the yard, he began to share some of his interesting stories, and when he spun a tale, he owned it and captivated the attention of anyone who stopped to listen. His gift for oral interpretation was undeniable. That's how he arrived on the commissary porch holding court over his fellow employees. Now,checking himself, he picked his story back up, partially in the vernacular and partially in the scholarly, descriptive language of his childhood. It was hard to break a good habit. "Now, boys, Mrs. Bell knowed something was up with that goofy girl by the way she was sliding her feet. She commenced to questioning Pony's girl. 'What's wrong, Nelly? How did your cake turn out? Did your daddy like it?'"

"Nelly's pumpkin head was as red as that old crane her daddy useta drive and she sputtered and stammered," Skipper pursed his mouth to imitate the girl's speech. " 'Mis' BBBBell, that there box lied! HHHHHit didn't have no cake in it like tttttthe pitcher showed. There waddn't....nuttin' but some flour in that damn box!' "She huffed and puffed like the big bad wolf." Skip snorted at his own impression. "Mrs. Bell had to turn away from the counter to keep from laughing in the girl's moon shaped face. Nelly stomped her flat feet and hollered at Mrs. Bell." He stood up, reached into his overalls, and checked the time on his father's old, scratched pocket watch. "Nelly grabbed the drawer to the cash register and reached over Mae Bell to dig out a dollar or two, hollering,'I want my money bbbbback. I had that same thang happen when I got that box with the mashed taters on the front, but I minded my manners and didn't kick up no fuss. You and Mr. CCCChuck gonna need to quit lyin' 'bout them mixes or I'm gonna quit tradin' in this here sssstore!'" The whole crowd, who began to stretch their legs and stand, too, anticipated the quarter till whistle as they shook with laughter. Skip just smiled slyly and laughed.

Finishing up the story, Skip wiped his eyes. "Rather than argue with her or explain to her that she hadn't actually paid for the cake mix, Mae just moved Nelly's grubby hand, and slid out the cash. She would explain it to Ponyboy later; he'd understand and pay the ticket. But, Mrs. Mae felt an obligation to instruct the girl how to use the mixes or she'd be back in the store with the same complaint." Skip stepped off the porch, readying himself for the dramatic finish, even though the story was as familiar to him as his own hand. "Mrs. Bell explained to Nelly like this: 'Honey, the picture on the front of the box just shows you how the cake will look like after you add water, butter, and eggs to the flour inside the little bag. After you mix that all together in your mixing bowl,—you know the one on the electric stand-you pour the liquid you just stirred up into two greased cake pans and bake on about 350 degrees for about 25 minutes. Then, you take them out of the oven and let them cool. Next, you take them out of the pans and make the icing for the cake, using the recipe on the side of the box. That's why you didn't have a real cake inside the box. You still have to make it, darling.'" Skip screwed up his baritone voice to imitate a female one. "Well, Nelly grabbed that money and headed back out the front door, almost colliding with Chuck who had been pumping Mrs. Barr's gas. Silly Nelly flapped those dry, crusted heels and toes against that loose gravel until she was clean out of sight. From then on, she stuck to ironin' and cleanin'. Yep, you could say that her cookin' was REALLY poison!" he concluded amid thunderous applause. The whistle blew as the thoroughly entertained crew walked onto the yard just in time. The light mood carried the men back to finish the workday.

"Hey, Mr. Grover," one of the younger men asked, "did Nelly ever git her a man, or did she jest give up on that, too?" He obviously wanted more.

"Glad you asked, Whippersnapper," Grover answered as he ran/walked to catch up with the faster, inquisitive worker. "Can you believe she finally caught old Midget Mike, and he was fool enough to marry up with her? They made an awkward pair-Mike as short as a dwarf and Nelly as tall as a tree. I even went to their hillybilly weddin'. I guess it takes all kinds, huh?" The eager listener backed away, disappointed in the ending. Then Skipper lowered his loud voice and whispered into the young man's ear. "He did find her one true skill.....and they went on to have seven wild brats! He came back from lunch every day with a smile plastered on his round face, and I can assure you that it wasn't 'cause of Nelly's culinary skills!" The young man folded over with laughter while the other men stared at him and wondered what old Skip had pulled on the unsuspecting greenhorn.

Most Americans are at least partially aware of the southern man's obsession with the sport of hunting. Some of the finest hunting land anywhere in the United States was and still is located in Alabama. Hunting clubs were formed and rites of passage for first time hunters are strictly but playfully observed. However, the depth of this devotion might be underestimated by those who were not personally committed to the hunt. The southern hunter did so for the game, but he/she also hunted to provide food for his family. The local butcher was usually overextended during hunting season when he was commissioned to process the deer meat in addition to his regular butchering job.

For example, during the legal season, the Red Hill commissary stayed backlogged with orders for deer sausage, deer jerky, ground deer, deer tenderloin, deer backstrap,and other varieties of cuts. Even old Tad, the taxidermist, enjoyed a boost in business for those hunters who displayed their kill; closely related to that trade, skilled leatherworkers painstakingly crafted smooth deerskin gloves, coats, hats, and buttons. Hunting was a booming business, and Mr. Bell was an expert in preparing deer meat for his customers-all done after closing time.

One bright Tuesday morning during deer hunting season, Chuck Bell was cleaning and sharpening his larger knives in anticipation of an "unannounced" visit from the county health inspector who was notoriously nitpicky with his citations at Red Hill unless Mr. Bell gifted the nervous little bean counter all dapper in a three-piece suit from Penney's with some of Mr. Bell's finest center cut pork chops or his leanest ground beef prior to the sanitation observation and ranking. Just as the expert butcher replaced the final knife in its side sheath fastened to the butcher block, Mrs. Bama Moore pulled up even with the nearest gas pump to the commissary porch (not an uncommon sight, as she came twice daily to buy $2 of gas each time). Strangely, today, she just called for the busy Mr. Bell. "Hey, Chuck, I got sumthin' for you to see out here; I don't need no gas. Can you come out here and look at it?" the pleasingly plump, friendly woman asked. "It's Bama, Chuck," she added as if there were any doubt of the identity of her signature screech owl voice. Chuck Bell wiped his hands on his white butcher's apron, lifted the straps over his curly head, and left the meat market. He liked Mrs. Moore, but she seemed to appear at inopportune times, and she owed quite a sum on her charge ticket; yet, she had just recently started paying cash for her current purchases, but at the same time, continuing to ignore her standstill, but substantial debt. The good-natured store manager ambled to the front of the store.

"Whatchaneed, Bama? I'm a'waitin' on that peckerwood inspector this morning. I ain't got no fresh pork chops to cut, so he's liable to be in a tizzy and write me up sumthin' fierce. Ham (the commissary manager at the sister plant in Oak Tree) jest called me from his office and told me the Man was headin' toward Red Hill...." Chuck stopped in midsentence, looking up as he let double doors slam behind him. "What the heck? Don't tell me that my eyes see what they *think* they are seeing." Mr. Bell quickly jumped off the side of the porch, not waiting to get to the stairs. Bama was standing proudly by the open back door of her brand new yellow Cadillac with custom leather seats. Resting lifeless on the beautiful back seat of that expensive vehicle was a six point deer weighing about two hundred pounds! Splattered blood was visible on the pale seat, the passenger's window, the back glass, and the customized floor mats. It took a few

minutes of walking back and forth and rubbing his wavy salt and
pepper hair before Chuck could find his voice again. "Bama, did you
hit this thing?" He actually meant *hit with the car*, but around the
same time as he asked the question, he noticed a small hole located at
the back of the deer's brain. The entry still held a clot of blood mixed
with fur dried around the wound. Chuck knew that Bama was an
expert shot, generally dropping a deer with one vertebrae shot. She
regularly used a .223 caliber rifle which had belonged to her marks-
man father, a renegade game warden of some reknown in Red Hill
and Bethsaida. Still she *could* have run over him as he fled after being
shot, but it wasn't likely. A deer, once hit, instinctively tried to move
off the road if it was at all possible. He didn't want to die in the road.

"Yep, Chuck, I shot him as I was a'drivin'. He was jest standin'
there eatin' in the ditch past the Edwards' place on the left. I had
daddy's gun beside me in the front seat, so I slowed down and rolled
the winder down. Then, I reached over and grabbed the gun with my
left hand and took a lucky aim. You know, I'm left handed. My daddy
always believed in a head shot over a body shot, so I aimed toward
his antlers. Daddy said the body shot was too risky, but if you aimed
jest below the back of the skull in the first four vertebrae of the spine,
you'd nail it ever time," she explained brilliantly to the growing crowd
which had gathered around the banana colored luxury car. Chuck
had guessed right.

Now, Bama was one of those southerners who had amassed wealth
but still lacked class. Her ambitious husband owned and operated several lucrative sawmills in the vicinity and had turned a fine profit early
in his life. Bama's father, it had always been rumored around Red Hill,
was frequently and privately employed by those shady, secretive citizens
who found themselves in need of a bounty hunter from time to time,
and he was considered one of the best gunmen around. So, Bama and
Slim got together, built an enormous Jim Walter home, and rapidly
produced four poorly groomed boys. Cleanliness was not next to god-
liness at the Moore home. It really shouldn't have surprised Mr. Bell
and the other onlookers when Bama pulled up with a deer in the un-
protected back seat of a Cadillac. She had brought him small game

catches in her big, plastic purse, right alongside her leather wallet and expensive sunglasses. Why would she all of a sudden be so preoccupied with guarding her vehicle's upholstery as to put a towel or blanket down on the seat before single-handedly loading up this buck? She had nice things, but she didn't know how to care for them properly, or perhaps, she wasn't concerned with the possibility of damaging her possessions. After all, she and Slim had more than enough money for repair or replacement.

"Chuck, I want you to grind all of this meat-ever bit of it-into sausage like you done for Jed Phillips. I done called Mr. Beaux to see if he'd let you butcher for a private citizen on company property, and he said you could do it after working hours if he got a pack of sausage out of the deal. You know Slim'll pay you whatever Braun pays you per hour, or even more 'caus this here gonna be some good grub to put in the middle of a cathead biscuit! MMmm! Now, take ye time; I got several in the freezer down at my honey's sawmill up on 13," she offered amiably.

So, Mr. Bell walked back into the store, rolled off several yards of market paper, wrapped the body, and with a little assistance from the railroad crew, hauled that monster to the huge porcelain cooler located in the back of the butcher section of the store. Mrs. Bell took a wet towel soaked in lye soap and wiped down Bama's seats and window. One of the teenagers watching the action volunteered to pump Bama's daily allotment of gas, and off she barreled through the dust and the gravel of the unpaved farm road which exited through the back of Red Hill. She left without paying on her bill. As for the dreaded inspector, amazingly, he was delayed at Slim's sawmill when Slim, who was cooking deer steaks on his garbage can grill near his office, invited the weasel to stay and eat lunch, thus making the inspection at the Red Hill impossible to conduct.

The following day, Mr. Bell unlocked the dark store from the back, heading straight for the meat market before dawn and long before opening to the public. He had already bled and cleaned Bama's kill directly after she had driven away and the commissary was closed for the day. Now, he commenced to divide and cut the venison, blending the lean deer meat with some fatter pork scraps for a good balance of lean and tender. He carefully mixed his own special spice combination, using the same recipe he had used for Jed's meat. Then, he stored the enormous trays of blended meat and the glass canister of spices in the walk-in cooler. He knew he could probably work on it intermittently during the work day, but he knew his brother-in-law's conditions concerning moonlighting, and he was unwilling to destroy that trust over a deer. Besides, the extra day would give the meat more time to blend flavors with the pork, and the spices would savor after mingling in the jar. The sun lit up the dark, creosoted floors, and Chuck unlocked the front doors to hungry customers already lined up on the porch.

When Bell returned home that evening from his extra long hours at the store, he collapsed in a kitchen chair where he methodically ate his supper of hamburger steak with gravy and onions, jojo potatoes heavily battered and fried, and a beefy ripe tomato. His only child, a thin, adoring girl named Nina, climbed into his lap as he inhaled his cold meal. "Daddy, momma told me what you have been doing with that deer of Mrs. Bama's. Can I go with you and help you in the morning? I won't mess up my clothes; I'll wear your white apron. Please, please, please, daddy, I can catch the bus at the store with Glen and his little sister?" She pleaded her case so well to the man who couldn't deny her anything within reason. He nodded and kept shoving food into his drooling mouth. It had been hours since his lunch of liver loaf and cheese. He thought of his wife. Mae had stayed with him until the final pole truck clocked in to be refueled. Kissing her husband's cold cheek, she walked home and cooked their supper, but couldn't wait any longer to feed Nina, so the two girls ate and made Chuck a plate, storing it in the breadbox for warmth. His exhausted wife had inhaled her food, had cleaned up the kitchen, and had fallen asleep on their double bed on top of the unfolded laundry she had dumped from its plastic basket.

Chuck kept nodding off even though he was famished. He was literally too tired to eat. He pushed his half-eaten plate of food aside and wrapped his strong, tattooed arms around Nina, gently placing her on his bony knees. "Okay, little bird, I reckon you can go, but you know you'll have to be ready at 2:30 in the morning; it'll be black dark at that time, but I've got lots and lots of work to get done before I start my regular day," he tweaked her nose as the rest of her face beamed with excitement. "Set you out some old clothes to wear; your momma'll get me if we mess up your school clothes. And then, get you another set of everyday clothes to change into before the bus runs. We won't wake ye momma; she has had a long day with me today at the store. We'll fix ourselves somethin' at the store, or we might just splurge and eat one of them sample Seven-up candy bars that the candy man left us to try." She nodded as he slid off of his lap and onto the cold linoleum floor. "Now, you go do what I said, and I'll tuck you in when you've brushed your teeth. Brusha, brusha, brusha," he began to sing a toothpaste jingle. She happily scampered off toward the narrow hall and stomped on the floor furnace just for good measure. "Nina, don't wake your mother. Go on," he mildly scolded.

Nina ran to the tiny bathroom which was too small to house the big claw-footed tub inside its walls. She had to lean over the water monster to reach her toothpaste on the shelf above it. The girl, banking on her father's approval, had already completed her homework, bathed, and even selected the two outfits her father had mentioned. She raked quickly through her snaggled teeth, common at her age, and hopped into her four poster oak bed and snuggled down between the thick handmade quilts. "I'm ready, Daddy," she called through the open bedroom door. Chuck tiptoed into her wide, cold room and tightly tucked her in, kissed her rosy cheeks, listened to her short, rote prayer, and closed the door almost shut, leaving only a slender crack for light to come through. Then, he dragged across the breezy hall to his own bed, made warm and toasty by the new electric blanket Mae had installed and had cranked up to high heat. He was fast asleep almost before his head make contact with the feather pillow.

The Seth Thomas alarm made a horrific, unwelcomed sound as it warped the night's silence. Chuck pried himself from the enticing warmth of the wrought iron bed and methodically pulled on his work pants and shirt as he stumbled toward the chilly bathroom. As he walked past the kitchen and into the Early American style decorated dining room, there sat Nina in the captain's chair of the dining set. She appeared to be wide awake and completely prepared; she held a small bag in her hand-her change of clothes. She spoke clearly, devoid of any sleepy slurred speech. "Hey, Pop. I'm ready to go. I slept in this chair all night. I slipped back out of my bed after you went to sleep. I watched the Pepsi clock all night so I wouldn't make you late. I even made you a piece of cheese toast for breakfast; I've already eaten mine," she reported cheerfully.

Sleepily, he patted her tousled, mousey, brown ponytail and headed back toward the bathroom. He grinned to himself as he thought about Mae; she would never be able to wake up that perky in the morning. Mae Bell unashamedly admitted that she was NOT a morning person like her sister Eula. When Eula had to phone Mae early for some reason she would, kiddingly, declare to her bubbly, older sister, "I just hate ole' cheerful people in the morning! What in tarnation do you want, Eula?"

Right now, Chuck commiserated with his wife, but he was thankful that little Nina wanted to be with him so badly that that she would stay in an uncomfortable chair all night just to go. He nibbled at the limp grilled cheese, which was really just a cheese slice inside two pieces of cold white bread, and the two partners in sausage making disappeared into the darkness of the wee hours of the morning.

Chuck, again, unlocked the back door of the commissary where animal feed, car/truck tires, and larger containers of supplies were stored. Holding Nina's hand still, father and daughter wandered through the dark until he made contact with the chain which hung from a single, naked light bulb in the middle of the storeroom ceiling. "Let's put a little light on the subject," he joked and Nina laughed readily as was her habit when her dad shared one of his corny jokes. "Now, baby, you go on through the door and stay back there in the market while I get the spice jar out and roll the meat cart out from the cooler," he instructed her with a kind voice. The willing child followed his directions without fail and came to a halt near the sliding glass cases filled with fresh meat. Her father soon joined her and slid the heavy deer meat from the stainless steel cart to the huge butcher block framed with various knives which rested in individual leather loops. He assigned Nina a few simple, but useful chores such as handing him items (towels, butcher paper, knives with the blades turned down, etc.) as he operated the powerful and dangerous meat grinder alone for fear of catching a straying finger of his beloved Nina who continued to climb on a wobbly chair to better position herself to the action.

By around five o'clock, Chuck had ground and re-blended the meats with the aromatic spices, dumping them into several number two washtubs which were scattered over the black and white tiled market floor. Holding his arms from the elbows up, he turned toward the back of the meat department to wash his greasy, spicy hands in a rust stained bleached enamel sink. "Oh, oh, no! Daddy, help!" Nina urgently howled. The child's bawl was followed by a thick, sickening, sloshing sound. Chuck, even though alarmed and curious, was slightly delayed in turning around; he dreaded the visual affirmation of his auditory assumption like he had done as a child at the Cane's picture show when he fearfully covered his eyes with his sweaty hands during the heart-racing drama of a Gene Autry movie and then slowly widened the gap between two fingers to verify the delicious details of the tragedy. Nina, as he soon discovered when he finally moved away from the sink, had tripped and fallen into a batch of sausage. The comical, but frustrating scene unfolded and featured Nina as the tragically humorous heroine wading awkwardly, (But then, how graceful could one be in this situation?), to liberate herself from the stringy contents of the tub.

She wailed and began to explain herself. "Daddy, I'm sorry. I'm sorry. I leaned over too far and fell in this one," she pointed to the tub closer to the butcher block. "And", she continued, "as I was getting out, I slipped again and fell in this other one," she nodded her head toward the tub which was still rocking from the invasion. Raw deer sausage dripped from her flattened hair to her discolored white PF Flyers. She moaned and wailed uncontrollably during the entire apology and explanation. Even her thick, cat-eyed shaped glasses were completely covered in grease and random spice flakes. When Chuck sized up the comical scene before him, his anger melted to laughter.

He gently sighed and patted her narrow shoulders. "Nina, honey, it's alright. Go back to the bathroom and clean up as best you can. Then change clothes and put your dirty clothes in the bathroom garbage can. Here, take off your shoes, first; I'll try to clean them up, or you might trip again and get hurt. Stop your cryin'. I ain't mad, but child, if you aren't the clumsiest little sapsucker," he encouraged the sorrowful little girl. He loved Nina, but he was all too aware of her clumsiness even in controlled environments, unlike this one which provided so many opportunities for her propensity to show up and to invite disaster. Chuck handed her the shoes, and she trudged back through the double doors of the supply room. He would call Mae later on. There was a more pressing matter as the opening time drew nearer in the near sunrise hours.

The sausage, he thought. What would he do? Would he just toss it all? He thought out the details logically. The child was clean; her clothes were clean, and she had fallen in. He made a quick and economically sound decision and stuck to it. Then, he called his wife to retrieve Nina so the child could fully cleanse herself before she caught the bus. He also shared with Mae his plan, urging her to keep the sausage caper to herself and asking her to please emphasize the need for silence about the morning's events when she spoke to Nina.. After restoring the messy market to its usual pristine condition, Chuck hurriedly wrapped the prepared meat into family sized packages and stored them on a steel tray in the refrigerated cases. He knew his meat was clean-cleaner than most fancy city markets' products.

Around mid-morning, Bama rolled up in her newly laundered Caddy, reupholstering it in new red dust and gravel specks as she squealed to a stop at the commissary from her home located on the Sullivan Road. And Mr. Bell, ever prompt, had just completed transferring the neatly tucked white market packets from the glass case to the rolling steel cart. He had fried a few sausages for Bama to sample, and they were still sizzling when she slammed open the double screen doors. She pushed the dripping sausage into a piece of white bread, folded the slice over and shoved the half-sandwich into her salivating mouth. She was ecstatic with the taste of Chuck's flavorful sausage. She paid him promptly and generously with a thick wad of grimy cash. "Mine is even better than the last batch I tasted! I a'gonna tell everbody 'bout how good you done on my deer. You'll git a lot bidness 'cause of this here mix," Bama talked with her mouth full as she continued. "Boy, Honey is gonna want this fer breakfast ever morning. Thank ye, Chuck. Ye done good, my friend. I better git on out of here. Oh, yeah, I need a couple of dollars of gas 'for I leave." Bama high stepped it down the stairs and toward the gas pumps. Perhaps it was the human factor which enhanced the flavor. Despite Bama's great satisfaction with the deer sausage and her free advertising, she continued to pay for her current items in cash, but she didn't pay her running ticket on that day or even when the store finally closed years later.

The Christmas season in Red Hill was celebrated and savored by the entire community, but its anticipated arrival actually fueled Mr. Beaux prematurely around Thanksgiving. In a time in history when holiday decorations traditionally were still in hibernation until mid-December, Beaux's personal obsession with rushing the season was markedly unusual and quite ominous of the sweeping changes that would soon characterize retail marketing years later when Halloween and Christmas trappings disturbingly co-mingle, ignoring the Pilgrim/Native American tradition except for an obligatory, dusty, tacky cornucopia and a set of cheap Pilgrim salt shakers hastily displayed and just as hastily removed.

Thanksgiving Day afternoon after the relatives had left and the house was cleared of debris, Ray disappeared from his preoccupied family and entered his organized tool shed, pulling down banana boxes individually labeled CHRISTMAS LIGHTS-EXTERIOR. Beaux then meticulously pilfered every box, checking the condition and effectiveness of each red, green, blue, white, and yellow bulb, replacing those ineffective lights with new ones. As he strategically placed the colored bulbs in an ordered sequence, he sang his favorite Christmas carols-off-key to himself. When the seasonally compulsive Beaux was satisfied with the color scheme, he grabbed a ladder and a sturdy flashlight and with the assistance of his little family, by dark that very Thanks-

giving night, he had joyfully strung the magnificent lights on an enormous cedar in the front yard of one of the two white company houses
Braun ever built in Red Hill.

Beaux generally nurtured a large, healthy cedar tree (sometimes
recently transplanted) located in the perfect spot near the right side
of his open garage; occasionally, if the weather had been unusually
frigid in winter or excessively dry in summer, the chosen tree did not
thrive, appearing unhealthy, weak, or even nearly dead. If the tree did
not weather well, Beaux and Rabon dug it up, chopped it up, and
placed in campfire position for the upcoming night when it would
warm the many Red Hill visitors who made the journey up the hill
on a tradition holiday night. Then a replacement would appear almost overnight to keep the holiday momentum going.

Once Beaux had gathered the necessary tools and supplies to complete the lighting of the tree, he called Eula, Jansey, and Rabon from the
warm fireplace to collectively assist him in holding the string of lights,
feeding them on command to Beaux who balanced precariously on the
aluminum ladder as he stretched to meet their hands. His excitement
was contagious, and soon, all four were singing and laughing as they
worked together to make Red Hill a festive place. Mrs. Beaux's additional job was to set up the stereo system on the wide screened porch at the
front of the boss's house. She dragged the oversized speakers across the
living room carpet and onto the wooden planked porch. After she positioned them on small marble tables, she selected various long playing
records of traditional Christmas tunes to echo across the valley of Red
Hill for all the residents to hear and to spark their holiday spirit.

Bells and chimes were Mr. Beaux's favorites, but he did allow Eula
to choose other genres. Mrs. Beaux loved Elvis's Christmas album,
but her husband frowned on Elvis's renditions of the classic tunes.
The Beaux children preferred Bing Crosby's classic holiday album,
and of course, the Caroleers' renditions of Johnny Mark's lively songs
were Jansey's favorites, as she periodically slipped the album in the 33
1/3 record stack. The residents chuckled when "Santa, Bring my Baby Back to Me" rocked Red Hill. Mr. Beaux, they figured, was either
too preoccupied with work to rectify the error, or he was absent on

business. Overall, though, Beaux was too elated about the whole Christmas season to stay angry at anyone, especially his beloved Eula.

Even though it wasn't a realistic goal, Beaux wanted everyone to share the spirit and his love of Christmas. He clearly and fondly remembered the meager Christmas gifts of his impoverished childhood, presents which consisted of a few pieces of fruit and a handful of homegrown pecans-all that his sharecropping father could spare for his large family during those extremely lean years. In his dirt floor sharecropper house, a small pine stuck in a lard can served as the holiday tree; it was sparsely decorated with holly berries and a thin strand of strung popcorn, but no presents rested at the base of the sad little native sapling. He wasn't bitter, and he knew it was the season for giving; he just wanted to protect the Red Hill children from experiencing the gnawing results of poverty that still gnawed at him even as a prosperous adult.

After the stereo system and its Easter Island shaped speakers were lovingly and strategically positioned, and the traditional exterior tree was decorated with perfectly staggered colors on each strand, then the interior tree and other household trinkets were pulled from the back of the tiny tool shed. Eula, who was gifted with the ability to creatively decorate and to recycle used wreaths, table toppers, etc., was responsible for placing her favorite items here and there throughout the rambling, perpetually remodeled boss's home. The children's unsophisticated handcrafted decorations mingled comfortably alongside expensive ornaments on the tree, and various, oddly shaped pieces unfit for tree hanging were unashamedly exhibited on strands of shiny tinseled ropes above the four Woolworth's stockings which swung from the mantle fireplace. It was suddenly cozy to sit in the usually cold, boring living room;Christmas was in the air!

The interior Christmas tree was visible through the wide picture window; it could be seen throughout the community at night. Some years the tree was an artificial evergreen with multicolored lights; other Decembers saw a silver aluminum tree with pink balls, no lights, and a multicolored reflector. And, spontaneously in some winters, the mistress of the house would choose a "back to nature" theme that required a fresh cedar which had been cut, soaked in water for a week, and placed in a large red or green pot. Only once did Eula downsize her decorations; she had accompanied Beaux on a whirl-wind pre-holiday public relations trip throughout Alabama, Mississippi, Tennessee, Kentucky, and Indiana in only a few days. Eula was pressed for time with all the other Christmas festivities at home, family, work, etc. The quick thinking lady ran to Dawn's Greenhouse and purchased an oversized Norwegian pine and deco-rated in Snoopy style with red bows and miniature gold bells. Mr. Beaux was not exactly pleased, but he understood Eula's plight well so he withheld any criticism. After all, his favorite Christmas icon was his exterior illuminated massive tree on Pine Straw Hill, and it had claimed its place long before the holiday rush.

The most anticipated event of Christmas in Red Hill was the grand entrance of Santa Claus into the secluded, rural settlement. Mr. Beaux actually owned and often donned the elaborate and realis-tic St. Nicholas' costume, complete with shiny black boots, a shiny belt to match, and a full, fluffy white beard. The costly suit was duti-fully taken to Morgan's Cleaners in town approximately a week before it was worn so that the experts there had plenty of time to restore its holiday luster. The identity of the jolly old fellow, (which switched from person to person and from year to year), was a well guarded secret to which even family members were not privy until after St. Nick had shared his ample lap with every child who wanted to tell his/her Christmas desires to the red suited hero; his voice might be faintly familiar but his anonymity was quickly accepted and unquestioned, allowing the "real Santa" to propitiate the delightful fantasy of the treasured moment for the little ones who stood pa-tiently in line on the Beaux's front lawn.

To prepare for this remarkable night with Santa, usually only a day or two before the big event, Ray Beaux, the perpetual kid during Christmas, left his bustling office a little earlier than the quitting whistle to head toward town for a private shopping trip. Before he left, he stopped Jansey's bus at the two-mile sign, and she hopped into the blue truck alongside her smiling father. She was his only shopping partner today, and they headed to town, laughing and sing-ing-she was on pitch and he was not. Their secret mission included purchasing a variety of small toys, an assortment of fresh fruits, and a variety of traditional holiday candies which would fill the small brown grocery bags for distribution by Santa's elves on the big night.

Jansey, his beloved daughter, was relieved when her father asked the bus driver if he could take his daughter with him. She, earlier in the ride, had barely contained herself before her father had interrupt-ed her bus route to include her on the yearly trip. She had silently cursed the substitute bus driver today because the lady was unfamiliar with the route, a fact contributing heavily on the tardiness of her eventual arrival in Red Hill. She had unrealistically feared that her punctual father would just leave her behind. Beaux gave Jansey a strict cost cap on the toys due to his usually accurate estimation of the large number of Red Hill children expected to show up for Santa. She began figuring out how much could be spent on each gift as soon as she slammed the door to the truck. Upon arriving at the local dime store, Beaux backed up the company truck, its bed laden with sturdy boxes for transportation, to a parking spot nearest to the en-trance of the store. Jansey and her father separated company to make the most of their shopping time before the large department store closed for the evening at 5 pm, as most retail stores did not offer ex-tended shopping hours then.

Once Jansey and Beaux were satisfied with their gender specific toys, bustling store clerks, ready to end their work day, checked out the presents, loaded the crates or boxes, and even assisted in transfer-ring the fairly inexpensive, but numerous items to the truck bed. The two happy, secret shoppers leaped into the cab and headed for the wholesale grocer who had previously filled the fruit order, (usually apples, oranges, tangerines, and bananas), and the candy request (chocolate cream drops, Circus peanuts, and King Leo peppermint sticks in small bundles), by telephone when Mrs. Beaux had called in the order earlier in the day.

With their exhausting and exhilarating mission complete, father and daughter automatically headed for the Dairy Queen for their yearly reward-supper out together. Now was not the time for nutritional concern; Jansey was allowed to eat whatever her chubby little self craved with no questions asked and no suggestions offered. The two left the friendly restaurant wearing onion ring breath and sporting chocolate malt moustaches. Mr. Smit, an older teenager who managed the restaurant, had never forgotten his own storybook childhood in Red Hill. He went the extra mile for the two because Beaux went the extra mile for his employees.

Eula and Rabon joined the rest of the adrenalin-fueled family in unloading the sagging truck bed and in quickly organizing an assembly line of toys, candy, and fruit on long tables on the front porch. Steadily filling the brown grocery bags with the assortment of goodies, the family then covered the gift bags with a bright green canvas tarp which, when removed on Santa's night, revealed the presents for the children of Red Hill. The festive mood was contagious, and it took some time for the Beaux family to settle into their individual cozy beds for the night. Tomorrow, after school and work, the day would rapidly develop into a busy afternoon and evening. The glorious time for Santa drew near. Beaux was more excited than Jansey about the night of his own childhood dreams.

School dragged by the next day for Jansey, and it seemed, once again, the substitute bus driver, Mrs. Long, ignored every bus stop on her route even with the protests from the riders; then she grudgingly backed up the bus to liberate the rioting children from their yellow prison onto their usual stops. If the usual driver, Mr. Wall, had been at the wheel, thought Jansey, he would have had all the stops memorized, and he'd known to speed through paths for her and for the other Red Hill children anxious to get home, to hurriedly swallow their evening meals, and to bundle up for the walk to the big house on the hill where Kris Kringle would soon greet them with "Ho, ho, Ho," as he rounded the corner of the Beaux's front yard. He knew his Red Hill kids, but Mrs. Long, who lived near the highway, was not aware of the magnitude of this particular day and the importance of a speedy journey. Finally, the new driver signaled a left turn toward the Two Mile sign. Jasey realized her hand had been gripping the seat in front of her so hard that it had caused it to cramp and to sweat; so, she eased up on herself and leaned her wide back against the hard, green plastic seat. After all, the bus was on the last leg of the journey before heading toward the Farm Hill. Red Hill riders were the next to the last to disembark in the afternoons and the second group to reload in the mornings.

After slinging on an extra thick jacket or wrapping up in a cozy quilt before the sun set, the children and their parents walked under the few street lights as they formed a line that snaked around the Beaux's dirt driveway and swirled around the side yard near the perfectly lit Christmas tree. For the Christmas rookies, the older children explained and modeled the usual procedure, and with each added detail, the ingénues squealed and jumped with excitement. The darker the sky became, the noisier the crowd became, but it was a cheery, spirited noise which signaled their enthusiasm and eagerness, not one of chaos and of disruption. The joy of the occasion illuminated the sky's darkness and slightly lifted the spirits of the gentle, simple people of Red Hill-if just for this holiday season. The benevolence generally characteristic of the time of year infused renewed hope and produced feelings of good will even in the adults who knew the magic was a temporary smokescreen for their problems. Suddenly, squeals in unison announced, "Look, I see him. I see Santa!" Santa mysteriously arrived, stomping his patent leather boots around the far side of the house. It seemed as if he just materialized from the darkness in the east and emerged under the flood lights that brightened the Beaux's front yard.

"Ho, ho, ho, and Merry Christmas to you all," the jolly one wished the bystanders in his slightly disguised, grandfatherly voice. The Red Hill Santa was one of few words by necessity in a deliberate effort to blur his identity as most citizens knew each others' voices all too well. Either Mr. Beaux, his son, a new crew member, or a visiting family member was roped into playing the part of the holiday hero. It was hard to refuse such an offer: Eula's delicious supper, release time from work if the actor worked for Braun and who solemnly vowed to keep the secret, and the unabashed adoration and hearty welcome of an entire community. Some thespians such as Mr. Bell or Mr. Barr required extra body padding for their slim bodies, while others like Little 'Un Lloyd were naturally equipped with the girth necessary for the job! Besides, the lights on that side of the house were kept dim for more than one reason—to showcase the tree lights and to camouflage the face of Santa as well as his body shape. Everyone played along because they all wanted to believe. Perception is reality; it has been said.

One by one, each anxious child perched on Santa's lap and rattled off a gift list. Then Old St. Nicholas asked the inevitable question: "Have you been good this year?" Before the child could respond, peals of good-natured laughter arose as volunteered tales of misbehavior erupted from the jovial group who surrounded the tree and the goody table which had been uncovered and placed outside. Regardless of the "goodness" factor, the child was handed a candy cane and directed to collect his "happy sack" from the table which was manned by the Beauxs and the Bells.

After all the children had been processed, the satisfied families headed back down the slippery hill, almost marching in step with the familiar carols and hymns which rang out loud and strong all over the settlement. (Beaux was too preoccupied to strictly govern the song selections, so an occasional Elvis would bellow out among his chime albums.) Santa's disappearance was equally as puzzling as his arrival. He slipped back around to the darkness as the party dispersed. The momentary magic was soon replaced with reality as cold as the December night became when the families moved away from the warmth of the camp fire, but it was a reality refueled with joy and tinged with hope like fresh dew temporarily refreshes dying plants in a neglected garden during a devastating drought.

The Beauxs gathered up any extra sacks of toys, fruit and candy and stacked them inside the living room. Beaux sought out needy families in neighboring communities who might not have Christmas gifts and covertly delivered the extra bags to these individuals in the following days before December 25. In addition, during the Santa night, Beaux stationed himself nearby, when he was not playing Santa himself, to eavesdrop on children whose lists included necessities such as shoes, coats, blankets, food, etc. so that those basic needs could be met, too.

He never distanced himself from the little dark-headed share-cropper's son with a wide gap between his front teeth, with ragged clothes on his malnourished back, and with calloused and split feet lacking any shoes for protection; his heart remained tender toward impoverished children for the rest of his long, fruitful life. Tonight had been his night as well; for, the clever leader of a large, successful company righted the wrongs for that barefooted child of long ago who reported frequently to a freezing bed and whose sleep was disturbed by the plaintiff cry of a hollow and unappeased belly.

Poverty had not extinguished his desire for success; conversely, its impact had done just the opposite. As a holiday revisionist, he fashioned this Christmas and all other Christmases past and present into the ideal Currier and Ives portrait for Red Hill children and for himself. Although poverty did, however, eat straight to the bone and affect people's confidence and well being, during the Christmas season, he felt that, at least, he had been its formidable competitor.

On the one holiday which encouraged selflessness and promoted the celebration of a King, no bible was ever distributed. No sermon was ever preached. No judgment in regards to choices about cleanliness, child-rearing, thriftiness, sobriety, purity, greed, or any other organic topic was meted. But Biblical principles were being practiced. Just an ordinary man performing ordinary deeds for under-ordinary families, creating extraordinary memories, and exemplifying pure generosity-giving without expecting a gift. Red Hill took care of its own.

After a few days off for Christmas and New Year's holidays, Red Hill settled back into a comfortable, familiar routine. Abandoned toy boxes, softened by morning frost, and wet household garbage, increased by their additional seasonal visitors, lay temporarily forgotten in the marshy back yards, awaiting incineration-the acceptable method for waste management at the time. Dry, brittle Christmas trees lined and cluttered the thick ditches between Mrs. Barr's yard and the community center in hopes of trapping fish and enriching the nutrients present in the slender pond. Plastic decorative wreaths were stripped from the sides of the pressure treated houses and front doors and were now neatly stored in the distant corner of the least used closet space, becoming dormant until next Christmas. The children were still interested in their new play things: riding their Panther I Schwinn bikes up and down the recently re-paved front streets; playing cowboys and Indians with new Daisy guns; or strolling along the neighborhood with Chatty Cathy as their new best friend. The holiday afforded tired and sometimes discouraged residents a much needed respite from the weariness of Red Hill life which, despite its benefits was characterized by smothering poverty and sheer ignorance. Besides, everyone knew no earthly respite is permanent.

25093142R00119

Made in the USA
San Bernardino, CA
18 October 2015